"Fast-paced, c.̶ ̶.̶ ̶.̶" —John J. Lamb, author of *The Treacherous Teddy*

"[A] new exciting . . . series . . . Part of the fun of this solid whodunit is the vivid description of the Renaissance Village; anyone who has not been to one will want to go . . . Cleverly developed." —*Midwest Book Review*

"Joyce and Jim Lavene have teamed up for yet another terrific mystery series . . . A feast for the reader . . . Character development in this new series is energetic and eloquent; Jessie is charming and intelligent, with . . . saucy strength." —*MyShelf.com*

"A promising new series set at a Renaissance Faire . . . Interesting juxtaposition between the present and the past and the real and the fantastic . . . Entertaining and vivacious characters." —*Romantic Times*

"I cannot imagine a cozier setting than Renaissance Faire Village, a closed community of rather eccentric—and very interesting—characters, [with] lots of potential . . . A great start to a new series by a veteran duo of mystery authors." —*Cozy Library*

Praise for the Peggy Lee Garden Mysteries

POISONED PETALS

"A delightful botany mystery." —*The Best Reviews*

"A top-notch, over-the-fence mystery read with beloved characters, a fast-paced story line, and a wallop of an ending." —*Midwest Book Review*

"Enjoy this pleasurable read!" —*Mystery Morgue*

continued . . .

FRUIT OF THE POISONED TREE

"I cannot recommend this work highly enough. It has everything: mystery, wonderful characters, sinister plot, humor, and even romance."   —*Midwest Book Review*

"Well-crafted with a satisfying end that will leave readers wanting more!"   —*Fresh Fiction*

PRETTY POISON

"With a touch of romance added to this delightful mystery, one can only hope many more Peggy Lee Mysteries will be hitting shelves soon!"   —*Roundtable Reviews*

"A fantastic amateur-sleuth mystery."   —*The Best Reviews*

"For anyone with even a modicum of interest in gardening, this book is a lot of fun."

—*The Romance Readers Connection*

"The perfect book if you're looking for a great suspense."

—*Romance Junkies*

"Joyce and Jim Lavene have crafted an outstanding whodunit in *Pretty Poison*, with plenty of twists and turns that will keep the reader entranced to the final page."

—*Fresh Fiction*

"Complete with gardening tips, this is a smartly penned, charming cozy, the first book in a new series. The mystery is intricate and well-plotted. Green thumbs and nongardeners alike will enjoy this book."   —*Romantic Times*

PERFECT POISON

GHASTLY
GLASS

Joyce and Jim Lavene

BERKLEY PRIME CRIME, NEW YORK

THE BERKLEY PUBLISHING GROUP
Published by the Penguin Group
Penguin Group (USA) Inc.
375 Hudson Street, New York, New York 10014, USA
Penguin Group (Canada), 90 Eglinton Avenue East, Suite 700, Toronto, Ontario M4P 2Y3, Canada
(a division of Pearson Penguin Canada Inc.)
Penguin Books Ltd., 80 Strand, London WC2R 0RL, England
Penguin Group Ireland, 25 St. Stephen's Green, Dublin 2, Ireland (a division of Penguin Books Ltd.)
Penguin Group (Australia), 250 Camberwell Road, Camberwell, Victoria 3124, Australia
(a division of Pearson Australia Group Pty. Ltd.)
Penguin Books India Pvt. Ltd., 11 Community Centre, Panchsheel Park, New Delhi—110 017, India
Penguin Group (NZ), 67 Apollo Drive, Rosedale, North Shore 0632, New Zealand
(a division of Pearson New Zealand Ltd.)
Penguin Books (South Africa) (Pty.) Ltd., 24 Sturdee Avenue, Rosebank, Johannesburg 2196,
South Africa

Penguin Books Ltd., Registered Offices: 80 Strand, London WC2R 0RL, England

This is a work of fiction. Names, characters, places, and incidents either are the product of the author's imagination or are used fictitiously, and any resemblance to actual persons, living or dead, business establishments, events, or locales is entirely coincidental. The publisher does not have any control over and does not assume any responsibility for authors or third-party websites or their content.

PUBLISHER'S NOTE: The recipes contained in this book are to be followed exactly as written. The publisher is not responsible for your specific health or allergy needs that may require medical supervision. The publisher is not responsible for any adverse reactions to the recipes contained in this book.

GHASTLY GLASS

A Berkley Prime Crime Book / published by arrangement with the authors

PRINTING HISTORY
Berkley Prime Crime mass-market edition / September 2009

Copyright © 2009 by Joyce Lavene and Jim Lavene.
Cover illustration by Ben Perini.
Cover design by Lesley Worrell.
Interior text design by Laura K. Corless.

ISBN: 978-0-425-23030-5

BERKLEY® PRIME CRIME
Berkley Prime Crime Books are published by The Berkley Publishing Group,
a division of Penguin Group (USA) Inc.,
375 Hudson Street, New York, New York 10014.
BERKLEY® PRIME CRIME and the PRIME CRIME logo are trademarks of Penguin Group (USA) Inc.

PRINTED IN THE UNITED STATES OF AMERICA

10 9 8 7 6 5 4 3 2 1

Dedicated to our sister-in-law and friend, Marcia Koch: We know you would have loved Jessie and Chase! We miss you!

J & J

One

"Hear Ye. Hear Ye. Death stalks the streets of Renaissance Faire Village. Run for your lives."

"Would it hurt him to add some inflection?" A fairy, waiting in the costume line ahead of me, rolled her eyes and watched the Village crier go by on the cobblestone street.

"I'll add some inflection, dearie," the little man in the dwarf costume responded as he walked by, "when *you* take some acting lessons."

Standing between them was making me nervous. The Black Dwarf, alias Marcus Fleck, was holding a long pole with a swinging lantern on one end. It was pointed at me instead of the fairy.

"Acting lessons?" the fairy shot back, her translucent wings quivering. "I've been in dinner theaters across the south."

He snorted. "So has roast beef. What's your point?"

The fairy (I'm not sure if I know her. Fairies all look the same to me) made a noise somewhere between a screech and a howl. "I'll show you my point, little man," she threatened the dwarf, long red fingernails poised in his direction.

I was still standing between them. "Could you take this somewhere else?" I was hoping for a quick resolution to the problem since it looked like rain and I was still a good twenty minutes from the inside of the Village costume shop.

This was the first year ever that Renaissance Faire Village and Market Place in Myrtle Beach was decking itself out for Halloween. I'd wrangled and made promises to everyone but the devil to be here for the eight full weeks of the Halloween season and to continue my research on Renaissance crafts. Of course, I could continue my research next summer, and I probably still could, but I *really* wanted to be here for Halloween. I'd heard tales of all the fantastic stuff the Village theme makers had lined up for the season. I couldn't wait!

"Jessie!" A former student of mine at the University of South Carolina at Columbia hailed me. Debby had dropped out during the last semester to work the Renaissance Village full-time. Some people came to the Village and couldn't go home again. "I was wondering when you were going to get here. We're roomies!"

She hugged me and I absently patted her shoulder. I looked around at the crowds of actors and students ready to trade in their traditional Renaissance Village garb of knaves, varlets, wenches, and ladies for their special Halloween costumes.

I'd hoped to see Chase here. Actually, I'd hoped he'd be

waiting at the gate with breathless anticipation of my arrival. Chase Manhattan was the Village bailiff but also my main man since July. I hadn't seen him in a few weeks. My promises and commitments to be here for the next two months had really dragged me down for a while. But I was firm in my belief that he was probably, *hopefully*, still my man. You never know for sure. A few weeks can be a lifetime.

I was hoping not to need a roomie or Village housing because I'd be staying with Chase. But maybe not. I wouldn't know for sure until I saw him, hopefully not wrapped around some smug little fairy or one of the story-book characters that inhabited Renaissance Village.

"I'm glad to see you, too." I smiled at Debby. The line for costumes had moved closer to the shop, and the Black Dwarf had moved on with his cheery message.

But in fact, the Village crier was right about Death stalking the Village. I was looking right at him. Complete with black robe and huge scythe, he was Death incarnate. He was tall, too. Or on stilts.

Debby laughed at me when she saw I couldn't take my eyes from the character. "You just got here, right? Let me introduce Ross, or as we like to call him, Mr. Big." She turned to the spectacularly frightening figure of death. "Ross DeMilo, meet my good friend, Jessie Morton, of late apprenticed to Mary Shift at Wicked Weaves. Jessie, this is Ross. And he's gonna get you if you don't watch out."

Ross pulled back his black hood, frowning at me. His brown hair was greased back from his narrow, skull-shaped face. He wasn't on stilts. He was just tall and thin, his ribs showing beneath his black Renaissance Village T-shirt.

"Welcome to Renaissance Village, a horrible place to live but a worse place to die. I am Death, the original dark stalker. My scythe will separate your body from your soul."

As terrifying speeches went, it was pretty good. He had a deep John Carradine voice that added a certain monster charm that worked even in the bright September sunshine. I didn't want to think what it would do after dark.

"Hi. That's a great costume." I smiled at him, then he moved away, mingling with the crowd. I turned to Debby, who was in a red wench's costume. "Where's your scary outfit? I thought everyone was dressing up."

"Today is the last day to trade in your non-Halloween costume for the scary one." She shrugged. "I figure why do anything right away when you can wait until the last minute. There are plenty of people who say they aren't dressing up for Halloween. Robin Hood and the Merry Men aren't into it, and neither are some of the Craft Guild. They want the dancing girls at the Caravan Stage to dress up like witches. Kind of corny, huh?"

I should mention that a lot of people at Renaissance Village take their roles very seriously. They live and work here all year and sometimes get a little weird. Robin and his Merry Men tend to be that way more than most since they hang out in Sherwood Forest dispatching brigands and stealing toaster ovens from the rich to give to the poor.

"How do the people from Adventure Land feel about people *not* dressing up?" I looked around at the milling crowd of residents and visitors. Adventure Land is the owner of the Village and supposedly dictates the rules and regulations. "Has Robin told Livy and Harry about this?"

"You are behind the times, I fear, good lady. Queen Olivia and King Harold are on the royal outs. Neither one is taking visitors or problems. It looks as though they're leaving that to our good bailiff, Chase Manhattan. Methinks you know of him. Tall fellow who has shoulders like a Viking and tends to be good at most sporting events?"

Yeah. I know him. I glanced around at the crowd forming outside the costume keeper's shop, hoping to see his handsome, smiling face. No such luck.

I stood in line behind the fairy talking to Debby about her life at the Village. I was surprised she wasn't living with Fred the Red Dragon, but she laughed when I mentioned it. "You were so right about not getting involved with any of these guys on a permanent basis, Jessie. I'm over Fred. Now I'm seeing the new blacksmith. His name is Hans Von Rupp. He's from Latvia or Germany. Somewhere in Europe. He's *big*, too." She giggled. "All over. He can lift me with one arm and—"

"Sounds like fun." I cut her off, not wanting to hear so much that my ears started bleeding. Why do people always feel they have to give you more information than you need?

I wished I could just ask if she'd seen Chase with Little Miss Muffet or one of the underdressed woodland creatures. I couldn't. I wasn't willing to sound that needy. I was really sure everything was fine anyway. It had only been a few weeks since we last saw each other. No reason to panic just because I'd been here an hour already and hadn't seen him.

The fairy in front of me was at the window where Portia the costume keeper handed out daily apparel to those of us who didn't own the costumes we wore everyday. "I hope I'm not going to be one of those dead people walking around," the fairy told Portia. "I didn't come all the way from Texas to be a zombie."

Portia put a gauzy, gray garment in front of her. "All fairies are wraiths for the duration of the Halloween season. Please turn in your wings when you exchange costumes. Wraiths do *not* fly in the Village."

"What? This is big and long," the fairy complained. "My legs are my best feature. I can't work like this."

"Then go back to Texas," Portia recommended, sounding tired as always. "Next?"

Debby smiled at the unhappy fairy/wraith. "Look at it this way, wraiths don't have to wash their hair or dye it. You'll save time and money during the next few weeks."

The fairy, about to turn wraith, hissed at Debby, "Stay out of my way or I'll take you straight to hell."

Like I said, an intense group of people. While Debby and the fairy-turned-wraith argued about what the other deserved, I stepped up to the window and smiled at Portia. "This is exciting, huh? The first Halloween in Renaissance Village. I'm really looking forward to it."

She glanced at me. "Where are you working, Julie?"

"Jessie." I smiled again. It hadn't been *that* long. What was wrong with everyone? How could they all just forget me? "I'm apprenticing at the Glass Gryphon until Halloween. What kind of costume do you have cooked up for me?"

Portia yawned. Her graying black hair was pulled starkly away from her thin face. "Craft Guild has a choice between ghosts and witches."

Ghosts and witches? Neither one sounded appealing. "What does the ghost costume look like?"

"If I take it out, it's yours for the duration. I'm not dragging costumes out for everyone to look over at this point. Ghost or witch?"

I tried to imagine which one would be less likely to catch on fire since I'd be working with flame as an apprentice glassblower. I tend to have a little bad luck when it comes to my apprenticeships. I didn't want to catch on fire, no matter how memorable that might seem to some diehard Ren-Faire visitors.

"Ghost. I look better in white."

Portia lifted a black costume complete with pointed hat.

"Sorry. Fresh out. Try again at the beginning of the week. Good to have you back. Enjoy your stay."

Was it just me or did everyone seem to have a bad attitude about this venture? Where was the spirit? Where was the excitement?

"Next." Portia looked past me at Debby. "All bawdy wenches are the undead."

"The undead what?" Debby demanded. "You mean vampires? Or zombies?"

"I'll see you later." I tactfully sneaked away before it got any worse. This visit to Renaissance Village wasn't turning out the way I'd envisioned. No Chase. No excitement. I was disappointed to say the least.

"Greetings, good lady!" A handsome lord doffed his large feathered hat in a deep bow. "Might you be the apprentice for the Glass Gryphon?"

My heart sped up a little when I took in the excellent attributes that even his lordly apparel couldn't hide. His hair was thick, chestnut brown, gleaming with red highlights in the sun. His smiling blue eyes looked me over from the tight jeans to the low-neck green sweater I'd worn for Chase, who wasn't around to appreciate me. All in all, a sweet welcome package.

"I'm Jessie Morton, good sir. Who might you be?" I dropped him a little curtsy that showed off a couple of my attributes.

"I am Henry Trent, nephew of Roger Trent, owner of the Glass Gryphon. My uncle sent me to meet you and escort you through the Village to the shop. Are you ready to go?"

I knew I should get my bag from the car and settle in with Debby, but this seemed a good opportunity to meet Roger again and go over my responsibilities as an apprentice glassblower. You had to be careful in the Village or the craftsman you served would have you running errands and picking up laundry from the Lovely Laundry Ladies instead of learning the craft.

Since I'm already working on my dissertation, which I hope will become a book someday, my research here has become very important to me. I've titled my dissertation, "Proliferation of Renaissance Crafts in Modern Times." I've already apprenticed with a Gullah basket weaver at Wicked Weaves and Master Archer Simmons at the Feathered Shaft. This time it's glassblowing. Who knows what it will be next summer? I've talked to a few other Craft Guild members like the Hands of Time clock shop and Pope's Pots pottery shop. I'm ready for anything.

Especially if a good-looking man comes along with the project. It can't hurt. "Lead on, good sir."

Henry swept me another elegant bow, then took my hand and laid it on his forearm as we started walking through Renaissance Village.

The Village is situated on the site of the old Myrtle Beach Air Force Base. Most of the shops have living quarters above them for the full-time merchants. The rest of the space is filled with part-timers like me, about three hundred of them at any given time.

Unlike most Renaissance faires, this one goes on every day except Christmas day. It's open from morning to evening seven days a week with the King's Feast held at the castle every Sunday night. Hundreds of thousands of visitors come through the main gate every year to be delighted and swept back in time, with Shakespeare walking the cobblestone streets reciting odes, King Arthur retrieving Excalibur from the stone every two hours, and fantasy creatures ready to have their picture taken. The experience is nonstop fun, excitement, and good food. Adventure Land, the parent company, says it will be so, and it is.

"How was your trip to the Village, my lady?" Henry asked as we walked past the first fountain toward the hatchet-throwing contest.

"It went well, thank you. How is your uncle?" The monks were chanting in the Monastery Bakery, a good sign usually because it meant they were baking instead of getting into other kinds of trouble. Their bread is to die for, but their quasi-religion of the Brotherhood of the Sheaf is a little strange.

"My uncle is quite well. I am here visiting him because I am opening another shop for him outside the Village." Henry smiled at me, his big blue eyes crinkling at the corners. I *love* men with crinkly eyes.

We were passing the elegant houses on Squire's Lane, which are eclipsed only by the sight of the castle rising above Mirror Lake where the pirates live. There was loud laughter coming from Peter's Pub, a favorite of Village residents after hours. It was Friday and there was a good crowd around.

Lady Godiva rode by with her body suit and butt-length blond wig. I didn't have to look closely to see that Arlene, the last Lady Godiva, had been replaced. Everything here is transitory. People come and go all the time. Even shops and restaurants change from time to time. Nothing like a real Renaissance village where the same families lived and died for generations.

"Hail to thee, Mistress Jessica!" Alex, one of Robin Hood's Merry Men (and a former summer love of mine), walked by us quickly. "I see you have selected a new gentleman friend."

I knew this was a jab at the many years I'd been coming to the Village and seemingly finding a new love interest each time. I wanted to set that rumor to rest before he spread it everywhere. "I'm working with Henry and Roger during the Halloween season. That's it."

Alex laughed, nearly unsettling his forest green hat from his blond head. "Of course, good lady. Who would think otherwise?"

I was about to protest on my own behalf when Henry swept me down into his arms and planted his mouth on mine. It was only an instant before he set me back on my feet. *All right*. I said he was interesting. But not *that* interesting. At least not in the first twenty minutes of meeting him.

I was about to wipe the grin from both their faces when someone behind me cleared his throat. I didn't have to look. It was Chase, of course. He might not have been there to greet me in the first hour when I didn't do anything but look for him. But he managed to be there for the split second I got into trouble. Why do things like this always happen to me?

All four of us stood there as though time really had stopped, just as the ads for the Village promised. I guessed Alex and Henry were waiting to see what would happen next. It suddenly occurred to me that Henry may have been in the Village long enough to know about me and Chase. Had he seen Chase coming as I spoke to Alex and purposely tried to break us up? I didn't want to judge him right away, but my relationship with Chase could be on the line.

Without hesitating (any further), I hauled back and slapped Henry. His head jerked back, and he looked at me with real hurt in his eyes. "Sorry, my lady. I could not resist your tempting lips a moment longer."

I glared at Alex. He laughed and trotted off toward Sherwood Forest. I turned my attention back to Henry, who was still standing there. "I'll meet you and your uncle at the

Glass Gryphon shortly, sir. Please give him my regards while I take care of another matter."

Henry bowed, seemingly chastened, but the evil little smile on his face told me otherwise. "I will take your message to my uncle." He nodded at Chase. "Good day to you, Bailiff."

When we were finally alone (except for the hundreds of visitors, wandering knaves, and a few serfs), I turned to Chase. "Hi there."

"Hi." He was staring at me in an un-Chase-like way. Normally he'd be running up, throwing me in the air (not a small task since I'm six feet tall and not at all waiflike). There was no big grin on his handsome face, no big kiss coming my way.

I couldn't decide which course would be better. You know how sometimes when you defend yourself it makes you seem guiltier than when you keep your mouth shut? I didn't know which way to go with this. No matter what, it was only a stupid kiss. How upset could he be?

Before I could ascertain whether he was really upset, a varlet, now dressed all in black instead of varlet brown, came breathlessly running up. "Bailiff! It's happened again! Except this time it's Death."

Chase frowned. "What are you talking about, Lonnie? Did another visitor collapse?"

"No. It's Death. Really."

"You mean another one died?"

"No. Really, Chase. Death died."

"I think he's talking about Ross." I pushed into the conversation before I had to hit one of them. "You know, the tall guy with the scythe."

Chase glanced at me as if he'd forgotten I was there. "Oh yeah. Where is he?"

"In the Village Square," Lonnie replied. "One minute he was threatening a few visitors and telling them he'd take their souls, and the next minute, boom! He was on the cobblestones for the count."

"Let's go," Chase said.

"Me, too." I started running after him. "Have visitors died in the Village? How did I miss that?"

"Too busy, I guess," Chase returned as we cut through the alleyway between Squire's Lane and Harriet's Hat House. "Too busy to watch CNN, or call anyone."

"CNN was down here covering visitor deaths?" How had I missed that?

"Yep." Lonnie's little ratlike face twisted up as we ran across the cobblestones. "That's why I left Sir Latte's Beanery. Chase needs all the help he can get."

"So what killed them? It was probably the heat, right? Lots of visitors wear those heavy clothes and get heatstroke over the summer." I looked from Chase to Lonnie.

"We don't know for sure yet," Chase finally answered.

A large crowd of visitors and residents had gathered near the Good Luck Fountain right in the middle of the Village Square. I stayed next to Chase, almost having to push Lonnie out of the way as we broke through the crowd to take a look at the man on the ground.

Ross's black robe had fallen open around his bony body, but his hood covered his face. The scythe lay beside him, not too far from his reach. There was blood everywhere and something sticking up out of his chest. Everyone was whispering around us as Chase knelt beside the giant's form.

"Call the police," Chase said finally. "He's dead. And I don't think it's heatstroke."

Two

"Yep." Detective Donald Almond took another swig from his Cheerwine. His white shirt had a brown food stain on the front, and his suit jacket looked slept in. "He's dead all right. Looks like that steel reinforcing bar went right through his heart. That makes three this month, right, Manhattan?"

Chase and his helper, Lonnie, had their hands full keeping people away from the dead figure of Death on the Village Square, until the police took over. The media swarmed around like mosquitoes before a storm. Even though we were away from the main area and behind a temporary stage, visitors knew something was going on when they saw all the TV cameras.

I kept trying not to look at Ross's dead body. I'd just been through a similar experience over the summer and I was beginning to stress out. It was terrible thinking he'd just been alive while I was waiting for my costume. What had happened to him?

"I'm afraid so. But this one is different." Chase frowned as he looked at the dead body, covered now by a Renaissance banner.

Chase is not only the bailiff for the Village, he's also judge and jury when it comes to vegetable justice in the stocks. The Myrtle Beach Police Department had officially appointed him an auxiliary police officer for his role at the Village. A lot depended on him to keep the peace, including turning over shoplifters and other petty crooks to the authorities. Besides that, he's a good jouster.

"I don't know." Detective Almond scratched his balding head. "Could be an accident, I suppose. We'll have to check it out. Are you sure this boy's name and information are accurate?"

Chase nodded. "It's what Adventure Land has on file for him. Will you contact his family?"

Detective Almond said he would. He used his gloved hand to uncover the dead body again. "What do you make of these words on his robe? *Death shall find thee*. Is that some Village saying?"

"If it is, it's the first time I've ever heard it." Chase asked Lonnie, who'd been standing really close to the body (too close if you ask me), if he knew what it meant.

"Maybe it has something to do with him being Death," Lonnie suggested.

Both Chase and Detective Almond seemed to disregard that idea. Roger Trent (hopefully my new mentor) joined us. He had once been the Village bailiff before Queen Olivia and King Harry decided he was too old, despite his police experience from his former life. Roger didn't seem to care. He tried his best to keep everyone on the straight and narrow while amusing all of us with tales of his youthful exploits as a cop. "Did you get the autopsy results back on those other two visitors who died here recently?"

"Hi, Roger." I smiled. "It's good to see you."

He glanced at me but didn't return my smile. "Jessie."

"Not yet," Detective Almond responded to Roger. "The Horry County medical examiner thought something might be suspicious with two visitors dying from heatstroke in only a couple weeks. He sent his findings off to Columbia. Might be months before we hear back."

"That's not good enough," Chase told him. "What if there's something more going on?"

Detective Almond seemed to give up on his cute idea of pacifying Chase with silly answers. "Look, Manhattan, it might be the food or it might be the excitement. People die, son. It happens everyday. There was no sign of trauma on the other two. And until I think otherwise, this boy's death could be an accident. Maybe you should give OSHA a call. I think you're taking this too personally. You do a good job here. We'll get this sorted out."

"Thanks." Chase's voice was deadpan. I knew he was humoring the detective in return.

"Okay, boys," Detective Almond called to his officers. "Let's get this cleaned up so these nice people can get back to doing whatever it is they do. Mac, call in those crime scene boys. We'll need this area cordoned off until we say it's okay."

It was like being dismissed in school. No matter what was going on, you were supposed to take the hint and get out of there. Roger stood beside Chase, the two of them talking about what had happened, no doubt. Henry had sneaked up and managed to get close to me again. It was an unpleasant sensation. I just didn't want to snarl things up any further with Chase.

I moved away from him, over to Chase and Roger. I

was right. They were talking about the three people who'd died.

"It's not like Ross was a visitor like the other two," Roger said. "If something bad was going on, the killer would keep going in his same pattern. That's how you can tell it's different."

Roger was a plain-looking man in his fifties with a shaved head. He always wore a leather jerkin, leather britches, and a blousy shirt with the neckline open. He wasn't very tall, but he'd stayed slender (for the most part) since his long-ago police days. Despite his tendency to be melodramatic, and the stories I'd heard every summer since I got out of college (I don't want to think how long ago that's been), I'd always considered him an okay guy.

"I still don't like it," Chase said. "Livy told me our numbers are up, but part of that is probably due to curiosity. This isn't a good way to bring in more visitors."

"Maybe it is." Roger shrugged. "After all, this is Renaissance Faire Village Halloween. What could be scarier than Death dying here? We'll probably have buses of teenagers dying to get in."

Chase didn't respond, and Roger nudged him. "Get it? *Dying* to get in?"

"Maybe we should think about hiring a few more security guards," Chase suggested. "Something about this doesn't feel right to me."

"Don't worry so much, Chase. Look! Jessie's here. She's going to apprentice with me through Halloween. I'm sure everything will be fine. Just try to relax and let the police do their job."

Henry smiled and offered Chase his hand. "I'm Roger's nephew. We haven't met as yet, good sir. I hope we haven't gotten off to a bad start."

All three men looked at me. I ignored them and watched

the crowd of onlookers leaving the Village Square. There was nothing for Chase to be jealous of and less than that for Henry to think was going on between us. Better not to say anything. *At least for right now.*

"Yes. This is Henry." Roger completed the introduction. "Jessie, if you're ready we can get you settled in at the shop. There's plenty of room upstairs if you'd like to skip Village housing and stay with us."

I was caught between the sword and the stone, so to speak. I didn't want to tell Roger I'd been expecting to stay with Chase in case Chase had other ideas. Of course, if Chase *had* other ideas, staying above the glass shop would probably be better than staying with Debby. Maybe Roger would even consider feeding me for the time I was here. Food and other common necessities could become very dear with the Village's tendency to accidentally forget paychecks.

I glanced at Chase without moving my face or even my eyes. I have very good peripheral vision. It came from trying to communicate with my twin brother, Tony, after our parents had died and we felt we couldn't be ourselves with strangers. We were both pretty good at it, and for a while, we always seemed to know what the other was thinking.

Now I tried to use that skill on Chase. Would it work? Or did it only work because Tony and I were twins?

"No need for that." Chase grabbed my hand. "Jessie's staying with me at the dungeon. She'll be at the Glass Gryphon first thing in the morning. Thanks for your help, Roger. See you later. Nice to meet you, Henry."

We walked together down the King's Highway past the Village Madman, who was taking dirt out of a pot and smearing it on himself. As visitors walked by, he held out his hat, begging for coins as he spouted gibberish. I didn't remember his name, but I recognized him as one of the Merlin's Apothecary servants from last summer. I wasn't sure if being recast as the Madman was a step up or down.

I glanced at the side of Chase's face as we headed toward Brewster's Tavern. He hadn't said a word since we'd left Roger and Henry in the dust as we hot-footed across the crowded center of the Village. I was perfectly happy with the resolution he'd presented to Roger. He didn't seem as happy.

The King's Tarts, next door to the tavern, were in rare form, actually trying to lure visitors into their bake shop by standing outside flirting with them. That tactic usually wasn't necessary since the combination of pie and low-cut dresses seemed to coax people inside all the time.

Once inside the tavern, I sat down across a small wooden table from Chase. I didn't know if I should wait or jump right in like I usually do. I decided to give him a minute to see if he'd get the conversation started. I wouldn't wait any longer than that. I was tired, hot, and hungry, among other needs. The dungeon was a long walk from here.

"You don't have to stay with me," he said abruptly.

"Beer?" Jake called out from behind the bar.

"Two." Chase held up two fingers.

"You know I want to stay with you." I revealed my heart above the rush-strewn floor.

"Chips?" Jake yelled.

"Nothing for me." Chase glanced up. "You?"

"No. Thanks." I tried to gather my thoughts again. "You know I care about you."

"Wings?"

I glared at Jake. "Will you please stop that? I'm trying to have an important conversation."

The tavern keeper shrugged his broad shoulders and laughed, making his little belly jiggle. "Sorry, Jessie. Go on."

The moment was totally spoiled. I grabbed Chase's hand and pulled him out of the tavern to a bench outside. It was one of the few spots in the Village where a large tree had been planted. I sat down beneath its gold-red leaves and asked Chase to join me. I *dared* Jake to walk out the tavern door with our beer before we were done talking.

"What's the problem?" I got up and paced the cobblestones as soon as Chase sat down. "Aren't you happy to see me? I waited by the gate for you for a long time. Where were you?"

"You didn't say what time you were coming. I tried to keep a lookout for you, but I had other things I had to do."

I thought back to my last e-mail. He could be right. "I'm sorry. It's been really hard coming up with the time to be down here during Halloween. I'm exhausted. I was hoping you'd understand."

"I do. Or at least I *did*."

"You mean Henry?" I guffawed. That's allowed in Renaissance Village. Unfortunately, the rest of the modern world has all but outlawed a good guffaw. "You know he doesn't hold a candle to you, right? He just saw you coming and wanted to cause trouble. Believe me, that tarted-up Craft Guild dandy means nothing to me."

Chase jumped to his feet and picked me up, turning both of us around until I thought I might vomit. But it was good. We were okay. "You know I would've made that guy joust me for you, right? And I don't mean one of those jousts for a flower or a handkerchief. I mean a joust to the *death*."

I eyed him carefully. Was he losing it? Sometimes the playacting in the Village got to people and they couldn't differentiate real from Renaissance anymore.

"Just kidding. But I *am* the bailiff. I would've demanded

vegetable justice for the fraud perpetrated on my heart." He shrugged and smiled at me before giving me a long, slow welcome-back kiss. "That was good. Let's head over to the dungeon. The Village can live without us, at least for the rest of the day."

We stayed glued to one another as we covered the ground from Brewster's to the dungeon, kissing and panting the whole way. I vaguely heard a few people call out to us. Bo Peep had misplaced one of her sheep again and wanted Chase's help finding it. Little Jack Horner had his thumb stuck in a pie and was looking for help getting it out. The Lovely Laundry Ladies, all garbed in black now, wiggled their pieces of laundry at us.

It seemed to take forever to cross the King's Highway and get past the line of visitors waiting at the privies before we finally reached the dungeon. Chase put his key in the door and kicked it open without ever losing lip-lock. Now *that's* talent. But before we could step inside, there was a terrible screech from within the two-story building.

"What was that?" I looked up before the scream had dribbled down to painful-sounding pleas for help. "Is that in here?"

The dungeon where Chase lives and dispenses court has a series of almost-authentic cells that wind through the bottom floor. Outside are the stocks where visitors (and sometimes residents) can pay to throw vegetables at someone else. That's vegetable justice. The upstairs of the dungeon is Chase's apartment. Kind of small, but in this case location was everything.

"That's my banshee. You like her?"

I shuddered. "It's *awful*. How did you do it?"

"I didn't. I got it off eBay. Sounds creepy, huh?"

"You could say that. I suppose the whole Village will sound like that by tomorrow."

"You bet. Wait till you see all the stuff we have going on. Dead Queen Elizabeth will be riding through the Village twice a day, her ghostly features gazing out at us from her carriage window."

I supposed this was what I'd worked so hard to accomplish. I wanted to be here for the Haunted Village and here I was. Chase closed the door behind us, and I followed him up the winding staircase to the dungeon's tower.

The amorous mood had dissipated with the banshee's wail. We sat around and talked about all the tricks and treats visitors could expect to find and what had been going on during the weeks we'd been apart. I wasn't mad at Chase for the abrupt change. I felt the same. But I thought we might have to disconnect the banshee if we were ever to be in a romantic mood again.

"I got something for you!" He jumped up from his chair and went to the table in his cramped kitchen area. It was fine for a man who thought making Pop-Tarts was home cooking. Not being much of a cook myself, I never encouraged him to feel any different. I was excited about the gift. The spontaneity was contagious. What could it be? I'm not much of a jewelry person, but a jeweled dagger with a sheath would be nice. No well-dressed Renaissance lady should be without one.

The wrapping paper was a brown bag with *Ace Hardware* printed on one side. He handed me the package then hovered anxiously, waiting for me to open it.

I smiled and took the pair of elbow-length gloves from the bag.

"They're flame retardant. Maybe you won't get burned so much when you start working with the hot glass. Do you like them?"

It wasn't a jeweled dagger, but Chase's handsome face looked so worried that I had to love his gift. "They're wonderful! Exactly what I need. Thank you." I kissed him slowly and all those warm thoughts that had brought us to the dungeon returned with a vengeance. He picked me up and was heading toward the bed when his radio went off.

He started to ignore it. I could see him struggling with the decision. Unfortunately, it was one of those stupid radios that starts talking without anyone flipping or pressing anything.

"Chase, we need you over at the Caravan Stage. We've got a group of rowdy young guys on stage with the dancing girls. Chase? Can you hear me?"

I looked at him. He looked back at me. It was his job and the Village depended on him. "Don't worry about it." I almost meant it. "I should go over and check everything out with Roger before tomorrow anyway. I'll meet you back here."

"I'm sorry." He kissed me. "I'll make it up to you. No banshee when we come back."

I agreed to that and some pasta from a new restaurant, Polo's Pasta. We left the dungeon together, splitting up at the tree swing next door, to go our separate ways.

Life was good. Even the fairies (dressed like wraiths) made for a feeling of happiness. Usually they were the ones wearing less than anyone else. But for Halloween, they were like the rest of us, covered from neck to toe.

I managed to get past the Three Chocolatiers and Fabulous Funnels without buying anything, even though the scents were wonderful. I waved to one of my previous teachers, Gullah basket weaver Mary Shift. She was sitting on her steps across the way from the Glass Gryphon, a sweetgrass basket balanced on her knees.

Before I had a chance to go and talk to her, Henry grabbed me and brought me quickly into the glass shop. "There you are! I knew you'd change your mind." He kind of whirled me into a corner between some glass horses and ships. He put one hand on either side of me and stood there, grinning like the Village idiot.

"I think you should move," I told him. "We don't want to break anything."

"That's what I like, a feisty woman! I couldn't wait to see you again."

I was about to show him what I'd learned in self-defense class a few years back when Roger came into the display area. "Jessie! I'm glad you changed your mind. There's so much to show you."

Henry moved aside but not before his predatory eyes told me we'd be back in the same circumstance again sometime. *Bring it on*, I mouthed at him before going to join Roger. No way was this loathsome Lothario going to ruin *my* time in the Village. Roger was right. I needed to learn enough in the next few weeks to use in my dissertation. Henry wasn't going to get in my way.

"I'm glad to see you're dressed sensibly," Roger said. "We have to wear very plain, craftsman type of clothes here. Everything we wear while we're working with the glass should be made of cotton or leather, and no open-toed shoes. Blowing glass and even doing these ornamentals can be dangerous. I see you've brought some gloves. That's a good idea. You can't wear them out here for demonstrations, but you can wear them in back with the furnace when we get it working again."

"I can't wear jeans and a sweater when I'm working," I explained. "Portia would only give me a witch's costume."

"I'll talk to her and we'll get something set up, even if you have to dress like a boy." Roger shook his head. "I voted for this idea about Halloween. Visitors are always a little slack this time of year. Now I'm not so sure. Some people seem to have gone overboard with it. I hear there's a falconry show where the falcon actually flies into the audience and pretends to pluck out someone's eye. It's a resident planted in the audience, of course. But it's pretty gross just the same."

Henry laughed. "My uncle's a little old-fashioned, Jessie. He thinks Halloween should be all pumpkins and black cats. I heard they're doing the jousts to the death complete with fake blood."

I shrugged. "None of it's real. I guess it doesn't matter much what they do."

"But some of it is real, at least lately," Henry said. "Like Death dying today."

"Now that was an extreme circumstance and a terrible accident, I'm sure." Roger said it like he was reading a press release. "This hot weather can get the best of anyone."

That and a little rebar. We walked over to one of the workbenches where I'd be learning my craft. "So what will I do first?"

"First of all, I want to make sure you understand that you won't be a certified glass worker when you finish this apprenticeship. It took me more than ten years to become a master glassblower, and that's only in the states. In Europe, it's much more difficult. There's a formal program a person has to pass before earning the title."

"I understand. And you know what I'm looking for out of this. So where do we start?"

"Good enough." Roger nodded. "We'll be doing lampwork while you're here, unless we get the furnace working. We'll start with the basics. This will be your workbench. Keep it clean and free of unused material. Remember you'll be working with flame and it can be dangerous."

"Yes it can," Henry added. "You can look at either of our arms and see what he means."

Henry rolled up his sleeves. Roger did the same in grand dramatic fashion. Both of them had scars on top of scars crisscrossed from their hands to their shoulders. It was pretty effective as a safety lesson. It might be manly to be scarred that way, but the only scar I wanted was a pirate tattoo.

Roger had just begun explaining about the process of removing stresses introduced into glassware during the glassblowing process when the door to the shop flew open and the Black Dwarf all but fell across the threshold.

"Someone help! Call the bailiff. There's another death in the Village!"

Three

"Where at?" Roger helped the Black Dwarf to his feet. "I saw him near the fountain at the Hawk Stage. Is the bailiff here?"

"No, but I used to be a police officer. Lead the way." Roger sounded suitably impressive using his TV police voice. I wondered if they taught all officers to talk that way.

"We'll just stay here, and I'll help Jessie with whatever she needs." Henry leaned toward me and smiled in an unwholesome manner.

"No way! I'm going, too." I took out my cell phone (I was allowed to have one on me since I wasn't technically working yet). "I'll give Chase a call as we're going."

"I don't need Chase!" Roger ran out the door before me. "I have years of experience at this kind of thing. Chase is a pretty face they set up here to *pretend* they have some law enforcement."

I'd bet he wouldn't be willing to say that to Chase's *pretty* face.

Chase finally answered his phone as we ran by Pope's Pots and veered around the long lines of people waiting at the privies. "Come to the Hawk Stage. There's another death."

"I'll be right there. Have you called 911 yet?"

"No. Roger's on top of it."

"Great."

I thought maybe some of the crowd was there to gawk at the dead person, but once we got past the privies, the street was relatively clear. The Hawk Stage was occupied by another bird of prey show where the trainer was trying to get a bald eagle to come down from a parapet. He wasn't having the best of luck despite holding out some kind of meat in his gloved hand. The audience sat craning their necks, watching the bird. There was nothing unusual going on here.

Next door, kids were climbing on elephants and camels for a ride around the animal enclosure. A group of teenagers dressed like knights were waiting their turn, laughing as the elephant lifted sand with his trunk and sprayed himself and his riders.

"I don't see anything." Roger turned to the Black Dwarf, who'd come up panting behind us at that moment. "Where did you see this death?"

The Dwarf pointed toward the fountain. (I call it the Lady Fountain because the water is gushing up and down some poor Renaissance woman's gown. Who'd think of such a thing? It makes me uncomfortable every time I see it.)

"He was right there, big as day. Bigger than the old Death. I don't think there was *anything* under his black robe. His scythe was *huge*. He started to swing it toward me, but I ran away. He could be anywhere by now." The Black Dwarf seemed sincere in his fright. His little white goatee trembled, and his eyes were huge beneath his black stocking cap, which swept the ground behind him.

I could see Roger was angry at chasing an apparition rather than finding another dead body. "You might've mentioned that, Marcus. We ran here in this heat for a costumed character." Roger started walking back toward the Glass Gryphon.

Chase came tearing up at that moment. He could really move considering he had serious muscles and a broad chest. Most runners are skinny, but not him. No wonder everyone said he'd turned down all kinds of scholarships in college to play football. A thrill of pure delight ran through me when I saw his sweaty face. "What's going on?" he asked.

"Nothing." Roger kept walking. "But if there had been, I could've handled it. Jessie doesn't have to call you every time something happens."

"I *am* the bailiff. That's my job." Chase smiled at me quickly then turned back to scowl at Roger.

"I *was* the bailiff before you showed up," Roger reminded him. "I've had *real* law enforcement training. What've you had? A few weeks riding around with Myrtle Beach's finest?"

The two men, totally unequally matched, advanced on one another. The Black Dwarf went to hide behind a flower cart being pushed by a comely maiden dressed in what looked like cobwebs. *Hmm, where'd she get that costume?*

Putting my costume envy aside, I stepped between the two men and held out my hands. They both walked right into them and pushed toward each other. "Come on, boys. There's no point in fighting over who gets to see the dead body first."

Chase's head jerked up. "Where's the dead body?"

"There isn't one," I told him. "It's a figure of speech. The Black Dwarf told us he saw another death. We assumed he meant another dead person. But I guess he just meant they already gave that poor dead guy's role to someone else. It's awful, I know."

Roger laughed. "That's right. Nothing to see here, Bailiff. Go back to your dungeon and find some tomatoes for the next vegetable justice."

"Sorry." I ignored Roger. What was wrong with him anyway? He was usually a pain in the butt. This was worse than usual.

"That's okay." Chase glared at Roger one more time. "Are you finished at the glass shop?"

"Almost. I'll meet you back at the dungeon."

I could tell Chase left reluctantly. Roger was already down to Fabulous Funnels. I had to run to catch up with him. There was something going on that wasn't right, and I knew I wouldn't be happy until I found out what it was. "That was intense." I matched his stride since I'm a few inches taller than he is and I have size twelve feet. They make for better balance. "Is something wrong that I should know?"

He glared at me, never losing his stride. "Why don't you ask your boyfriend? He's the one who took my job as bailiff."

"But that was years ago," I reminded him. "You can't still be that angry about it."

"Yes I can. There's no reason for me *not* to be angry about it." He ducked into the Glass Gryphon and I followed.

Henry was sitting at one of the workbenches using a burner to heat a glass rod that he was applying to what looked like the beginning of a dragon. "So you found another dead body? Uncle Roger, I think you should've told me how dangerous this place is. I might not have come."

"Leave then!" Roger started up the stairs that led to his apartment above the shop. "I don't care."

I heard the door slam above us and looked at Henry. I didn't want to encourage him, but I needed to know what was going on. If things were as bad as they seemed, maybe it would be better if I worked as a flower pusher or even a drudge. My time here was short. I wanted it to be educational and fun. Foregoing the educational part, since I couldn't get an apprenticeship on this short notice, I could at least have fun. Maybe Chase could hire me as some kind of aid to the Bailiff. I could even put people into the stocks for him.

"He's been like this since I got here." Henry glanced toward the ceiling. "He doesn't talk to me. I don't know what's wrong with him."

"Maybe you should ask him."

"Maybe *you* should ask him. I don't really care." He looped the hot glass into an elegant tail for the dragon. I didn't like Henry, but I had to admire his artistic hand.

"But he's *your* uncle." I kept watching like I was hypnotized by his movements. The dragon's body was already formed, but Henry was adding detail. I wondered if I'd be able to do anything like that with the short amount of time I'd have here.

"And I'm watching his shop here and opening a second shop for him near the Pavilion. I think that's enough for me."

I couldn't think of anything else to say. My eyes continued to follow his movements. He had wonderful hands. His timing was perfect, never allowing the hot glass to go anywhere he didn't want it to go. I could understand why demonstrations like this drew a big crowd.

"Would you like to try it?" He looked up at me through his safety glasses.

"No. I'd only make a mess of it. I've read a lot about it, but I haven't tried it yet." I said no but I really meant yes. I'm sure my eyes gave me away.

"Come on. It's simple once you get the hang of it. Stand right over here by me. I'll guide you. You'll be fine."

Without thinking of the consequences, I did as he suggested and moved to stand between his parted legs and the workbench. He put one arm down so I could position myself in such a way that his arms were around me with the burner and the glass in front of us.

"Here, you hold this." He handed me the glass rod he was using to detail the dragon. "I'll hold the dragon and we'll manipulate the glass together. See that crest I'm starting on his head? That's where we'll work, building it up."

The heat from the burner was intense, like standing beside a small campfire. I couldn't move back since I was already practically in Henry's lap. I was afraid to look at the burner or the glass without safety goggles. In all, it was a bad position to be in. And then I managed to burn myself as he guided my hand. I yelped and dropped the rod, which, of course, shattered all over the floor.

"Look out!" he called too late as I tried to catch the glass rod.

"I'm sorry." Turning fast, I accidentally pushed his other hand and the beautiful dragon ended up on the floor, too. I was ready to cry. I had destroyed the dragon and burned myself in less than five seconds. Imagine if I'd had a whole day.

"It's okay." Henry turned off the burner and removed his goggles. He put his arms around me. I was already in a vulnerable position. Being Henry, he made the most of it. We went from him patting my back to kissing me and nuzzling my neck in less time than it took for me to kill the dragon.

"Now that's *hot!*" he said with an evil glitter in his eyes.

The shop door opened, and I prayed it was some unsuspecting visitor who would only imagine what had gone on in the last few minutes. But I'd left my lucky shamrock at home, so it was Chase. "I thought maybe you'd be ready to go. I was making my rounds, so I stopped by," he said.

Henry made a big deal about moving his legs so I could get out from behind the workbench. Honestly, if there hadn't been glass all over the floor, I would've climbed *under* the bench rather than go through that elaborate charade. I couldn't say it wasn't what it looked like, especially not in front of Henry, who seemed intent on ruining my love life. I thought I should save the long version of the explanation for when Chase and I were alone. Maybe it wouldn't make any sense, but at least I wouldn't be pleading my case in front of Henry. It wouldn't take much more for me to hate this man.

Chase didn't say anything as he walked out the door. Henry waved and grinned as I closed the door to the shop behind me. What had I gotten myself into this time? Roger was a surly ass, and his nephew was a pain in that same general area. How was I going to learn anything about glassmaking with the two of them?

The Village was closing down around us as Chase and I cut across the King's Highway toward the dungeon. Already there were signs that things were changing over for Halloween. A few shops were decorated with black bunting. It made them look like they were in mourning. Jack-o'-lanterns were glowing in the twilight.

A group of vampires (once the king's acrobats) walked past us with a nod at Chase. A few fairies had already donned their wraith costumes. There was no flitting, thank goodness, although they were a little pitiful in their gray shrouds. I could almost feel sorry for them and forget all their evil tricks—and their flirting with Chase.

That thought brought me back to the man at my side. He was walking right next to me but hadn't looked at me since we left the Glass Gryphon. I tried being cute and sassy, nudging him with my hip and winking when he looked my way. "So I hope you managed to turn off the banshee today."

"Yeah."

"Great! I'm looking forward to tonight."

"Jessie—"

"Chase, he means nothing to me."

"That makes me feel *so* much better." He kicked an empty popcorn container instead of picking it up and putting it in the trash. He was *really* in a foul mood.

"That's not exactly what I mean."

"So he *does* mean something to you?" He stopped walking and confronted me right outside the Mother Goose Pavilion. The old goose keeper was finishing off one of her tales for the last group of children that evening. Although it was only around six P.M., it was getting dark. That felt a little weird to me since I usually spend my time here in the summer, when it doesn't get dark until nine.

I was thinking of the past summer when Chase and I had finally gotten together after years of just being friends. It was so much more than any summer fling I'd ever had at the Village. I hated to see that look of betrayal in his beautiful dark eyes.

"I just met the man, Chase," I said, trying to reason with him. "How could he mean anything to me? He's good-looking and he's got great hands, I'll give him that much. But what else does he have? He's opening a shop at the beach for Roger. So what?"

"I hope that was supposed to make me feel better. Can't you see what's happening? Henry knows we're together and he wants to split us up. He doesn't care about you. Hell, he probably doesn't even think you're attractive!"

That kind of pushed a few bad buttons for me. "We're just not communicating. We both know what Henry is. I know I could've handled the situation better. I don't know what I was thinking."

"Or not thinking," he muttered.

"Excuse me? Are you the same Chase Manhattan I saw kissing Princess Isabel after the joust last summer? You knew I was standing there and you let her lip-lock you. I thought I was going to have to get something to pry her off your face."

"You knew why that happened."

"And I forgave you." I lifted my head and looked him right in the eye. "Now you have to forgive me."

"There's nothing to forgive." He started walking again. "Like you said, we both know what Henry's all about. Just try to stay away from him while you're here."

I kept up easily with his rapid strides. Being tall isn't good for much, but I can walk faster than most men. "That's fine. But you have to say the words."

"What words?"

"What words indeed, Sir Bailiff?" Da Vinci, one of our Village artists, dropped into our conversation as we were walking by him. "A picture is worth many words, my friend. Perhaps I could assist you by drawing the picture in your heart for your lovely lady."

The short, old guy (at least I think he's really old—either that or he's always in character) smiled at me and held his pen at the ready to create a picture of what Chase wanted to say. His robes were still gray and white. I wondered what he'd be wearing tomorrow. He was a member of the Artist

Guild, which prided itself on its division from the Craft Guild I belonged to. Artists, it seemed, did not want their work confused with crafts, although I have a hard time defining the difference.

"I don't think the lady would like to see the picture in my heart right now, Sam. Maybe later." Chase nodded to him then kept walking.

"Methinks Sir Bailiff is in a foul mood, good lady. Perhaps a glass of ale might be helpful. One never knows the trouble another has until one has sat down with him over ale."

I didn't know what to say to that philosophy. I smiled, nodded, and ran after Chase. There are all kinds here in the Village. The monks at the bakery based their philosophy on bread. The pirates that sailed Mirror Lake set their sails by the rites of pillage. I guessed Da Vinci was into ale.

"Wait, Chase!" I had almost caught up with him when Lonnie came out from behind the tree swing, near one of the old huts, and stopped to chat. *Great!* Just what I needed.

"Hey, Chase. I've been looking for you everywhere, man. I heard something went on by the Hawk Stage today. I hope it wasn't anything bad." Lonnie's beady little eyes lit up with hope as he shifted an enormous keg. It was hard for me to believe that little guy could carry something so heavy.

"No, nothing really happened. Thanks for stopping by. Where are you taking that keg?"

"I'm just taking it over to the Pleasant Pheasant for a party. If you need me for something, I'll be back in a few minutes."

"No, that's okay. Enjoy yourself. We're done for the day." Chase walked up to the dungeon door and opened it. Immediately, the banshee began to wail.

"Oh, yeah." Lonnie laughed. "I noticed that was broken this afternoon, so I fixed it for you. Nice, huh?"

Chase put his head against the door. I knew exactly how he felt. It had been a bad day.

"Look, I'm going to get my stuff," I told him quietly. Lonnie still stood there, taking it all in. Tomorrow the Black Dwarf would be announcing it all over the Village. "It's been that kind of day. I'll be right back, and then we'll have some dinner and talk. Okay?"

"That sounds good." Chase took my hand. "I'll walk over there with you."

"I'll be fine. Maybe you can silence the banshee again. Let's eat at the Pleasant Pheasant, huh? I hear they have a full keg tonight."

He laughed. "All right. Hurry back."

As I started to walk away, Chase yelled out, "I forgive you."

It made me feel better. There were always going to be complications with a man like Chase. Maybe even with a woman like me. Being here made me philosophic. The Village might not be real as far as existing in the past, but it gave me a sense of all those lives that went on before mine. It's what I love best about history—that feeling of connection with those people who have lived and died for generations before me.

Only a trickle of visitors were walking out the main gate past the turrets where the minstrels played and sang their good-bye songs. Flower girls tossed petals at their tired feet, and ladies of the court bid them adieu. Tomorrow night, the first official night of Halloween, Renaissance Village would be open until midnight. The mist would cling to the streetlights and pool in the shadows. Shopkeepers would hang their lanterns in the doorways to welcome visitors.

God, I love this place!

I walked quickly through the large visitors' parking area to the smaller parking area for residents. It seemed strange and almost spooky being here this time of year, and I hadn't even seen good, dead Queen Bess drive by yet. The summer brought the visitors from the beach and the hotels along the Grand Strand with their countless accents and languages from all over the world. The fall would be the same, I supposed, but the difference in the air was more than just a few trees shedding their leaves. It was a good idea to deck the Village out for the holiday.

I picked up my two bags (no point in bringing more since I'd be wearing a costume every day) and locked my car again. Plenty of other cars remained in the residents' lot, but the visitor parking was empty on this side. The only way into the Village was through the main gate, even for residents. The single entrance was supposed to cut down on shoplifting, but Chase didn't find that to be the case. Occasionally, someone got in through a hole in the eight-foot-high wall that enclosed the Village just as one would have in Renaissance times.

I walked back thinking about Chase, swinging my bags and deciding which cute nightie I would flaunt that evening. A loud baying sound caught my attention and made the hairs on the back of my neck stand up.

It sounded like a wolf. Of course, I assured myself, this was Renaissance Village. What did I expect? There was bound to be a werewolf or two here for Halloween. Just like Chase's banshee. It wasn't real. No doubt the last time anyone had seen a real wolf in this starkly urban area was when Sir Walter Raleigh first got here.

Still, I walked a little faster. I heard the wolf again and laughed out loud. "Good one!" I said for the benefit of anyone who might hear me. I was completely alone, but the jaunty tone seemed to help.

I could see the gate from the parking lot now. All the day's visitors were gone, as were the minstrels, who had probably set out in hopes of free food from one of the many pubs and restaurants that served the residents leftovers after hours.

The shadows grew longer and deeper as I neared the gate. I walked even faster, though my reasonable assistant professor's brain told me this was all being set up for the visitors. Wasn't this what I'd worked so hard to be part of? And here I was, about to be in the Renaissance version of *A Nightmare on Elm Street*.

A wolf (I swear it sounded like a different wolf) howled again, and I noticed a full moon rising over the castle and Great Hall, visible from the parking lot.

That was it. I clutched my bags and ran for the gate. I wasn't sure what was going to save me once I got there, but being inside the Village wall seemed safer than being out here alone in the parking area.

I pushed open the heavy portal that would be locked for the night at some point, and a hand came down on my shoulder. I'm sure my scream made a few other residents pause and wonder if it was real or theater.

Four

"Hey! I didn't mean to scare you." Detective Almond cleared his throat and moved his hand. "I'm looking for Manhattan. It seems I was wrong about death stalking the Village."

"What are you talking about?" My heart was still pounding and I was breathing hard. Terror does not become me.

He pointed behind me. "Death stalking the Village, like the poster says. Only in real life."

I turned around to study the recently hung poster, which said that Death would be stalking Renaissance Village. There were other references to ghosts, goblins, witches, and demons. I hadn't noticed it before.

"Don!" Grigg, an ex–Myrtle Beach police officer turned Village resident, greeted his former boss. "I got your message. What's the problem?"

Grigg was looking very much a part of the Village.

He'd started as an undercover officer for the police but had enjoyed the Village so much he'd decided to stay. He'd spent some time as the Piper's son but had evidently graduated to become one of the pirates. He wore an eye patch, bandana, and shiny gold earring. I wouldn't have recognized him if I hadn't seen him with Detective Almond.

"Grigg. There you are." He looked his former officer up and down and pulled at his pants, which always seemed to be sliding down. "You look like you've gone native, boy. I need some help here. Are you feeling up to it?"

"I'm a pirate now." Grigg showed him the required pirate tattoo on his right arm. "Where's Chase? I'm sure he'd be glad to help you out."

"That's just the problem." Detective Almond glanced around, saw me, but continued anyway. "Manhattan is a fine young man, but he doesn't have your experience. He needs a hand here, Grigg. There's likely been a murder."

Grigg and I exchanged looks. "You mean one of the heatstroke victims?" Grigg asked.

"No, I mean that tall boy that was pretending to be Death or whatever. The ME's preliminary showed the chances are good it wasn't an accident after all."

I heard a footstep before I saw Chase. He didn't look happy. "And why aren't you telling me about this, Detective? I'm responsible for what happens here. I had to put Grigg in the dungeon twice last month for stealing."

"Stealing?" He stared at his former officer. "You've been taking things that don't belong to you?"

Grigg laughed. "It's all part of living here, Don. I know you don't understand, but it's a great life. The Merry Men steal toaster ovens and the occasional loaf of bread from the bakery. The pirates steal more personal things, items closer to the heart."

"Like underwear from the dancing girls at the Caravan

Stage," Chase continued. "And garters from the Lovely Laundry Ladies. Sometimes the wings right off a fairy."

Grigg burst out with a hearty combination laugh and pirate yell. "That's what we do! It makes the place worth living in."

Detective Almond shook his head. "You people are all crazy! If workers are stealing, Manhattan, why aren't you turning them in?"

"We handle our own internal problems, sir," Chase said. "I only give you visitors who create a problem."

"That's why Chase is your man." Grigg clapped his ex-boss on the shoulder. "Avast, ye landlubbers! We set sail at high moon."

We all watched Grigg dart away and blend into the shadows. Garbage trucks collecting the day's trash and electricians setting up new lights for the Halloween season were moving through the streets, making his departure even harder to track.

Chase looked back at Detective Almond. "If you'd like to join Jessie and me, we were about to have some dinner at Peter's Pub. We can talk over whatever you like there."

"Peter's?" I wondered what happened to the Pleasant Pheasant.

"The Pheasant's out of food already." Chase shrugged, taking my bags from me. "It's the extras. Everyone has to be fed."

"But does everyone have to eat *together*?" I linked my arm in his and gave him what I hoped was a meaningful look. After all, this was our first dinner together in a month. Surely we deserved some alone time.

"Jessie!" My brother Tony decided to join what was becoming a parade through the Village to Peter's Pub. "I didn't know you were here yet. You could've called."

I noticed his arm was looped around a slender wraith

whose lipstick was way too red to be on her pale face. That never changed. Whether they were fairies or wraiths, Tony was bound to have a female with him at all times.

"Sissy, this is my sister Jessie. Jessie, Sissy. Sissy's the sexiest little wraith in the Village." Tony gave her an extra squeeze at the thought and Sissy giggled. "Where are you guys headed? Maybe we could all have dinner together."

So Tony, Sissy, and Detective Almond all fell in line behind me and Chase. "This isn't exactly what I had in mind for tonight," I told Chase.

"Me either. I was wondering what was taking you so long."

I told him about the weird wolf howling while I was in the parking lot.

"I heard it, too. I guess it's some kind of Halloween thing. It's going to be a strange couple of months. Stranger than usual."

We trooped into Peter's together and managed to find a table big enough for all of us. There was no menu since the food was free. Whatever was left over from the day's visitors was what was offered after the Village closed each night. Tonight's fare was some kind of stew with bread from the bakery and apple pie, and there was cold ale to wash it all down. A good supper, even considering the crowd.

"What happened to the guy playing Death that made you suspicious?" Chase asked Detective Almond.

"The ME says it's the angle the rebar entered your dead man." He belched and excused himself. "Also the force with which it entered. There are hundreds of smudged fingerprints on the rebar, but there are two or three clear prints we might be able to lift. That might tell us something else. I guess it *was* suspicious from the beginning, given that weird crap written on the dead man's chest."

No one laughed, so Detective Almond went on to

explain his attempt at humor. "Get it? Dead man's chest? Pirates? Lord, you people have no sense of humor."

As if on cue, the door to the pub blew open bringing in a gust of rain and cooler air. It left behind the scent of the ocean, only a few miles away, even after one of the waiters closed the door.

"I guess we should get going." Tony tickled Sissy and they started kissing. "I wouldn't want my little wraith to get wet."

"Yeah." Detective Almond lumbered to his feet, tossing some change down on the old oak table for the waiter. "I guess this party's over. Just keep your eyes open, Manhattan. It may be nothing, or it may be something more."

The big pub door blew open again. How did they get something like that to happen? I was amazed and scared at the same time. I knew no one had a secret button that made the door fly open every time a dramatic statement was made. It was as if the Village *knew* what was going on.

"I'm really tired." I stood up and glanced at Chase. "I have to go to bed before I start wondering if the stuff around here is real."

"I'm right behind you," he said with a grin.

"If I could have a word." Detective Almond leveraged himself between us as the rain began to fall more steadily on the roof of the pub.

"Go ahead. I'm going on to the dungeon," I said to Chase. "I'll be fine. You disconnected the banshee, right?"

"She's gone." He snickered, then sobered. "No, really. There shouldn't be any more howling or evil laughter. I'll bring your bags."

I saw the look in his beautiful eyes and my heart responded by pounding faster. Even though the day had been a total mess, the night was going to be perfect. With that exciting, yet soothing assumption blanketing me from

the real truth of life in Renaissance Village, I ran out
through the rain to the dungeon, only a short walk away.

But what a walk! The black bunting was everywhere.
There were glowing eyes peering through holes in the brick
wall that surrounded the Village. A group of laughing
vampires wearing long black capes ran by me as I passed
the Dutchman's Stage.

Good Queen Bess, her white face staring at me through
the glass window of her black carriage, rattled by the privies. I don't know where they found such a faithful replica of
a funeral carriage from the 1500s, but it was frighteningly
realistic. What made it even worse was that they had somehow managed to make the two horses that pulled it look as
though they were headless.

It was awful, terrifying, and would probably increase
the visitors to the Village by several thousand or more in
the next few weeks. I'd been to Disney World and Knott's
Berry Farm at Halloween. Neither one had anything on
Renaissance Village. I was proud to be part of it.

Soaked by the time I reached the dungeon, I opened the
door to run inside and was met by the banshee. After hearing the wolf in the parking lot and seeing headless horses, I
couldn't help but jump at the banshee screams. How was it
that Chase could be so incompetent in this matter? Maybe I
was wrong about what was going to happen tonight.

Ten minutes later, Chase came whistling up the cobblestone street with a bag in each hand. I was sitting in the tree
swing as he opened the dungeon door and the banshee wailed
for him, too. He swore and ducked inside for a moment
before he came back out and looked around. "Jessie?"

"I'm not going in there with that thing." I twisted the
swing that hung from the old oak tree that had somehow
managed to survive everything this land had gone through
between being an Air Force base and then the Village.

"Obviously you can't control her like you thought you could. She and I can't stay in the dungeon together."

He walked up to me and pushed back the swathe of wet brown hair that had fallen into my face. "Let me make it up to you. She doesn't mean anything to me. You're the only lady in my life."

I looked up at him through the steady rain and felt that excitement again, despite the banshee that wanted to come between us. "I'll give you one chance. After that, I'm staying with Debby. She may not be as exciting, but at least she doesn't scream when I open the door."

Chase swept me off the swing and into his arms where I lay helpless against his broad chest. Oh, the fantasies I could weave with, or without, the Village.

The next morning, the sky was clear and the air cool. There was a faint smell of wood smoke billowing through the streets. Autumn had reached the Village at last, and the residents were happy to see it after the long, hot summer.

"Make sure you wear your gloves." Chase kissed me on the lips then kissed each of my hands. "I don't want to see burns instead of grass cuts this fall. Burning is a bad thing. And don't let me catch you anywhere near Henry's legs again. Inside or outside. The next time I won't go so easy on you."

I smiled in a dreamy, goofy way. It had been an exceptional night the likes of which I knew we might not share again. No one had come yelling about some problem they needed Chase to resolve, and the banshee had stayed asleep. Chase was all mine and I was all his for a full, wonderful eight hours. "Don't worry. If Henry tries anything again, he won't have any legs left."

"That's what I like to hear! Do you have your cup?"

I held up the cup that meant I could get free drinks all day, a Village standard for residents. "I'm going to try to have lunch around noon. Maybe at Fabulous Funnels. Maybe you could be there, too."

"I'll try." He clipped his mug to the black belt around his waist. This morning the Bailiff was in Halloween black with a touch of red at his throat.

"If you'd get me a radio like yours, we could talk during the day."

"If you get a job with security, I can do that. Until then, we'll have to do the best we can." He kissed my forehead. "I'll see you later."

I was late as usual, with Chase and breakfast and everything. I still had to turn in my witch's costume and pick up something made of cotton to stay in line with Roger's decree. I was surprised there wasn't a long line at the costume shop. The Village wasn't open to visitors yet, which probably worked to my advantage. From what I could see, the residents were already decked out in their evil attire.

Portia, of course, wasn't thrilled to hear I needed a different costume. She took the witch's black dress with a shake of her head. "Now we're going to be short one witch. How's that going to look? And what's wrong with the costume?"

"I need cotton that doesn't have billowy sleeves or a full skirt," I told her again. "I'm going to be working with hot glass and flames. Roger doesn't think the combination would be very safe."

"All right. I think I have exactly what you need." She took out a green costume that was in two parts. "This should do it."

"What is it?" I looked at it but couldn't decide which part went where.

"It's a demon costume. I didn't give you the mask. It's made of cotton. No billowy sleeves or skirt. Exactly what you need. Next?"

Since there was no one standing behind me, I decided to argue the point. I was going to have to spend a lot of time for the next few weeks in this costume, or one just like it. I *really* didn't want to be a demon. "Don't you have a Craft Guild costume for a man? Cotton trousers, shirt, boots. You know, something normal."

"We're not doing normal right now. Look around you." She gestured. "Does anything *look* normal?"

"Nothing ever looks normal around here, Portia." I leaned on the counter. "Couldn't you *please* find me something I can work in? I don't think a demon costume is going to cut it."

"Cheer up. You don't have to wear the red contacts that go with it. How's that for helping you out?" She leaned toward me. "I heard the man playing Death was murdered. What've you heard?"

"Can you get me a shirt and a pair of pants?"

"Maybe." She narrowed her eyes. "Come on. You're with Chase. You know what's happening."

That's all it took, I'm ashamed to say.

I spilled everything I knew for a pair of brown cotton britches I had to tie around my waist with a rope. I even made up a few things and got a peasant shirt that fit me closely. Portia threw in a hat, and I told her about things that *might* happen. She loves gossip, and she doesn't care where it comes from.

I took what I could get and hurried away. Portia waved before turning to share her news with the three seamstresses who worked on the costumes. It was worth it anyway. There's so much gossip all the time flying through the Village that there was no way of knowing how it would actually end up.

The main gate had just opened, and musicians had taken up their seats to serenade the first crowd of visitors. I could see by their werewolf, vampire, and Renaissance costumes that they were in the Halloween spirit. A few resident demons with red eyes wandered by, challenging each other to a duel. A group of witches ran through the street asking visitors if they were in need of a spell.

Other than that, it was the usual chaos of horses, sheep, and chickens mixed in with black-garbed fairy-tale folk playing in the streets. The Wandering Madman kept asking everyone he met if there was a bird on his head. The Pied Piper, dressed in deep purple (obviously he couldn't wear *black*), walked along playing his pipe, a group of adult-looking children following him.

I took a deep breath and smiled. It was good to be back.

Roger and Henry were waiting for me at the Glass Gryphon after I'd stopped and changed into my costume at Debby's since Chase was still working on the banshee problem. Henry went to talk with a few visitors while Roger sat me down behind the workbench again. "I want you to get a feel for all these tools, Jessie. You'll be using them shortly. You can move things around, left and right, however you feel comfortable."

I looked at all of the tools. Some I recognized. There was the hot glass rest, the lapping wheel, a tungsten pick, and a torch. I knew the torch could be moved around the glass, unlike a stationary burner. "Okay. I'm ready."

He laughed. "You're not, but we'll get you started anyway. First thing we're going to do is light up your torch. We're going to practice sealing or joining two pieces of glass together. It'll give you a feel for working with it. Just take these two pieces and use the torch to heat up the ends until you can fuse them."

I followed his instructions exactly and ignited the gas torch with a flint lighter. "How big should the flame be?"

"Should be less than an inch. You can leave it on at this level and put it in the holder over there while you do something else. But shut it off before you leave the bench."

He had me practice flame control by changing the setting on the gas and oxygen valves. I made a really large flame that I thought might've singed my eyebrows, and then I made a tiny little flame I could barely see. "How's that?"

"Pretty good. Now let's see what you can do with the glass."

I picked up the two clear glass rods and held them together in front of the torch. They heated up right away, and I dropped one.

"Not like that," he said, correcting me. "You'll have to hold it like this and melt the two pieces so the ends join. It'll get pretty hot, so you might have to hold it with this clamp. Henry and I are used to it, but a newbie like you will need some time. And remember to wear your goggles. The glass can shatter. I had some taken out of my eye once. Not a pleasant experience."

I moved the pieces of glass together so the ends would get hot. I was concentrating so hard on what I was doing that I didn't notice Henry bringing his two winsome lasses closer to my workbench until the first one said, "Ooh! That looks hot!"

I glanced up, making my safety glasses fall off my face. The glass rod heated up too much and melted on the bench. I moved the other rod quickly away, narrowly missing the torch held in the clamp. Unfortunately, my sleeve didn't miss the torch, which blazed a black hole in the fabric. Guess it could've been worse. At least I didn't have to stop, drop, and roll.

"Henry, move the visitors away from Jessie's work-bench. She doesn't need to be nervous."

"Sorry, Jessie." Henry smiled. "Let's come this way, ladies. Methinks there may be something of interest to you on yon table."

I watched them walk away, glad to see them go. That's the only problem with apprenticing in a shop that relies on the public watching what you do. Half the fun (and there-fore the appeal of the products) has to do with seeing how the craft is done. But the audience puts a lot of pressure on the apprentice.

I cleaned up my mess and checked to make sure only my sleeve was burned. I was going to go through a lot of shirts this way, but at least I wasn't hurt. I tried again with the glass rods, this time wearing the elbow-length gloves Chase had given me. I found out quickly that it was almost impossible to hold the glass and manipulate it wearing the gloves. Too bad, because they would've protected me.

I concentrated on the glass rods, watching the ends turn red as they heated up. I carefully put them together and hoped they'd seal. That would be one task down and about a billion more to go before I could create anything. I knew I wouldn't be able to make dragons or other pieces that required a lot of training, but I was looking forward to making something small and easy, like a cross or a boat. That didn't seem too much to ask by the end of October.

A few more visitors wandered into the shop, fondling expensive pieces of glass with careful hands. Roger and Henry waited on them while I continued sealing pieces of glass together. I was getting the hang of it, I thought, as the Royal Trumpets sounded outside announcing the entrance of the Royal Court.

Surprisingly, Princess Isabel entered with her entourage of ladies-in-waiting, fools, and jugglers who accompanied her everywhere she walked in the Village. "We have witnessed something strange outside your door, good craftsman." She approached Roger with a puzzled expression on her face. "Could you tell us what you are about with such a sign?"

Roger bowed low, edging Henry out in that department. "Of course, Your Highness. How may I assist you?"

The entire group made for the outside of the Glass Gryphon. On the side wall facing the King's Tarts shop was a gruesome warning written in what looked like blood. *"Death shall find thee,"* Roger read aloud. "I wonder how that got there?"

Five

"Obviously someone's idea of a good Halloween scare." Chase examined the writing on the wall. "Look around you, people. Everything is set up to make an impression."

"True, Sir Bailiff." Isabel managed to stand close enough to Chase so she could wrap her hands around his arm. "But with blood? We do not find this to be appealing and do not think the visitors will either."

"Blood?" Chase reached up and stuck his finger in the red lettering then licked it.

"Eww!" The action grossed Isabel totally out of character. "Chase, you shouldn't eat that stuff!"

"It's just strawberry jelly."

I stepped between the princess (who was about to lose her lunch) and my boyfriend, who said, "It's just a prank. Someone's watching us right now, having a good time."

Everyone turned to look at King Arthur, who was about to retrieve the sword from the stone on his usual quarter-hour basis. He glanced up to see all of us staring at him and stepped back. "What? You think this is an easy job and any of *you* could do it? You think I don't wish I had something with more meat, more passion? Well, never mind. You do what you're supposed to do, and I'll do what I have to do."

"Someone needs some oatmeal for breakfast." Roger shook his head and looked back at Chase. "So you think this is just a prank?"

"Or a bad decorating scheme," Chase replied. "Why? Do you think it's something more?"

"It seems odd to me that it would be on *my* shop," Roger continued. "I didn't really even know Ross that well. Why would it be here? Any other reports of the same thing around the Village?"

"None that I've heard. Look, Roger—"

"None on the dungeon, I bet."

"I'm sure it's not personal," Chase argued. "What's wrong with you anyway? It's like everything I say is wrong."

"*Everything* is personal." Roger stalked back into the shop. A few seconds later, he bellowed my name.

"I guess I better go," I told Chase. "Did you *know* that was strawberry jelly or did you just guess?"

"If you look close, you can see the little strawberry seeds. It didn't take a lot of brainpower. I'm sure we'll be seeing more of it since the press played that phrase up big time." He looked at the burn mark on my shirt. "You haven't been wearing your gloves."

"Bailiff!" Princes Isabel's voice was demanding and a little whiny. "We believe we shall need your escort back to the castle. We are feeling rather faint after this ordeal."

Chase bowed (at least ten visitors' cameras flashed) but smiled at me around her. "Yes, Your Highness."

Isabel put her delicate little hand on his forearm, and they fell in step as her courtiers hastened to go with them (more camera flashes here). I watched them go a little longer than I should have.

Henry was at my side with an evil smile on his face. "I bet Chase *hates* that."

"Stay out of it," I warned, walking past him to go back into the shop.

Roger was at my workbench. The look on his face boded no good for me. "You left your torch on to go outside, Jessie. That's inexcusable, even for a newbie. I'm afraid there's only one way to learn a good lesson on that."

"Uncle Roger, you can't put her in the stocks because she made a mistake."

"Shut up, Henry." Roger handed me a broom. "You'll have to spend the rest of the day cleaning up. That's what happens to lazy apprentices. An apprenticeship with an important craftsman is sought after, even fought over. A single mistake like this could cost your life."

I didn't want to spoil the theater, especially with a couple of visitors in the shop. I took the broom and the punishment without saying a word.

"I thought you told me the stocks were the punishment for making a mistake," Henry continued. "You made me spend a whole night out there when I first started."

Roger ignored him and went back to working on a large fairy with delicate wings. The two ladies followed Henry to his workbench and watched him start a new piece.

I swept toward the back door, glancing up occasionally to make sure no one was watching. Did Roger really make Henry spend the night in the stocks? Was Henry crazy enough to do it? It wouldn't surprise me. People here actually took care of a lot of problems that developed. I wouldn't have done it, but I wasn't inheriting Roger's glass shop either.

Sweeping the trash out the open door, I accompanied the little bits of hay and leaves that had found their way into the shop. The weather was glorious. Deep blue sky above me and cool breezes swaying through the small trees. It would be great if you could make glass figures outside. That torch was hot even when you stood away from it.

There was a smaller building behind the glass shop. I decided to check it out and found it was used as a supply area. The broken furnace was in there. There was also an oven that was used for annealing. I'd read about the process during my research before coming down here. The process took out the stresses, tiny fractures in the glass that happened when the glassmaker worked with it. I'd hoped to use an annealer. But not while I was in the doghouse. I had to admit it was careless to leave the torch on. I'd remember next time.

"Hello, Jessie." Master Archer Simmons from the Feathered Shaft walked by and smiled at me. "Another apprenticeship?"

"I'm learning glassmaking this time," I told him. He made me long for the familiar, for something I was good at. When I had been his apprentice I'd done very well almost from the beginning with making and shooting arrows. I had a feeling working with glass was going to be harder.

"Good luck to you. I hope to see you at dinner one night, even though we'd be crossing guilds to sit together."

"I'm sure it would be okay for one night. It's good to see you." Master Simmons belonged to the Weapons Guild like Daisy, who made swords, and Hans, the blacksmith.

Glassmaking, pottery making, and basket making all belonged to the Craft Guild.

It was true the people from each guild tended to hang together. I didn't live here all the time so I tended to ignore it. This wasn't the real Renaissance—things had changed since then.

"Jessie!" Roger yelled from inside the shop. "What are you doing out there?"

I ran inside with my broom and found him frowning at the back door. The breeze I'd thought of as glorious had blown sand, leaves, and hay into the shop while I was outside. "Sorry. I was just pushing the last of the sand and stuff out the back. Who knew it'd blow right back in?"

I smiled, but he didn't smile back. "You know, an apprentice during the Renaissance would be beaten for letting something like this happen."

I glanced around the shop. It was just me, Henry, and Roger. I'd had just about enough of him treating me like a servant and quoting references from the Middle Ages about my position. "I really want to learn what you know about glass art. I know I made a mistake with the torch and some stuff blew in the door, but honestly, Roger, if you don't start treating me like a person from the twenty-first century, I'm walking out and not coming back. I was led to believe this would be a good time for you because of the crowds they expect during this Halloween thing. If it's not, let me know now."

Henry smirked but went back to his work when Roger looked his way. I felt like I was trapped in a Scrooge movie marathon, only at Halloween instead of Christmas.

"I appreciate your help and your willingness to learn, Jessie." Roger turned back to address me. "But if I can't have authority here in my own shop, where will I have it? Now, let's get back to work. You tidy up and then report to my workbench for further instruction."

That didn't sound like much of a compromise between his need to lord it over me and my need to be a person, despite being his apprentice. I handed him the broom and saluted him smartly. "I believe, good sir, you will need to find another apprentice to harass."

I turned on my heel and strode out the back door with a confidence I didn't necessarily feel. I'd never get another apprenticeship at this point. It had been hard enough to get this one. I'd have to spend the next few weeks in the Village zipping MasterCard numbers across the Internet or waiting tables at one of the food vendors. I didn't want to do either, but I seemed doomed to it. I refused to let Roger treat me the way he apparently treated Henry. There had to be another way.

I was kicking rocks across the cobblestones when I noticed Mary Shift sitting outside her shop across the street. She was weaving a large sweetgrass basket. My memories of the pain and bloody fingers I'd experienced while working with her suddenly disappeared as I considered that she might take me on for the season.

"Hi!" I sat down next to her on the back stairs like I was working there again. "Nice day, huh? How've you been doing? Do you ever hear from Jah?"

Jah was Mary's son she'd rediscovered over the summer. They'd been apart for many years. She narrowed her dark eyes, and smoke puffed from her corncob pipe. "Throw you out, did he?"

My shoulders slumped. Everyone in the whole Village would know within a few hours. Everyone would feel sorry for me. "I quit, if that makes any difference."

"Not to me." She shrugged and addressed the basket she was working on. "Might matter to you, though. It'll be hard to get an apprenticeship now."

"I know." I stared at the old plum tree that was losing

its leaves. "You could let me work here until Halloween. I know the business. I could even make baskets. I got pretty good there at the end."

She laughed, the sun picking out the web of wrinkles in her dark skin. "That's the funniest thing I've heard since last week when the elephant trainer mistook the camel for his animal. Jessie, child, you were good when you were here. But I got a new apprentice now."

A handsome, young black man stuck his head out of the back door and smiled at her. "Mary, there's a customer who'd like to meet you."

"See what I mean?" She put her basket down and told the young man she'd be right inside. "Damian's a sweetheart. I hope he never leaves. Unlike some people who get a mite cranky when they think they aren't the only one in your life anymore."

"Are you talking about Jah?"

"You're a slow top today, missy. Is that the *only* person you can think of who might mind Damian being here?"

A dim light was forming in my brain. Roger and Mary had been a couple for a long time. Was he worried about this young man in her life?

"I can see you got it now." Mary laid her pipe down in a bowl next to the door. "He's been like a bear with a thorn stuck in his paw for the last few weeks. He thinks there's something going on between me and Damian that ain't baskets. He told me to get rid of him or he'd break it off. I told him where he could put that notion, and the sun don't shine there."

I jumped up, suddenly understanding Roger's horrible surliness. "So he's all alone and missing you. *Are* you doing something with Damian besides baskets?"

She snorted, a terrible sound no human should make. "I'm not going to answer that. He's a fool to think I'd fall for some young, pretty face after all this time. But I'm not crawling back to him. He'll have to come to *me*. Excuse me now. I have to sell some baskets. Good to see you, Jessie."

"But you'd take him back if he was willing to make the first move, right?" A plan to save my apprenticeship, and Roger's heart, formed in my brain.

"I'm not saying until I see him on his knees right here." Mary pointed to the grass outside the shop.

I watched her walk inside and close the door behind her. I could do this. All my friends said I was the best matchmaker in the world. If I could do *anything*, I could get Roger and Mary back together. It would be good for them and good for me. Now that I understood the problem, I definitely had the answer.

I decided to wait until morning to implement the first step of my plan. I'd have to do some crawling first to get back in Roger's good graces. But it was absolutely necessary if I was going to save him. I had to be close at hand to make things happen.

"You seem lost in thought, my dear." William Shakespeare, aka Pat Snyder, addressed me as I walked by his usual spot for creating odes. "Dost thou wish for an ode or a sonnet to cheer you?"

I'd known Pat since the first day I'd been in the Village. He'd created a sonnet about my eyes, comparing them to a summer's day. Not terribly original, but it had cheered me up after getting my first assignment, which was to be a servant at the castle. A drudge, at that. I'd wanted so much more, but I'd worked myself up to being a varlet in no time. I always thought about Pat when I remembered those days.

"Yes, good sir." I sat on one of the chairs in his gazebo. "I am feeling rather blue and would enjoy any kind word."

"Prithee, allow an old man to remark on your beauty and charm. Yon sun shines the more brightly for you being here, fair maiden. Pray tell me what causes your sorrow?"

"I can help with that." Henry had zoomed in on my location and was standing too close for my peace of mind. "She lost her apprenticeship with Sir Roger of the Glass Gryphon. Not much an ode can do for that."

"Go away." I turned my back on him. "Pray continue, Sir Shakespeare."

I should've remembered one of the first rules of modern warfare, which is: never turn your back on the enemy. It will only bring you grief.

In this case, it brought me Henry wrapping his arms around me with his hands in questionable positions on my chest. Shakespeare laughed and strolled away, probably thinking we were having a lover's quarrel. I was so astonished that Henry would do something so blatantly stupid, it took me a few seconds to get my elbows ready to crunch him. Once he was bent over in pain, I planned to use a knee maneuver I'd learned in self-defense class.

"Jessie! I can't believe I'm seeing this!"

I thought at first it was Chase. But I was spared that embarrassment only to see Portia's unhappy face before me. The biggest gossip in the Village saw me with Henry's hands on my breasts. It might as well have been Chase.

I reacted by painfully gouging Henry with my elbows, then using my knee to crunch him in the chest as he leaned over. "See?" I turned to Portia to make my case and try to stem the tide of mouth-to-mouth that would spread through every guild by closing time. "I didn't ask him to do that. You can report that I hurt him for touching me. This doesn't have anything to do with me and Chase. We're just fine. Henry is an idiot."

Portia nodded slowly. "Poor dear. I guess we all have

our problems. Is that a burn hole in that shirt? You know we frown on that kind of thing."

We talked for a few minutes about costumes and what it took to maintain them for residents and visitors. I sympathized with her problems, then offered to buy her chocolate at the Three Chocolatiers shop. After that, I walked with her as far as Kellie's Kites beside the jousting Field of Honor at the far end of the Village. I prayed every moment that she'd take my gesture of fear and false friendship as the real thing and not spread rumors about me and Henry.

Only time would tell. I took a deep breath as I watched her walk away toward the Mother Goose Pavilion where Red Riding Hood was having a costume issue. I'd know within the hour how well I'd accomplished my goal.

Naturally, I was starving and thirsty after talking with almost hurricane-like force to try and distract Portia. I was close to the Pleasant Pheasant, which was too expensive during the day, but one of the carts carrying pizza slices from Polo's Pasta was coming my way and the price was right. As a rule, I try not to buy food in the Village, but sometimes emergencies present themselves.

I glanced over at the dancing girls on the Caravan Stage, then walked over and slid into an empty seat in the back row. Normally these nubile ladies danced in harem outfits, silks, and scarves with bangles and beads. For Halloween, they were all garbed in black and red silk. The music was almost tortured as they danced across the stage, which was covered in black bunting. It seemed like overkill to me. I mean, what difference did it make what color their costumes were?

But there was an added dimension to their usual dance routine. A man dressed in a skintight red suit with a pointed tail and little horns on his head joined them. Now *this* was interesting.

Every woman in the audience perked up. It was hard to

tell what the Devil really looked like under the gold and red mask, but his body language spoke for him. He advanced on the dancing girls, tossing some of them up in the air as though they weighed no more than the silk they wore.

"He's really something, isn't he?" Maid Marian of Sherwood Forest settled down beside me, tucking her green cape around her. This Marian had been at the Village for a few years now. When I'd first started, there was a new Marian every few months. Those Merry Men could get a little too merry.

"Yeah. He's interesting all right." I watched as the Devil sidled up to one of the dancers and pulled her against him, running his hand down the length of her body.

Marian cleared her throat and moved her cape around again. "I *love* to watch him dance. He's a real artist."

I had to agree with her. Both of us were lusting for him in our hearts. By the time the dance was over and the Devil disappeared in a puff of red smoke, leaving the dancing girls prostrate on the stage, Marian and I were fanning ourselves with our hands.

"I wish I could teach Robin to dance like that." She sighed.

"First you'd have to paint him red. I don't think the Devil was wearing any clothes, do you? Maybe just red paint."

"Except . . . well, you know." Marian actually blushed, and we both laughed.

"I know where I'm coming for lunch from now on."

"He does an evening show, too. He looks even better with some shadows around him."

I was wondering who the likely dancer was playing the Devil when I caught a glimpse of red leaving the back of the stage. Marian was already on her way back to the forest. Probably just out for a little shopping, maybe some spying. I think Robin had assigned her the job of locating the toaster ovens the Merry Men often made off with; she also kept her finger on what was happening in the Village to report back to him.

No harm introducing myself to the sexy Devil and finding out who he was. I mean, it wasn't being disloyal to Chase just to talk to him, was it?

The dancing girls were getting to their feet again and complaining about different aspects of the performance as well as various aches and pains. I skirted around the stage and picked up on the bright red Devil as he cut through the open space behind the privies and the tree swing where the old storage huts were located. "Excuse me!" I said before I lost him. He was tall and long-legged, so he moved fast. "I just wanted a minute of your time. I was watching you dance. You're really hot."

Some people might think this was a little forward, especially since I already have a boyfriend, but life is short. Getting to the point is always the best way.

He stopped and turned to look back at me. Marian was right. He was painted red from head to toe. His only clothing was a small band around his groin and a cape draped down his back. He was in great shape. Not better than Chase, but there was something about him that was incredibly fascinating. Maybe it was the same charisma that always accompanied the Prince of Darkness.

He laughed. "You think so?"

I knew that voice! Suddenly I was totally disgusted and felt like taking a dozen hot showers. "*Tony?* Is that *you* under there? When did you start dancing?"

"If you would've paid any attention to me at all last night at the pub, you would've known. But then I would've missed this great opportunity to make fun of you for the rest of your life. You found your own brother hot. Your *twin* brother, no less. There's something totally wrong and revolting about that, don't you think? What do you think that says about you, Jessie? And how do you think Chase is going to feel after I tell him?"

Six

I couldn't worry about what Chase would think at that moment. I was too revolted by what I'd thought. I couldn't believe I thought my brother Tony was sexy doing *anything*. I couldn't believe Marian and I were drooling over him. I felt like I needed therapy or something. It was awful.

He just stood there, looking like the Devil, and gloating. I decided retreat was my best way out of this. I didn't want to talk to him about it anymore. Especially with him still wearing the almost nothing I'd found so attractive. Who knew (besides the fairies) that he was hot?

"I'll see you later." I turned and walked away, but he wasn't going to let me go that easy.

"Maybe we should do lunch some time. We could make it a threesome; you and me and Sissy."

"Shut up! Do you *hear* yourself? That's just sickening."

"Come on, Jessie. You didn't think it was so bad when I was up there dancing."

That was it. No one knew how to make me mad better than Tony. I turned to face him and pushed my finger into his chest. "Okay, I made a mistake. *You're* just as disgusting talking about it."

He pushed back. "Yeah? Well coming from Little Miss Perfect, that's a hell of an admission!"

I pushed him again. He pushed me again. We glared at each other like pit bulls.

"Hey there!" Master Armorer Daisy Reynolds came from her shop where we'd ended up confronting each other. "If you two want to put on a show, let's do it."

I hadn't realized that we'd drawn a crowd of visitors. The flashing cameras finally gave me a clue. Sometimes it was hard to remember that anything you did could be completely fascinating to the people around you. We were in Renaissance clothing (at least I was). That meant we were doing something that could be seen only in the Village. I supposed Tony would stand out anywhere dressed as he was.

"What did you have in mind?" I asked her.

Daisy was a large woman with muscled arms from her time as sword and weapon maker to the Village. She wore a breastplate with an image of a phoenix on it. Her badly dyed blond hair was wild on her head, giving her the look of a Viking war goddess. No one ever argued with Daisy.

She held out two wooden training swords. Tony snatched one, and I took mine, too. I suspected I was more reluctant than Tony to actually battle, even with a fake sword. But the crowd was really pressing in with the possibility of a show. I guessed we'd have to oblige them.

"I'll keep score," Daisy said. "Whoever nicks the other three times with the sword is the victor. Are you ready, *gentlemen*?"

Until then, I'd forgotten I was dressed like a man in the Craft Guild. I wondered if it would make any difference to the crowd. They looked fairly bloodthirsty. Probably not. Who wouldn't want to see a good fight with the Devil?

"It's like on TV," one little boy close to me said. "Who do you think will win?"

His friend grinned and said, "I'm betting on the Devil. That other guy looks like a girl."

Before we could take up arms, Chase and two security guards arrived to see what was happening. Daisy explained that she was in charge of the pseudo-match and would coordinate everything.

Chase glanced at me. "Are you sure about this?"

"Not really, but my stupid brother seems to be."

"Is that you, Tony?" Chase laughed. "I'm not surprised. I always thought you had a little devil inside you."

Tony gave his evil Devil laugh. "That's right. And I'm betting gold I can best this craftsman. Then we'll talk."

"Okay. Let's make it a fair fight," Chase reminded him.

"Oh, it'll be fair all right," Daisy said. "Or I'll take something out of someone's hide."

"If I win, you confess to Chase," Tony snickered.

"And if I win, we never talk about this again," I rejoined.

So my twin brother and I faced each other, with the crowd from the Pleasant Pheasant and the joust that had just finished watching us. I'm sure we seemed equally matched to the visitors' eyes. We were both right at six feet tall. Tony was broader in the shoulders and chest. I'm sure I appeared more lithe.

Before anyone could say go, Tony swooped in and nicked me with the point of his sword.

"Hey! That wasn't fair. That shouldn't count. Daisy didn't say we should fight yet."

Daisy shrugged. "It's not a running match, Sir Craftsman. No one has to tell you it's time to fight the Devil."

That made me mad. Or madder. The whole thing was
stupid. Unfortunately, I tended to forget that when at the
Village personal issues should be dealt with behind closed
doors. Anything outside in the street was fair game to be
turned into faire entertainment. "Cheater!" I taunted him.

"What did you expect? I'm the Devil. I don't play fair."
He tried to get past my guard for another nick.

I moved away quickly and spun back to catch his arm
with my sword. It reminded me that during the Renaissance
fights like these were all too real. These nicks meant nothing to us, but had this been a real sword fight, we'd both be
bleeding, possibly dying, before the cheering crowd.

"A point for the craftsman!" Daisy called out. "They
are fairly matched."

The presence of the bailiff and his security men meant
an ever-growing crowd of watchers. Not only visitors
joined us but also at least ten residents that I noticed. Tony
came close to catching me again with his sword. I decided
I'd better pay attention.

We feinted, parried, dodged, and whirled around each
other to the delight of the crowd. Tony's long red cape
punctuated his every movement. You might think most
people would be on my side, but there were as many people
cheering for the Dark One.

Too bad for Tony that he hadn't bothered taking the free
fencing lessons given by the master swordsman who'd been
in the Village two years ago. His movements were a lot
of jabbing and twirling while mine were actually skilled
efforts.

I gave him a second nick as he worried more about how
his cape flew out around him.

"Second blood goes to the craftsman!" Daisy called.

Tony glared at me, and I smiled back at him. "Just luck," he said. "I have longer reach."

"Whatever. We're the same height. That means our arms are close to the same length. With my added skills, I shall smite thee down, Satan."

I went in for the kill but realized my mistake a moment later as Tony tagged me again with his sword.

"Strike two for the Devil!" Daisy addressed the crowd. Half of them booed while the other half cheered. It was like being at a joust without horses. I noticed King Harold standing on the sidelines watching. He was surrounded by his courtiers, as always. A few new female faces were at his side (maybe the rumors were true about him and Livy breaking up).

The event that had started so innocently was about to be over. I'd noticed Tony's propensity for overcompensating because he liked to make his cape swing out. I went in for the pseudo-kill and stepped on the edge of his cape as he got ready to twirl it around for show. This made him step back and turn toward me, but his sword was in his left hand (Tony is a southpaw like our dad, while I'm a righty like Mom). I brought my sword in quickly, tagged him, then moved quickly out of his reach.

"Score! The craftsman wins the match!" Daisy called out and held up my sword arm. The crowd went wild. Even the people who were for Tony were applauding me.

Tony snarled and swept his cape around him as he dropped his wooden sword and stalked away from me.

Of course, I'd never hear the end of this. Just one more thing I did better than my brother, which included most life skills. But I'd never be able to dance the way he had at the show. Maybe that was where his true talent lay. I knew he'd keep his mouth shut now. He never went back on a bet.

The king came up and joined the event. He called for his

squire to give him one of the gold plastic medallions they awarded from time to time, usually to visitors. "For ridding our Faire Village of the Evil One, we salute you, Sir Craftsman, and would know your name so it might be heralded throughout our kingdom for all time."

"I am Jessie the Fearless of the Village Craft Guild." I held up my sword, and the crowd shouted, "Huzzah."

"We thank you for your good work, Jessie the Fearless. We invite you to join us for our feast tomorrow evening at six P.M. at the Great Hall in the castle near the main entrance. Tickets for the event are available at kiosks around the Village. Huzzah!"

I was less than impressed by the king's commercial. Still, a personal invitation to the feast meant I didn't have to worry about what role I'd have to play there. I'd been everything from a kitchen scullion to the jousting knights' squire in the tournament.

"Thank you, Your Majesty," I responded as I thought appropriate. "I shall attend thee at the feast on the morrow."

King Harold thanked me loudly for the benefit of the crowd, then whispered, "I'm sorry to have to do this to you, Jessie. No frills tomorrow. You'll have to ask Portia for a gentleman's feast attire. Can't have the crowd expecting a hero and getting the belle of the ball. See you there."

"Of course, Your Majesty." I inclined my head toward him in deference to his station, but my mind was already playing with possibilities that might surprise him.

The event was over, and the crowd began looking at their Village maps again, deciding where to go next. Daisy whacked me hard on the back and told me I'd done a good job as she took back her swords. "The king thinks we should schedule something like this every day," she told me. "What a crowd!"

Chase was waiting for me after all the well-wishers had moved aside. "Are you okay?"

"I'm fine. I beat the Devil. I think I deserve a tankard of ale."

"What happened? Did Daisy ask you and Tony to fight like that?"

Not wanting to admit how it all started, I shrugged. "You know how it is. Sometimes you're in the wrong place at the wrong time here. I guess that's what happened." I hoped he'd never find out the truth.

"Aren't you supposed to be at the Glass Gryphon?"

"Give me a tankard of ale and five minutes and I'll tell you the story." I watched as two headless gentlemen strolled by. One of them had a hat in his hand that he tipped to me.

"I think I've got five minutes." Chase wrapped his arm around my shoulder as we walked. "I got a call from Detective Almond earlier. The red gooey stuff on Ross's body was really blood. His blood. I guess it's hard to tell the real stuff from the fake."

"What about the rebar? Did they ID the fingerprints?"

"I don't think so. Almond has been kind of shifty about the whole thing. I can't figure out if he doesn't know much or doesn't want to tell me."

"Why wouldn't he want to tell you?" We entered the Peasant's Pub for that tankard of ale. Several people who'd watched my match with the Devil shouted, "Huzzah," and thumped their empty tankards on their tables to show their approval.

The Peasant's Pub was decked out in spooky spiderwebs, and the bar wenches were dressed like ghosts. A spider and various other unusual items along with the traditional pumpkin decorated each table. It was a nice effect, overall. It worked inside where the sunlight didn't reveal the flaws.

That's why the Village was waiting for dark to bring out the really interesting stuff.

"You're a hero!" Chase ordered us both a tankard as we sat at the big wooden bar.

"A heroine, please." I smiled anyway.

"Whichever you are this day, Craftsman, you are welcome at the Peasant's Pub, and I would like to give you a free tankard. On the house!" Hephaestus, a big bearded man who probably resembled the Greek god he was named after, bellowed out his praise. That started another loud set of huzzahs with more tankard thumping.

I was about ready to be done with all of that and start being an anonymous craftsman again. The huzzahs can get to you after a while, and tankard thumping gets to me right away.

"Maybe we should've gone somewhere else where you weren't so famous," Chase said. "Although free ale is nice."

"I know. I've been thinking about visiting the Lady of the Lake Tavern. I haven't been at that end of the Village for a while. You know how the pirates are sometimes."

"Tell me about it." Chase nodded to Hephaestus, who personally served us. "I had a run-in with the Pirate King last week."

"What happened?"

He blew off the head on his ale. "It's a long story. Let's get back to why you aren't working. Did Roger throw you out?"

"No. It's hard to explain." I wasn't sure what to say about what had happened at the glass shop, especially with my recent revelation about Roger and Mary. I didn't want Chase to disrupt my matchmaking plan. In my experience, men seem to have a thing about women interfering in love affairs, even those that are going badly.

"Did it have anything to do with Henry grabbing your breasts?" Chase didn't look up from his cup.

I swear I could've killed Portia at that moment. I could've looked at her unhappy, dead face in the Lady Fountain and been happy. She must've gone right to Chase for him to know so quickly about what had happened. The woman had no decency when it came to gossip.

I tried quickly to think of a good spin to put on the story. My mouth even opened a few times, but the brain-mouth connection didn't seem to be working. "Chase, I don't know what to say."

"Maybe it's a good thing you quit."

I didn't want him to think that way since I planned to beg Roger's pardon to get my apprenticeship back. "I can handle Henry. I know you know this isn't the first time some stupid jerk has tried to maul me."

"So you didn't quit because of that?" He finally looked up at me.

I could see his eyes were serious. He was really concerned about this thing with Henry. I felt as though I were walking on those shards of glass I'd broken earlier at the shop. I didn't want him to be angry, but I didn't want to give up my apprenticeship either. Well, I'd already given it up, but I was pretty sure I could get it back.

But what to say in the meantime? Something thoughtful and intelligent. Something that would tell him he was my number one and had nothing to worry about with Henry.

"Hey!" A tall, thin wraith hailed me as she walked by. Her makeup was *really* good. In the dim light of the pub, she looked dead. Her long white wig around her ghostly gray face made me wonder if theater had gone too far.

"Hi there." I thought she was one of the swordplay audience.

"I caught your attack on Sir Henry of the Hot Pants and

Heavy Breathing." She held up one artificially (I hoped) white hand. "You go, sister! He only hits on his subordinates, girls he thinks he can intimidate into keeping their mouths shut. He wouldn't stroll up to Daisy and do what he did to you. I only hope he can't walk for a while after that. You should be teaching girls to do that stuff. That was awesome! I caught part of it with my cell phone to post on YouTube." She glanced at Chase as she held out the cell phone. "You aren't going to turn me in, are you, Sir Bailiff?"

Chase laughed. "Nope. Sounds like Jessie was doing my job for me."

"Well, it was great watching it. See you, Jessie."

I played with my tankard and took a sip of ale. Were these the right words to convince Chase I could handle Henry no matter how it looked to Portia?

"Why didn't you tell me?" he asked when the wraith was gone. "I guess Roger kicked you out because you went barbarian on his favorite nephew."

Could I let that supposition stand? It would make things easier between us but wouldn't do anything for me going back to work there.

"That's not what happened. I quit because Roger was treating me like an apprentice from the 1500s. The thing with Henry happened after that. But I plan to get my apprenticeship back. Believe me, I can handle Henry *if* he ever tries anything again. Portia only saw what she wanted to see. *And* she's got a big mouth."

Chase finished off his ale and looked at me like he was searching my face for something only he could find. He finally nodded and stood up. "Good enough. If something happens that you *can't* handle, Jessie, you know where to come."

"And I appreciate that offer." I smiled and stood up

beside him, kissing him on the lips right there in front of God and sundry.

"Methinks the craftsman and the bailiff may be a little odd." The knave sitting next to us at the bar offered his opinion.

Chase picked me up (he has a bad habit of doing that) and grinned at the pub full of residents and visitors. "Methinks you should mind your own business unless you want to face the wrath of vegetable justice in the stocks."

The huzzahs and tankard pounding started again. Thank goodness Chase carried me outside and put me down on the street. I couldn't have taken another round of that. I was a little light-headed from the ale and dizzy from him picking me up. But I was very happy. I had to find a way to get through the fall with my apprenticeship and my relationship intact.

"I'll see you later." Chase kissed me good-bye. "I hear the Lady of the Lake is having a buffet for residents tonight. Something about food about to go bad in the freezer if they don't cook it and serve it. Your wish to visit that end of the Village is granted, milady."

"Thank you, sir. I would gladly pass the evening with you."

Two visitors wearing matching I Love Myrtle Beach T-shirts stood watching us. The woman smiled, but the man muttered, "Can't get away from that stuff even in the past," before he pulled the woman away. She managed to get a photo as she left.

"Is there any way we could negotiate with Portia or Beth to get you a *female* craftsperson outfit you can work in while you're here?"

"Not that I know of. I was offered a demon costume, but that was as good as it got," I explained. "Of course, being the bailiff and a highly respected Village official, maybe you could change that. I have nothing against looking like a craftswoman, but there are specific clothes requirements for the job. We don't want a skirt going up in flames, do we?"

"Of course not. Think of the work that would mean for the costume makers." Chase kissed me again and promised to find me when it was supper time.

I had a whole afternoon to wander through my favorite place on earth. No one telling me what to do or when to do it. No worries about what I was missing in my apprenticeship. It was fabulous.

I walked through every shop catching up with people I knew and introducing myself to some shopkeepers I'd never met before. I browsed the scarves, jewelry, incense, and all the other wonderful things sold throughout the Village. I indulged in some really good chocolate fudge at Frenchy's Fudge. Frenchy offered me an apprenticeship there, but I had to refuse. I might be able to pass off roasting turkey legs as an authentic Renaissance cooking skill, but there was no way making fudge fit that bill. It was tasty anyway.

I hit Cupid's Arrow up by the Merry Mynstrel Stage and talked to Adora the shopkeeper. She had everything that could make a man love any woman. Love potions, Renaissance lingerie, even chastity belts. She offered me a love potion for Chase, but I told her it wasn't necessary. We jumped around laughing for a few minutes in the excitement of celebrating true love.

"Let me give you this special incense anyway," she said. "I've had it on good counsel that this is the same incense the Queen of Sheba used with Solomon. And you know what kind of trouble *that* made."

I thanked her for the gift and tried my best to think of some way to apprentice with her. She was such a fun, free spirit. Nothing ever shocked her or made her think less of someone. You have to like that in your exotic-love-potion procurer.

She wrapped my gift, and I promised to wander down that way more often. I walked back out into the fading sunlight, feeling good about everything in general. I turned toward Baron's Beer and Brats and saw the familiar red writing and catch phrase on the wall.

Death shall find thee.

"Not again."

Seven

Two of the scullery maids from Baron's came up behind me and gasped. "That's what was written on that Death guy who was killed," one said.

"It was written in blood," the other added with a shiver. "Is that blood?"

"It's just strawberry jelly." I stuck my finger in one of the words as Chase had done outside the Glass Gryphon. It didn't feel like strawberry jelly and it smelled bad. I started to put it in my mouth, like he had, but then decided against it.

"Strawberry jelly?" one of the maids asked with narrowed blue eyes. "Are you sure? I'm in pre-med at Duke and it smells like blood to me."

I decided to put an end to the discussion. If it *was* blood, Chase should be here. If it wasn't, it didn't matter. "You know it's hard to tell the good fake blood from the real thing anymore. I'll just get something and wash this off."

Both maids seemed satisfied with that and walked back into Baron's through the back door. I paced in front of the writing on the Village wall for a few minutes. This was one of those times I *really* needed a cell phone or a radio to call Chase. How could I leave the message? What if someone else messed it up? On the other hand, what were the chances Chase would just drift by? Especially since I wasn't doing anything I didn't want him to see?

"If Henry was here grabbing my butt, Chase would show up like a lightning flash," I muttered.

I heard the trumpets announce that one of the Royal Court was taking a stroll through the Village. Obviously they were close by. I normally avoided all the cameras and visitors that accompanied the royal personages, but in this case, it could be a good thing. I hoped it would be King Harold as he'd be less squeamish.

Instead it was Queen Olivia, out for her afternoon stroll. There were fifteen people with her: someone to hold the pink parasol over her head, three ladies in waiting, three jugglers, a knave or two, and several fools with bells on their pointy hats.

The crowd parted as the queen came through, hundreds of flashes going off and some visitors bold enough to ask for her autograph. She was dressed in a full regalia of red velvet over a wide hoop. There were pearls around her neck and in her red hair. She was like an old luxury liner steaming through the Village, giving pleasure to the little people. This was heaven for Livy. She enjoyed the pomp and circumstance of her royal role better than anyone else.

Livy was also too squeamish to flick a bug from her hair. Once after a joust on the Field of Honor, she nearly fell from the twenty-foot dais trying to get away from a mosquito. She'd probably faint if she saw the words on the wall.

But there had to be someone in that group who could either take a message to Chase or stay here until I took a message to him. I searched all the faces of the ladies, knaves, fools, and jugglers, but there was no one I recognized. I needed someone I could trust. Someone who wouldn't faint or scream, alert everyone else, and generally cause a panic.

I stood there, hoping someone else would go by in the queen's wake, but the procession came to an abrupt halt in front of me.

"Are we interrupting your day, young craftsman?" Livy smiled at me and batted her artificially enhanced eyelashes.

I seriously hoped there was a young craftsman behind me. But there were only the bloody letters on the wall. I bowed, playing the game. *Of course she'll recognize me. Of course she knows I'm not a man she can flirt with.* "Of course not, Your Majesty. I am only awestruck by your beauty."

Two of the ladies giggled. That wasn't a good sign. I knew that giggle. I'd done it myself a few times. This looked very bad. I didn't want to imagine what would happen if it went any further.

"You shall join our royal parade, young man, and tell us about yourself. Where do you hail from?"

"I am from a goodly distance away, Your Majesty, and sworn to wait here for my master." She couldn't really believe I was a man, could she? I mean, I'm tall and everything, and I was wearing a man's outfit. But really . . .

"Never mind your master." She waved her heavily ringed hand in dismissal of my absent master. "You shall come with us. There is a party at the castle this eve. A *private* party."

This couldn't get any worse. I knew I was in serious trouble when Livy adjusted her large bosom, precariously set in the low-cut square neckline. She *was* flirting with me. What was the penalty for pretending to be a man during the Renaissance? What was the penalty for misleading the queen in Renaissance Village?

"There you are, you scamp!" Merlin was walking by in his starred, purple robe. He'd obviously been listening to our conversation. He might be the only one who could get me out of this mess. "I told you to wait over *there*. What are you doing over *here*?"

"Prithee, Master Sorcerer." Livy sidled up close to him, her wide hips swaying beneath the hooped skirt. "We are taking this boy with us. He would better serve the Village under our tutelage."

Merlin raised one shaggy white eyebrow. "Good heavens, woman! This lad is barely old enough to be away from his mother. You can't mean to dally with him! That would be *most* obscene."

I wasn't sure at first what Livy's response would be. I knew Merlin did as he pleased in the Village. I'd never heard of him being summoned or cajoled into doing anything the king or queen wanted. He'd been here since before Livy and Harry took up residence in the castle. Maybe he had some kind of seniority with Adventure Land.

"Watch thy tongue, sir!" I could see by the look on her face that the queen was truly angry. "We shall not put up with your rudeness, sir, and shall speak to the king on this matter."

Merlin bowed low, his gnarled hand on his staff. "As you wish, Your Majesty. I would advise the king to tread lightly in this matter. Neither you nor he want to anger me."

The queen turned abruptly and reentered her group of courtiers. She gave me a very sweet smile before starting off again for her promenade. I realized I hadn't breathed since Merlin entered the fray, and now took a big, deep breath. "Thank you."

"You're welcome, I suppose. I could ask why you're dressed as a man, but I just passed what I believe to be a headless sheep. I may be incapable of asking such questions anymore. Who thought of creating a headless Halloween sheep costume?"

I couldn't help it. I laughed. It was good to be able to laugh with the queen out of my radar. "I suppose one could inquire what Bo Peep was wearing if she was herding headless sheep."

Merlin shrugged. "I don't want to go there, my friend. What brings you to the Village at this time of year, Mistress Jessie?"

"I thought the whole Halloween theme would be interesting. I'm apprenticing with Roger at the Glass Gryphon."

"That's not what I heard at tea today. Never lie to a wizard, my dear. We get very testy about such things. Who knows? You could end up a headless sheep yourself."

News, as always, traveled through the Village faster than bytes across the Internet. "Okay. I lost that position, but I think I can get it back. Roger really likes me, you know. And I think something else ails the glassmaker."

"Come tell me about it over some pizza at Polo's. I'm famished. Magic takes a lot out of you."

"I can't." I moved away from the writing on the wall. I wasn't exactly big enough to hide it, but I must've been doing a good job since no one in the Royal Court had noticed it. "I have to save this for Chase."

He glanced around. "Save what? Has another visitor had a heat spell put on them by one of those crafty fairies?"

I turned to make sure the writing was still there. Of

course it was. The red bloodlike substance was even beginning to ooze down the wall. It creeped me out looking at it. "The writing. Didn't you notice it?"

Merlin stared at it briefly, then looked back at me. "Must I relate the story of the headless sheep again to you, my dear? You know you seemed much smarter last year. A little faster on the uptake, if you know what I mean."

"This isn't part of the Village Halloween event." I finally understood his confusion. "Didn't you hear about Death getting killed yesterday? The same words were written on him. The police said it was real blood, too."

"Like the message written on the glassmaker's wall earlier today?"

"No. That was strawberry jelly. This is the real thing, I think."

"You *think*?" Merlin strode past me, his purple robe flying out in a way that made me avert my eyes. He was known for flashing a little occasionally. He walked up close to the wall and put his finger in the red goo, then put the digit into his mouth. "Hmm. Type A, I'd say. Of course, a good O can be difficult to pin down. Definitely from the area though. High salt content, you know."

I took back everything I ever said about Livy being squeamish. I almost lost it right there in front of the crazy Village sorcerer. It was bad enough when Chase had done it, but at least that had been jelly (which he'd said he could tell before he tasted it). "*Eww*. That is totally the worst thing I've ever seen."

"But now we know." He nodded his stately white head beneath the ridiculous purple pointed hat. "As you might suspect, we should call in the bailiff."

"I know. I'll go find him if you'll wait here so no one will bother the writing." As I was speaking, Merlin was pulling one of the Village-issued radios from somewhere inside his robe. I don't want to know where. "Oh, that's great. You get a radio. Chase gets a radio. Roger has a radio. Probably Fred the Red Dragon has a radio. I must be the only person in the Village that doesn't have a radio."

"Hardly. And the dragon doesn't have a radio. You can rest easier now, Jessie." Merlin explained the situation to Chase. When he'd finished, he said, "You'd better get over here, boy. Queen Olivia was here hitting on your girlfriend. Or is that boyfriend? In any case, you'd better get over here."

Chase arrived a few minutes later. Lonnie took pictures of the wall. "Detective Almond can't get over here right now," Chase explained. "He said to take pictures and save some of the goo from the wall."

"I feel certain this is nothing more than people with bad taste copying what you found on poor Ross's body," Merlin replied. "I believe you've both taken it too seriously. You know how it is around here."

I *did* know how it was: crazy. "So maybe we're looking for somebody with a bad sense of humor and not a killer." That thought brightened my day. I didn't care for the idea that there was a killer on the loose in the Village, especially not right now when the familiar had become unrecognizable.

"I hope so," Chase agreed. "Lonnie, can you send that picture to the police for me?"

"Sure, I'm good with computers."

"Thanks. I'll scoop up some of this stuff, and then I guess we can go. It's getting dark. I expect all hell to break loose once the night settles in. And I mean that literally."

Merlin said his good-byes and started back to his apothecary shop near the big first aid station and the entrance to the castle. Chase dispatched Lonnie with the red goo from the wall and the camera.

"What made you take Lonnie on as your assistant?" I asked as we strolled toward the Lady of the Lake Tavern. I could already hear the cannon fire, a nightly occurrence, from the pirate ship as they set off a few rounds at sunset.

"It wasn't my idea. I guess Livy and Harold decided I needed some help. Lonnie showed up at the dungeon with a letter from Adventure Land headquarters telling me that he was officially mine. He's a useful little guy. He can do almost anything I need him to do."

"He was at Sir Latte's for a couple of years, but they kept him in the back. Probably that snorty laugh. I guess that doesn't bother you."

"Not really. I thought they'd choose Jeff if they decided to pick anyone as my assistant. You know how well we worked together at the stocks last summer. But he walked off one day about a week after you left in August. No one's seen or heard from him since. No telling where he's gone."

"I'm sure there are whole files of people who've worked here and left." I watched as the pirate ship sailed across Mirror Lake, past Eve's Garden where they did demonstrations on plants and herbs used in the time of the Renaissance.

The full white sails billowed out in the breeze that rustled through the trees as the sun sank beyond the horizon. It was a thrilling sight, even in modern times. The pirate ship, the *Queen's Revenge* was as close to an exact replica as could be built. She was a fine piece of living history, except that her script called for several attacks on the tavern and smaller shops around the lake each day.

The anguished howl of the lone wolf sounded again through the streets and beyond. I shivered and moved closer to Chase. "You know that's a recording like my banshee, right?" He laughed at me. "You don't have to worry about being eaten on the way to supper."

At that moment, two tall, hairy, wolf-headed creatures wearing only ripped pants ran past us, slobbering and panting as they went.

"You were saying?" I moved to the inside of the street closer to the shops.

"You're going to let them eat *me* first?"

"You're the one who said they didn't exist."

"I think you have too much imagination for your own good, Jessie. Maybe Halloween wasn't such a great time for you to be here."

"Don't be silly! I know this stuff isn't any more real than Livy's red hair or Princess Isabel's bosom."

We'd reached the Hanging Tree near the tavern. Sometimes they hung a few pirates up in the tree, supposedly for the evil they'd done. It was a traditional warning to other pirates back during the Renaissance. Tonight, however, there were skeletons in the tree. The breeze rattled the fake bones (at least I assumed they were fake) above us and made the cages that usually held the pirates creak.

Imagination or not, this was scary. Maybe Chase was right. Maybe I was better off as a fun time, summer worker. I'd never imagined the terrible things the Village artistic directors could think of would be so real.

The Lady of the Lake Tavern was symbolized by a figure dressed in blue, half woman, half fish but not really a mermaid type creature either. She held a nasty-looking sword in one hand and usually a tankard of ale in the other. The wooden sign had been modified for Halloween so that the tankard was covered by a head.

"Oh, that's nice. Just what someone wants to see before they go in to eat." I looked around the building, which was painted a shade of blue to match the fish creature's dress.

There were wide windows on the ground floor with tiny panes of glass. Viewed through these multiple window panes, the lamp-lit diners in the tavern looked surreal.

"You know, maybe this is a bad idea," Chase said before we went inside. "We could grab a sandwich or something on the way back to the dungeon and eat there."

"Probably halfway there, someone would need you for something and I'd get stuck eating alone. At least here, there's bound to be some excitement."

He put his arm around me. "Don't worry. I'll protect you from the real, and the not so real. If I can tell the difference."

"Protect me?" I demanded. "I'm the man who defeated the Devil. Don't you forget it."

"Shh. Not so loud. You don't want to start the huzzahs again, do you?"

We were early for dinner (and we'd pay for it) as our hostess reminded us right away. Residents could get free food after the Village closed, but before then we paid like the visitors.

I slid into a small wooden booth in the darkened room. There were lanterns and candles everywhere. It's always amazing to consider how anyone got anything done before electricity. This place was darker than Peter's Pub or the Pleasant Pheasant. It was probably the big wooden beams that seemed to press down on the dining area.

Luckily, we got a window seat overlooking the lake. The lake was artificial, too, but like the pirate ship, it put on a good show. The rising moon was peeking over the castle, the entire picture reflected in the still water. Torches were lit on the ramparts and across the battlements of the castle and the Great Hall. It was an awe-inspiring sight.

"Good table, huh?" Chase mentioned as he looked at the menu, which was burned into a wooden slab.

"The best." I couldn't look at my food choices for gazing out at the scene spread before me. The pirate ship was docking, which meant they would soon attack the tavern. I could see a few pirates sneaking up through the fog toward the restaurant. "Chase?"

"Hmm?"

"Where is all the fog coming from?"

He looked up at me and grinned, his leather-thong-tied braid slipping over one shoulder. "From fog machines, where else? Believe me, Adventure Land spared no expense."

"Great! Does that mean I have to worry about a big fake dinosaur eating me or eating what's left of me after the werewolves are done?"

"How about a glass of wine tonight, my lady?" He touched my cheek. "I think you need to relax."

"Greetings and huzzahs to you my fine fellows!" The burly waiter approached our table. He glanced out the window and sighed. "Do they *have* to come and pillage us *every* night? They're cutting into my tips. Show-offs!"

Chase and I ordered pasta and mushrooms with white wine and the tavern's specialty dessert, which was cheesecake. The waiter took the order, complaining the whole time about the slow but steady advance of the pirates.

When he was gone, Chase took my hand and kissed my knuckles. "We really need to get you another costume. I don't mind people thinking I'm with another guy as much as I mind Livy hitting on you. I don't even want to think where that could end up."

"I'm sure as soon as she realized I wasn't a man, she'd be out of there really fast," I ventured after a sip of the cool wine.

"Not necessarily. I remember one night when there was more than that going on at the castle after closing time."

"Were you involved?"

"Let's just say I never fell for Livy's offer to knight me again."

I laughed as the pirates burst into the tavern. There were at least twenty sturdy lads and lasses dressed in traditional pirate garb of ripped pants, waist-tied shirts, and lots of bandanas. Each carried a knife and some sort of sword. Most had gold earrings, and chains around their necks.

It was a good show. The pirates came in through a hole in the floor as well as dropping down from the ceiling. They pushed their way past a waiter in the doorway and generally invaded the dining area. Only the placid, sometimes impatient faces on the waitstaff gave them away.

"Avast, me hearties!" I wasn't surprised that it was Rafe, one of my long-ago summer flings. He was as sexy as ever with long, black hair, a few gold teeth, and a killer mustache. "What have we here? I think we shall be counting these spoils for days, lads. Strip them of their purses. Let none survive."

One very dainty older lady who was sitting close to me and Chase grabbed her purse and pressed it to her chest. "You can't take my money, you scoundrel!"

I glanced at Chase. Was she an audience plant?

Rafe approached her with appropriate swagger and fingered his mustache while he looked down on her. "Madame, you do not know who you are toying with. I am the king of the Pirates from the *Queen's Revenge*. You will give me your valuables or dance on my gibbet."

"The hell I will!" The dainty little lady brought her foot down hard on Rafe's insole and had the pleasure of seeing the Pirate King shout in pain. "Are we going to sit here and let them rob us?"

"Is this supposed to happen?" I asked Chase.

Before he could answer, the tavern diners let out a

resounding "No!" Suddenly the pirates were being attacked by the visitors. Chase was on his feet running into the fray. A wooden chair splintered on the floor near my feet.

Obviously, this *wasn't* supposed to happen.

Eight

It was chaos in the tavern with visitors and residents throwing themselves into the battle. I'm sure the pirates were surprised to find such a lively audience. Usually they snuck in, sang a few pirate ditties, and took a few purses from other residents who were in the crowd. No one ever took something from a visitor. That was strictly taboo.

I couldn't help wondering if that old lady was as innocent as she seemed. I couldn't see her anymore, so I hoped for the sake of the Village that she was actually part of the plot. Only a few people each year actually got hurt or upset about the theatrics going on around them. Most came here to be entertained on a grand level. The Village provided that with nonstop craziness.

I saw Chase standing on the other side of the room. He was talking into his radio but not trying to separate the factions, which made me believe things were in order. A pirate

I didn't recognize sailed by me, and I saw the red letters painted on the back of his jerkin: *Death shall find thee.*

Coincidence? I thought not. I'm not a big believer in coincidence. I ducked and weaved trying to get across the room to Chase. He needed to see that jerkin.

I saw Rafe's grinning, gold-toothed smile only a moment before he hauled me up on his shoulder like a sack of feed for the elephants and sprinted toward the open hatch in the floor. I made eye contact with Chase, but it was too late. Rafe passed me off to the next pirate in their underground lair and before I knew it, I was headed for the pirate ship.

I'd been on the ship a time or two while I was seeing Rafe three years ago. It's big and kind of musty smelling. There's a lot of rope and buckets (the good ship has sunk a time or two). It was hard to protest as I was tossed from shoulder to shoulder through the lines of pirates making a ladder to the water's edge. I've only crowd-surfed at one or two concerts in my life. This was a lot worse.

By the time I was able to stand on my own two feet, I was aboard the *Queen's Revenge.* It was dark and smelly, alive with the clomp-clomp of large boots as the pirates set sail from that side of the lake. I could hear the cannon fire as residents sounded the alarm and supposedly took aim at the ship. Luckily, they used only blanks and smoke bombs now. A good thing, too. The first time the ship had sunk, it was due to technical error: someone had shot real cannon-balls at the wooden vessel. They'd obviously had uncannily good aim.

I wasn't alone in the dark hold. Three wenches were taken with me. They all took a seat around the area, knowing the routine. One of them, a big, buxom blond, took out her cell phone to complain about everything to her boyfriend.

"I've never seen them take a man before." Another

buxom blond came to stand beside me and actually put her hand through my hair.

Yuck! I pulled away. "I'm *not* a man. Rafe knows me. He probably thinks this is funny."

She laughed. Apparently she thought it was funny, too. My sense of humor was off due to the loss of a nice dinner with Chase. Not to mention a forced hour-long cruise across the lake.

"Don't worry, sweetie," the buxom blond closest reassured me. "They always let us go over by the climbing wall. You can get back home from there, can't you?"

I didn't dignify that with an answer. Instead I started pounding on the hold door.

"What's he doing?" Buxom Blond with Cell Phone asked Buxom Blond Number Two.

"He's a she, believe it or not. I guess she wants to get out."

"God, she's tall!" the third wench added. "Is she wearing heels?"

A pirate finally came to get us. I saw in the dim oil lamp light that it was Grigg. "Jessie? How'd you get down here?"

"It's a long story," I snarled. "Where's Rafe?"

"You have to refer to him as the Pirate King now," he explained. "He gets really testy if you call him Rafe."

"Not a problem." I smiled charmingly. "I'm sure what I plan to call him will be much worse. Just show me the way."

We walked upstairs to the main deck, which looked like a scene from a pirate movie. All hands were on deck making fast the lines and setting sail across the dark lake. Back when I was dating Rafe, I knew the names of all the lines, sails, and other gear that kept the ship afloat. There was the mainmast, mizzenmast, quarterdeck, steering wheel.

Or rather, the helm. It had a certain charm back then even though it was damp and we were likely to be interrupted a hundred times every hour by pirates who had to report where the ship was on the lake.

Grigg knocked on the door to the captain's cabin, then shrugged and left me to it. The pirates started singing and playing that infernal squeeze box someone suggested was used during the Renaissance. Rafe called out for me to enter. I shoved open the heavy wood door and stepped inside.

The pirate with the painted jerkin was with Rafe at the crude table. There were a few roughly made wood chairs and an oil lamp in the middle of the table. Rafe looked up and smiled brilliantly at me. I wished I had something to throw at him.

"Why am I here? I don't think I signed up to play Captured Female Number Four at the tavern."

"Jessie, as beautiful as ever! Especially when you're angry!"

"Besides being the lamest thing to say, I seem to remember you weren't particularly fond of me getting angry when we were seeing each other. Some kind of affront to your pirate manhood."

The other pirate laughed. "She's a feisty one, sir. Methinks we should keep her for the crew."

"Well, methinks you're gonna have some explaining to do when we get to the other side of the lake," I told him. "Where did you get that jerkin?"

"This?" He shrugged. "You like it?"

"I think your choice of slogan on the back is either inappropriate or involves you in a potential homicide." I stared at him as hard and seriously as I could.

He glanced at Rafe. "What'd she say?"

"She's a history professor," Rafe told him. "It could be anything. Smile and nod."

"I'm talking about the red writing on your jerkin that says *Death shall find thee*. Those same words have been written in various places around the Village as well as on the figure of Death as portrayed by Ross DeMilo. Would you like to explain that?"

"I think she's saying you killed Death." Rafe snagged an Oreo from a wooden box at his elbow. "What say you, me hearty?"

The other man looked surprised, then made a sudden run for the door. Rafe got to his feet and barked out orders to his other crewmen on deck, but they weren't fast enough. The pirate jumped overboard. I ran out of the captain's cabin in time to see him swimming away from the ship.

"Stop that man!" I ordered. No one moved. I turned to Rafe. "Tell them to stop him."

"How would you suggest we do that, Jessie? You know we don't have any real weapons. I could throw him a life preserver, but I don't think he'd take it, do you?"

We just stood there watching the pirate swim toward the shore. I remembered Buxom Blond with Cell Phone in the hold and ran down the stairs to borrow her unlawful apparatus.

She put up a little struggle; I'd interrupted her conversation, from which I gathered she'd just broken up with her boyfriend. But in the end, I was the faster sprinter. By the time she got on deck, I was already on the phone with Chase. Rafe held her off by explaining the situation while I explained to Chase what had happened.

"I was going to meet you at the other side," Chase said. "I guess I'll make for the Eve's Garden area instead. Thanks, Jessie. Sorry about dinner. I'll meet you back at the dungeon."

I couldn't say much with an audience of buxom wenches and bloodthirsty pirates standing over my shoulder. I briefly said good-bye and handed the phone back to the wench. "Thanks. Maybe we can take care of this problem now."

"Come and have a repast with me in my cabin," Rafe said.

I had to admit he was super sexy in his pirate gear with the moonlight on his dark hair, illuminating his handsome face. If it weren't for Chase, I might've said yes. But I had a good thing going, and I wasn't blowing it for any sexy pirate. *Been there, done that.*

"I think I'll just stay out here and look at the water. Doesn't the castle look romantic with the torches and the moon?"

"No one refuses the Pirate King," Rafe whispered close to my ear.

"I guess there's always a first," I whispered back. "You and I are so much history."

He sighed. "It doesn't look good to have something like this happen. It undermines my authority with the others. If you can say no, so can everyone else. That's what happened to the Pirate Queen, you know. She got soft. Actually, she got pregnant, then she got soft. There was no authority left. The men look to me for guidance and authority. I have to do what I think is right to maintain that."

I saw it coming with the moon shining in his eyes just a moment before he tossed me over the side of the ship. On my way down I heard him laughing. That stupid squeeze box was playing, too, and one of the buxom wenches was giggling.

Then I hit the water. At least he knew from our past history that I could swim. That's about the only good thing I could say about the situation. At least he knew I wouldn't drown. If I'd been dressed in a long gown, he wouldn't have thrown me over. I wanted to feel sure about that. Then I started plotting my revenge.

* * *

I swam ashore not quite knowing where I was until I saw the lights from the main gate and heard the music playing. I had no idea what time it was, but visitors were still streaming in through the gate, which meant it wasn't midnight yet.

One group of twentysomething visitors dressed as Renaissance trick-or-treat rejects saw me and started laughing. "Do you think she's supposed to be some kind of water spirit?" one of the girls asked her partner.

"If so, they sure did a good job on her makeup." That started them all laughing again.

I was too angry to speak. I wasn't sure what would happen if I opened my mouth. I ignored them and clung to the shadows, which were easy to find in the dimly lit Village street.

A long line of lighted pumpkins followed every shop and amusement. Lords and ladies dressed in ghostly attire, their faces painted a deathly white, strolled the cobblestones. The wolf howled and bats chattered through the streets. Halloween had truly come to Renaissance Village.

The hatchet-throwing area, located conveniently close to a first aid station, now offered scarecrows, rather than fruits and vegetables, as targets. Even the monks at the bakery went all out. Two of the brothers walked by me on their way from the building. When I looked at them, I saw that their eyes glowed red. Chase wasn't kidding about Adventure Land doing it up right.

I dashed behind the Honey and Herb Shoppe, which took me into a dark part of the Village behind the privies and the Dutchman's Stage. Apparently the Renaissance Faire Village planners had not put any lights back here because they didn't want visitors getting off the beaten track where they couldn't spend any money. It was a good place for me in my drenched, angry state. I could hear the music and smell the roasting turkey legs, but I was by myself.

At least I *thought* I was by myself. I heard a rustling sound and glanced over my shoulder. There was Death again, if possible, bigger than when Ross was playing the character. The sight put such a chill down my back that I had to stop and confront him or leave the Village. To my way of thinking, you can only be so scared before you have to fight back.

"You must be the new Death," I greeted the specter. "Nice robe. I think your scythe must be bigger than the first Death's. Or maybe it just looks bigger."

He didn't say anything, just stood there towering over me (not an easy thing to do). The figure had to be eight feet tall. I glanced down at the ground where his robe met the damp grass. There were no feet that I could see.

"You must be new." I held out my hand. "I'm Jessie. I've worked here for about the last five years on and off. I'm apprenticing with Roger at the Glass Gryphon right now. Nice to meet you."

There was no response for a moment, then slowly, a bony hand slid from beneath the dark robe. I don't mean bony as in thin either. I mean bony as in skeletal, no flesh.

That was it. Someone might laugh at me later, but I was terrified. I took off running past the actors coming out from behind the Dutchman's Stage, through the darkness to the front of the dungeon.

I stopped when I reached the lighted front door. I looked back to see where the figure was. He hadn't followed me. I even went back a little (not too far) to see if he was waiting around the corner of the dungeon, but he was gone.

Is it real? My pounding heart, tortured lungs, and

sweaty face said it was real. My brain denounced what my senses told me was true. *Of course there isn't a real figure of Death stalking the Village. He's an actor just like me, hired by someone at Adventure Land to scare the living crap out of everyone he can. He's somewhere laughing right now, repeating the story to other Halloween figures.*

Or maybe it *was* real. People had died here. Maybe there really *was* a figure that personified Death. Maybe that figure just met me in the darkness to let me know he was real.

I heard the tree swing creak, close to the dungeon door, and glanced that way. A terrible specter sat there swinging from the tree. She had long white hair and a horrible death countenance, her gray gown trailing on the cobblestones behind her. The wind lifted her hair as she held her horrible face up to the moonlight. The wolf bayed.

I'd had enough for one night. I opened the door to the dungeon and the banshee wailed. I couldn't take the sound, so I slammed the door, stormed over to the Pleasant Pheasant, and sat down in the closest chair. I dared anyone to mention that I was soaking wet as I ordered a tankard of ale.

Daisy Reynolds took up residence in the chair opposite me and slammed her own tankard on the wooden table. "This place has gone nuts. Have you seen all the stuff going on out there?"

Sam, the owner, brought my tankard to me without a word. I drained half of it in a single gulp. "Tell me about it."

Chase didn't get back until almost one A.M. I was still sitting in the same chair when he finally thought to look across the street for me. I don't know what inspired him, but he was a welcome sight.

Daisy had turned in after three tankards and a long bout of philosophy about the sword and how it had changed the world. Everyone else left when the Village closed at midnight. By twelve thirty, residents started coming in, whining about their long day.

"After I heard the banshee, I thought you might be here." Chase pulled up a chair. "What happened?"

"Rafe threw me overboard because I refused to obey his command to eat."

"That guy has gone too far." He started to his feet. "I'll fix it so he really needs those gold caps."

"Never mind. I'll take care of it."

"Jessie, this is stupid. Sometimes things get out of control here. Throwing you overboard is one of those things."

"If you get into a fight with Rafe and lose your job here, you won't be able to help me have the serious revenge I need to get on him."

He sat back down. "What's your plan?"

"I don't have one yet. I need a hot shower, dry clothes, and at least six hours sleep." I drank the last of my ale and put the tankard down hard on the table. "I saw Death."

"I know. I did, too. I can't believe they found someone bigger than Ross."

"No. I mean I *really* saw Death."

"How many tankards have you had?"

"I saw him before I got here." I told him the story. I could tell he didn't believe me. Not the way I wanted him to.

"It's just the new Death, Jessie. They were bound to hire another one. He's kind of the quintessential figure for this kind of thing. He's really good if he can scare *you* since you know he's not real."

"He had a skeleton hand and he didn't speak."

"Next time, run up and kick him in the leg. Maybe that will get his attention. Let's go home. It's been a long day."

I was exhausted, I had to admit that. And logically, I knew he was right. My clothes had dried on me, and my hair was down in my eyes. It was better to agree with him and go to bed than believe there was a real figure of Death stalking the Village.

We called good night to Sam, then went out the door and started across the empty street. The swing was empty now, too, although the breeze still stirred it, creating the squeaky noise the ghost had been making. I don't know why I could easily dismiss the girl in the swing as an actress (even though she was well costumed) but be so frightened of the figure of Death. Chase had disconnected the banshee wail once again, and we started up the stairs.

"Did you find the pirate with the jerkin I told you about?" I asked with a yawn.

"We did. He's new. I think you scared him. He just started today and was looking for something to put on his back to make himself look tough. He saw us looking at the words on Roger's shop and copied them. I don't think he had anything to do with what happened to Ross."

"Great! I went through all of this for nothing. I'd almost convinced myself that it was okay that Rafe threw me overboard because I'd found an important link to what was happening."

"Sorry." We reached the top floor, and Chase put his arms around me. "You're still damp."

"I know. I need a shower."

"Go ahead. I'm going downstairs to personally rip out that banshee thing. I'll be back in a few minutes."

The warm water felt fantastic as I tried to put the night's experiences behind me. Of course I knew none of it was real. And being scared was supposed to be part of the experience. I came to experience that experience, as corny as that sounds.

By the time I'd washed the lake out of my hair and put on my pajamas, I felt much better. I was calm. Everything was exactly as it was supposed to be. Life at the Village wasn't for everyone, but I'd decided a long time ago that it was for me, at least a few weeks every year. I wasn't an actor, but this was as close to reliving history, with a paycheck, as anyone could get. I was with Chase. Life was very sweet.

"Chase, is there any pizza left in the fridge?" I asked coming out of the bathroom as I wrapped a towel around my head. When he didn't answer, I looked up. What I saw made my heart stop beating and the blood freeze in my veins.

There was a scythe, Death's scythe, I'd swear it. It was lying across the bed with blood or something red on the blade dripping on the sheets. On the scythe were the words *Death shall find thee.*

Somehow I walked very calmly to the door of the dungeon apartment and opened it before I let out with a scream that put the banshee's wail to shame.

Nine

I couldn't sit in the room while Detective Almond and his police officers (including one with a German shepherd) poked through the bedroom looking for clues about who could've left the message and the scythe on the bed.

Debby was glad to have me spend the night with her. I don't think I was very good company, though, because she fell asleep in the middle of my second telling of my awful evening.

I stood looking out of the window for a long time until finally the sky above the Village began to get light. I knew half-awake residents would soon be stumbling from their homes above their shops or from Village housing like Debby's.

I wondered where Tony was staying now. It would've been nice to be with family. He's the only one I have left in that department. I thought about my parents dying so young and wondered if that was why the figure of Death scared me so much. I wished I had someone with me to talk to about it.

But it was me, all alone. Chase was helping the police with their investigation. It was for the best that he was with them. Still, I couldn't help wishing I were lying next to him, safe, pretending the Village was the same place for me now.

I'd never been afraid here before. Suddenly, that sense of security had been taken from me. Maybe it was a curse for coming down here instead of being at school. I'd told a few lies to maneuver my time off. Maybe it was payback for taking time off out of turn.

Whatever it was, I was afraid I might have to leave. I knew if I did, I'd never come back. I didn't believe that would be the end of me and Chase. But it would be the end of an important part of my life. I resisted that idea. How dare whoever was doing this, do this to *me*?

Debby slept on through my soul-searching. She even slept through Chase knocking on the door. When I opened it, he put his arms out and I clung to him, burying my face against his chest.

"What did you find out?" I asked.

"Not so fast," he said soothingly. "You've been through a lot. I've got something for you. I woke Portia and shook it out of her. You could say it's a one-of-a-kind costume."

He held out his answer to my wardrobe dilemma. It was a man's britches, but topping them was a black leather bustier with a short-sleeved, red ruffled blouse that went beneath it.

I tried it on, looking critically at myself in the mirror. With the top's push-up magic, no one would have any trouble deciding whether I was a man or a woman. The red ruffles in the bodice didn't do much to keep my breasts from plunging out, but at least the sleeves were short. It would be unusual to see short sleeves on a Renaissance woman. Nevertheless, the strange pirate/craftsperson look was odd yet charming.

The effect was definitely what Chase was looking for. His eyes lit up when he saw me. "You look great! Let's go get some coffee and we'll talk."

I looked at myself in the mirror one more time. Maybe if I wore a little more eye makeup I could pull it off. It definitely would suit Roger's requirements, and I wouldn't have to worry about Livy flirting with me again. The idea of that was still too vivid in my brain.

We walked across the Village to the Monastery Bakery. The monks had added a sit-down coffee and pastry area that I hadn't tried yet. If they were as demanding about their coffee as they were about their bread, the coffee should be exceptional.

Sunday mornings were quiet after the late-night revels on Saturday. The main gate didn't open on Sunday until noon. That gave residents a chance to relax and get ready for the rest of the week, including Sunday night's King's Feast, which required a lot of preparation.

During the Renaissance, it would've taken a month to feed the number of people who attended the feast. Fortunately, labor-saving devices were okay behind the scenes. If not, I'm sure there'd be far fewer job applications at the Village.

"You're sure you're okay?" Chase asked as he opened the front door to the bakery.

Already, mouthwatering aromas were wafting from the popular shop. A few monks in their traditional black robes, accented with the red satin sashes, were outside blessing the bags of flour before they were made into bread. They ignored us as we walked by. That's just as well since they get a little theatrical when they have something to say. And all I could think about was drinking a hot mocha and biting into a freshly baked roll.

"Good to see you this morning, Bailiff, Mistress Jessie." Brother Carl bowed a little as he greeted us. "What can I get for you?"

Brother Carl was the head of the bakery and of the Brotherhood of the Sheaf. It was unusual to see him taking orders behind the counter.

"Good morning, Brother Carl. I'd like a latte and a cinnamon bun," Chase said. "And Jessie wants a mocha for sure, and what are you eating?"

"I'd like a cinnamon bun, too." I smiled at Brother Carl. "I haven't seen you since I got to the Village. How are you?"

Normally I'd never ask a monk (or most of the other residents) this question. The answer could include massive drama that would be too much to handle this early in the morning. But something was up for Brother Carl to be out here waiting tables. The monks had a certain hierarchy that never changed.

"Things have been better," he replied with a sad smile. "I have been voted out of my position as head of the bakery and lead brother. My brothers have sent me a message of humility."

I didn't know what to say, and truthfully, I was sorry I'd asked. I didn't really expect him to be so honest with me. The monks are usually closemouthed about what's going on with their internal politics. "I—I'm sorry," I stuttered as he handed me coffee and bun. "I hope it all works out for the best."

"I'm sure it will." He glanced up as Brother John came in through the back. I could tell from the look Carl gave him who Carl's successor was.

He didn't say anything else, and Chase and I went to sit

down at one of the square block tables and chairs. They were crudely made but effective. I'd heard lots of people call them rustic and charming.

"What's up with that?" I whispered to Chase as we ate. "I wonder how John was able to overthrow Carl that way."

"Rumor has it that Carl ordered too many ingredients for the bakery in August and John jumped on him being irresponsible. The other monks were just ready for a change, I guess. Good cinnamon bun, huh? Kind of small though. I think I need another one."

I was watching Carl and John from a side angle in the back of the bakery. John seemed to be making his position felt in the new order. I shrugged and let it go. The monks were a strange group anyway. The chances were that no one besides the Brotherhood would ever know the difference.

"So what did Detective Almond find at the dungeon this morning?" The cinnamon bun was really good. I licked the sugar off my finger.

"He decided it was just a prank." Chase sipped his coffee. "Good coffee, too."

"What do *you* think?"

"It would be a lot easier to say it was something serious if hundreds of people hadn't seen the same phrase written all over the Village during the last few days. It wasn't blood like it was on Ross. I think it was the strawberry jelly again."

"Except for two major issues. Number one, that Death guy was really threatening behind the Dutchman's Stage last night. Number two, I was in the shower when whoever it was snuck in there and did his Godfather routine. I feel kind of front and center on this guy's list right now."

He nodded. "I know. I think the problem is that Detective Almond has a hard time deciding what's normal for us in the Village and what isn't."

"Which is where you come in, right? You're the Village law and you know what isn't supposed to happen. Like what happened last night."

He looked at me over the top of his coffee cup. "Exactly. I told the police that I think there's something more going on here. I also told them you're leaving the Village until we figure out what it is. I think it would be okay for you to work with Roger today and go to the feast tonight, but that's it. I'll stay close by in case something weird happens."

I could feel my eyes bug out and my mouth drop open. "What do you mean I have to leave? You don't realize what I went through to be here now. I made promises I'll never be able to keep and lied to everyone I know. I can't just *leave.*"

"Tell me you weren't thinking about leaving this morning while you were with Debby after we left the dungeon? I *know* you were scared. Your hands were shaking and your face looked like someone put ghost paint on you."

"I was scared earlier," I acknowledged. "But I'm okay now. No tall, black-hooded guy with a big stick is going to drive me off, Chase. You can't really want me to leave."

He took my hand and stared hard at me. "I want what's best for you. I don't want you to be that scared ever again. And I really don't want something to happen to you."

I took his other hand and stared right back at him. "And I appreciate that. But let's just think for a minute. Who'd want to hurt me? I can't think of anyone. And it can't have anything to do with Ross's death. I didn't even know him. How can I leave with something like this happening in my favorite place?"

"Jessie—"

"And how would I get my revenge on Rafe? There's too much to do. Once I talk Roger into taking me back this morning, I'll be heavily involved with making glass art, but I'm sure I can find some time to help you figure out what's going on."

He shook his head, dark eyes worried. "I can't let you stay like that. We thought the message at Roger's was just a copycat. But you were in the building at the time. You found the same message, probably in blood, outside Cupid's Arrow. It could've been written while you were shopping in there. Don't you see the pattern? This guy might be after *you*."

I shrugged. "Why don't we go and pay the new Mr. Death a visit and find out what's going on? I can go see Roger after we do that."

I could see he wasn't happy with my idea, but I talked him into it. We finished our coffee and breakfast, then headed for Death's Village housing.

"I don't see what this will prove." Chase continued to argue even as we walked across the King's Highway toward Sarah's Scarves. He had a listing in his Palm Pilot of where every resident was living in the Village. "Unless you immediately recognize this guy as a former assailant or lover, what are the chances it was really him in the costume last night?"

"We can check to see if he still has his scythe," I suggested. "If he lost his, or we find some large amounts of blood or strawberry jelly, we'll have him. End of investigation, right?"

He smiled and kissed me as we walked. "You're completely insane. You know that?"

"Of course. Why else would I be here?"

I told him I needed to get Roger and Mary back together as we passed several green trolls swinging their clubs as they walked. One of them nodded and winked at me. I adjusted my revealing bodice. "I think that's why Roger is so abrasive right now. Mary didn't quite say she'd be up for getting back with him, but I think everything will work out."

"That's a lot on your plate for right now, isn't it?" Chase smiled at a group of young witches who giggled as they walked by. "You're going to solve the mystery of who killed Ross, play matchmaker, and learn to do glass art, all while staying alive. Sounds like a full-time job."

"Maybe. But if I don't get Mary and Roger back together, I may not learn to make glass art, and if I don't find out who might want to kill me, well, you can see the outcome of that."

"Which is why my original idea of you leaving the Village until this is solved is workable."

I watched several of the fairies-turned-wraiths as they practiced being scary instead of prancing around with their little sparkling wings, flirting with male visitors. It was such a change of pace for them. I was surprised they could maintain the new role. They were better actors than I'd thought.

Housing for residents is located literally throughout the Village. Sometimes supply sheds are outfitted with a cot and a few other necessities if all the real housing units are full. The only residents guaranteed a regular place to stay are the shopkeepers, who traditionally live in the small apartments upstairs from their shops. Sometimes they even let their employees bunk there, too.

Death's place wasn't too bad. It was located between Galileo's tent and Sarah's Scarves, just off the King's Highway. I think it was once a thriving incense and candle shop that had closed. Of course, next year it could be a shop again, and the residents living here now would be looking for shelter someplace else.

Chase stopped and knocked on a door. "I'm looking for Bart," he told the young man who answered.

"Bart?" The young man yawned and scratched his head.

"Death."

"Oh yeah. Just a sec."

The young man disappeared, leaving the door partially open. I looked in and saw pizza boxes and dirty socks littering the floor. Costumes were thrown everywhere. It was enough to give Portia a migraine.

"Is this guy as tall as Ross?" I asked Chase as we waited.

"Not really." He shrugged. "Maybe. I didn't pay too much attention. Some of that might be prosthetics."

"You mean you haven't met him in person?"

"I don't screen employees, if that's what you mean. It's one of the few things I *don't* do around here."

The young man finally wandered back to the door. "I don't see him. He was here last night. I guess he's out getting something to eat."

"Thanks. I'd like to see his room."

"Is that legal?" The young man looked at me. "I mean, don't you need a warrant or something?"

Chase laughed. "This is Adventure Land property. I don't need anything to look around."

The young man scurried before us picking up leftover food and dirty clothes while shouting out a warning, "Look out! The queen's hired thug is here. Hide what you can."

I was proud of Chase that he didn't squash the poor guy like a bug. I thought I remembered seeing him waiting tables at the Pleasant Pheasant. Not a great job.

We finally reached Bart's room through the maze of small rooms that had been quickly converted to house dozens of residents. Chase thanked the young man, then closed the door, shutting him out.

"What's Bart's last name?" I'd dated a guy named Bart

a few years back. He'd played the Big Bad Wolf before graduating to being a knight. I hoped it wasn't the same guy.

Chase consulted his Palm Pilot and smirked. "It says Van Imp. That seems a little hard to believe. These Adventure Land people don't notice anything."

I looked through the clothes on the floor, the bed, and tossed over the chair and chest of drawers. I didn't see the big, black Death costume or the scythe. I opened the drawers in the chest. There was nothing in there at all. "No blood or jelly. Dead end."

"Recognize the name?" Chase asked as he looked around.

"No. Van Imp doesn't sound familiar to me."

"I don't see any blood. No costume or weapons. If he's the guy who left that message on the scythe last night, he must be a lot neater about hiding his trail than how he lives."

"Somehow this makes it much worse."

"How so?"

"Well, if our Death isn't stalking me, that means it's a strange Death. Maybe even one that isn't from the Village at all. That means it could be anybody."

"True." Chase put his arms around me. "Reconsider? I think you should leave. I don't like the idea of not being able to protect you."

"Not a chance. Maybe this wasn't the answer, but there *is* an answer. We have to find out more about Ross. Maybe if we know why he was killed, we can figure out why Death is following me around."

"Stubborn."

"But beautiful," I added as he kissed the corner of my mouth. The next thing I knew, we were on the bed even though it was littered with old, smelly clothes. Really, I didn't notice at the time. But a moment later when I looked over Chase's shoulder and saw at least six pairs of eyes watching us, all of it became clear to me.

I jumped up, kind of taking Chase with me. He ended up falling back on the bed while I stood facing our intruders—Death's housemates, I assumed. "What do you want?"

They ignored me, except to stare at my bodice. Chase got to his feet, and they hustled out of the way. Now *that's* power.

"Sorry." He grinned at me when we were alone. "Want to head back to the dungeon?"

"I wish I could, but as you pointed out, I have a lot to do and not enough time to do it. Maybe we could meet for lunch."

"Maybe. Have you decided on your costume yet for the feast tonight? I guess you have to be there so Harry can praise your efforts. Dressed as a man, I take it. I'm sure he doesn't mean to parade a woman fighter in front of the crowd."

I smiled. "I'm sure he doesn't. We'll just have to wait and see."

"I *know* that look. I'm glad I'm going to be there."

We walked back through what had become a dorm. Chase called out as we left, "Make sure Bart reports to me sometime today, or I'll be back."

"Do you think they'll remember to tell him?" We stepped into the sunlight and were confronted by several headless gentlemen complete with walking sticks and capes.

"Who knows. I have something for you. I don't give these out very often, but this is an extreme case." He produced a two-way radio. "If anything looks wrong or you see the wacky Death guy following you again, call me."

"Yes!" I had finally attained status in the Village. Only a handful of the chosen elite were allowed to carry these radios. I was finally one of them. "Aren't you going to give me a big lecture on using them in front of visitors?"

"No. I don't care who you use it in front of if you need it."

I kissed him and we whirled around a few times outside the Frog Catapult. Merlin pranced by and winked at me but didn't say a word. As we separated, I asked Chase, "Who is Merlin and why did Livy back off yesterday when he told her to? I didn't think anyone around here had that kind of power."

He laughed. "I'll tell you if you promise not to blab it around."

"You know I won't. Tell me."

"If I hear it from *one* person today, I'll lock you in the stocks tonight."

I wiggled my eyebrows. "Kinky! Tell me, Chase. I won't tell anyone else."

He glanced around. The street was deserted except for the Green Man, who was practicing on his stilts several yards away. Seemingly assured of secrecy, Chase leaned toward me and said, "Merlin is really the founder and chairman of the board for Adventure Land. He just enjoys being here."

"You're kidding me? I can't believe he's—"

Chase put his hand over my mouth. "I'm not kidding, Jessie. If anyone finds out, I could lose my job. Besides Livy and Harry, I'm the only one who knows. You can't say a word."

I promised not to say anything, even though it would be hard. We parted with a kiss in front of the Glass Gryphon. I saw Roger standing at the front door to the shop. The look on his face was anything but inviting. I took a deep breath and started toward him, all of the reasons he should hire me back bursting to come out. I'd rehearsed last night in the shower (including my needy speech that included not having enough money to get home), and I was ready to confront him.

But as I reached him and opened my mouth to speak, the large wooden sign above us creaked. I looked up and saw it plummeting down on us. I grabbed Roger by the shirt front and jumped out of the way. We ended up rolling across the cobblestones, finally stopping with me on top of him.

The heavy sign crashed to the street and smashed against the stones. It fell facedown. As people started to gather around us and ask if we were both all right, I looked and saw a now familiar phrase: *Death shall find thee.*

"I don't know about Death," I said, "but I feel a headache coming on."

Ten

"Are you okay?" I asked Roger before I rolled off of him. I could only hope he wasn't hurt because of me.

"I'm fine." He put his hands on my arms and gazed into my face. "If that crazy person who's after me hurt you, I'll never forgive myself."

I was leaning close to him, worried that I wouldn't be able to hear what he had to say. There was no way of knowing how badly he might be hurt. His words stunned me since they were what I was thinking, only the opposite way. But if I wasn't prepared for his words, I was totally unprepared for him lifting his head and planting his lips on mine.

Stunned, I didn't move for an instant. It was long enough for Mary Shift to fly out of Wicked Weaves across the street and push me roughly off of him.

"What's going on?" she demanded. "Are you trying to make time with my man?"

Taking into consideration that I'd almost had a sign in my head, my next words shouldn't be judged too harshly. "I thought you two had broken up."

I didn't mean it that way, of course. It sounded bad, like I wanted Roger or something. That was the farthest thing from my mind, or any other part of my body. Just the idea made me feel worse than finding Death's scythe on the bed last night.

"So you thought you'd move in and take him?" Mary's dark face was furious as she paced beside us where we seemed to be glued to the street.

"It's not what it looks like, honey," Roger assured her. "Jessie was here and I was . . . relieved. I don't care anything about her like I care about you."

"But you two can roll around in the dirt letting everyone else see your business while you accuse *me* of fooling around on the side." Mary stamped her foot. "I'm through with *both* of you, you hear? I don't want to see either of you again."

I managed to get to my feet without stepping on Roger as Mary huffed back to Wicked Weaves. At least thirty residents were standing around watching the drama. Chase came up with Lonnie beside him as King Arthur set down Excalibur and helped Roger to his feet.

"Are you hurt?" Chase put his arms around me. "I got here as fast as I could. I think the Village needs to buy me a horse."

"I'm fine. I pushed Roger out of the way as the sign was falling." I was a little bruised, but I didn't want to go into that. It was going to be hard enough convincing Chase again that I didn't have to leave the Village because of this.

"*You* pushed *me*?" Roger brushed the dust from his jerkin. "I saw the sign falling and pushed you out of the way. Lucky thing I still have those police officer reflexes."

"I guess it doesn't matter who pushed who," Chase intervened. "I'm just glad both of you are all right."

"I guess it wouldn't matter to *you*," Roger retorted. "As long as *you* look good, that's all you care about. This kind of stuff has been happening to me the last few days. Someone turned my furnace on in the shed last week, locked the door, and almost roasted me in there."

"You, *too*?" I looked at Roger. "Somebody's been after me, too. I thought the sign was headed for me. But maybe it was after you."

Roger puffed out his less than substantial chest. "I've made a few enemies in my day. Sometimes they come back to haunt you. Maybe whoever's responsible is after you because you're my apprentice."

I only picked up on one part of that statement. "You mean I can have my job back?"

"Sure. I was upset yesterday. I shouldn't have gone off on you like that, Jessie. Shakespeare told me that after you left. He also told me what happened with Henry. I had a talk with him. He won't bother you again."

"Thanks! I—"

"Never mind all that!" Chase glared at both of us. "This isn't the time to think about going on here as an apprentice or anything else. Somebody tried to kill one or both of you. I don't know if *either* of you are safe here."

Lonnie had shinnied up the drainpipe to the roof of the Glass Gryphon, anticipating Chase wanting to know how the sign fell. "Looks to me like someone cut through the chains that were holding the sign up here. Guess they were just lucky it fell when their targets were standing right under it."

"That sounds like a lot of guesswork." Chase appeared

to be unhappy with Lonnie's conclusion. "Otherwise that sign could've fallen on anyone."

"Maybe that's the idea." I felt a brainstorm coming on. I pulled Chase to the side of the group. "Maybe it just *seems* like someone's gunning for me or Roger. Maybe it's more random. Like you said, it could've been anyone."

"What are you saying? That someone has it out for the Village and you and Roger are convenient targets?"

"Maybe." I shrugged. It was a very miniscule brainstorm. More like a brain spurt.

"I don't know, Jessie. What's happened to you doesn't seem too random to me."

"What about me?" Roger interrupted. "Why does it seem like someone has it in for me?"

"What about Ross?" Marcus, the Black Dwarf, added his thoughts. "Somebody sure had it in for *him*."

The crowd agreed, talking urgently about the need for greater security in the Village after everything that had happened. The funniest part was watching the witches discussing security with a group of vampires. How often do you see something like that?

We heard the Myrtle Beach police car before we saw it. It sneaked in through one of the side gates reserved for emergency personnel. Detective Almond wiped his sweaty brow as he pushed out of the passenger side. An officer got out from behind the wheel to accompany him.

The detective waddled through the crowd as though they weren't there. "Now the place is falling apart, huh?" he said, taking in the fallen sign lying on the ground. "What's next?"

"It's been a rough few days," Chase agreed. "I'm not sure what happened here. It looks like someone cut through the chains holding the sign up there."

"Could've killed anyone then." Detective Almond nodded. "Not just your pretty girlfriend."

Chase didn't say anything, but I could see he was holding back. A golf cart came in through the same emergency entrance behind the privies and careened toward us. I recognized one of the reporters from the local news station right away. Lilly Hamilton. She's the worst. That's all we needed—more bad publicity.

"I want forensics up on that roof in twenty minutes," Detective Almond told the young officer with him. "I want to know for sure what happened up there."

Lilly Hamilton and her cameraman were already working the crowd of residents to find out what was going on. Chase told them they couldn't park the golf cart in the street, and she grinned. "It's important for people to know what's going on. You don't want to stand in the way of that, do you, Prince Charming?"

Chase explained that the police bringing in a vehicle that didn't fit in with the Renaissance Village theme was one thing, but a golf cart full of reporters was another. "I'll have to ask you to leave."

Lilly, a tanned little blond (I'm sure she's had nose surgery), rubbed her hand on his chest. "Why don't you just show me around? What's your name again? I can send Mark outside with the cart. You can give me a *personal* tour."

I didn't like the sound of that. I sure didn't like her and her fake nose. I went to stand next to Chase and smiled at her. "I think you can do your job and get out of here before we open for business. How about that?"

She glared at me. "How about you mind your own business? What are you supposed to be anyway, some kind of pirate reject?"

"Ladies, please!" Detective Almond interjected. "You with the golf cart, move it out of here. And you, Ms. Morton, I'll need your statement about what happened."

This wasn't exactly what I had in mind, but since he'd gotten rid of Lilly, I obliged him with a detailed statement of what had happened. He talked to Roger next, then said our statements were the same, except for who saved whose life.

"I don't know what to tell you about this, Manhattan." Detective Almond scratched his chin. "If this keeps up, we're gonna have to shut the place down until we figure it out."

There was a collective indrawn breath from the residents around us. Unfortunately, Lilly was close enough to hear what he'd said. No doubt his words would be on the news later.

We all stood around talking until the big bell at the main gate sounded, letting us know visitors were arriving. Everyone scurried to their prospective places. I kissed Chase for luck, then darted inside the Glass Gryphon before he could give me a lengthy sermon on why I should leave the Village.

I glanced around inside the shop and was surprised to find that Henry wasn't there. Roger was already at his workbench, putting on his goggles and heating up his torch. "Are we alone today?"

"Henry mentioned something about going into town," Roger explained. "Are you going to worry about him all day or are you going to get busy?"

Naturally this was all the encouragement I needed. I went back to my workbench and tried to remember how to light up my torch. After a moment or two, Roger sighed and came to help me. "Nothing fancy now. Just practice putting the glass together like I showed you, okay?"

"Yes. Thanks for giving me another chance."

"It's okay. I was kind of a jerk yesterday. This thing with Mary is driving me nuts. I know something is going on over there with Damian. I haven't caught them yet, but I can *feel* it."

I put on my goggles. "Roger, Mary thinks there's something going on between us. Things are not always as they appear."

"I suppose that's true. You know, that woman has been the queen of my heart since we first met. I don't want to lose her. I wish she'd marry me. Then I'd feel more secure about everything."

"Some things have to be taken on trust." I picked up two glass rods and used the torch to soften them and glue them together. At this rate, I'd never learn to make glass animals.

"I wish there was something I could do, some way to prove to her how much I love her."

I glanced up from my hot glass rods and studied his face. He wasn't a handsome man, but I supposed he was likable. Mary seemed to care a lot about him. Maybe there was some way to bring them back together. It would be easier with Roger being part of the plan. Just as well since I'd become the enemy as far as Mary was concerned.

A lady and gentleman entered the shop. Her dress was to die for. It looked as though it had been spun from real spiderwebs. I'd never seen anything like it. The gentleman wore a black cloak with a high collar that framed his gaunt, white face. I wasn't sure if he was supposed to be a vampire, but he sure looked like one.

"Just keep practicing," Roger said quietly before he went to bow before them and ask if there was anything he could help them with.

I mostly tuned out the conversation after that. They were visitors, even if they were dressed in Halloween garb. They were looking for a bird of some kind for the mantle in their house.

I was just getting the hang of fusing the glass rods together when several other visitors entered the shop. Roger glanced up at me and I knew what he wanted. I put my torch into the special holder and turned it off, then took off my goggles to wait on the two ladies dressed in rich satin and fur.

Funny how visitors never come dressed as peasants. Everyone wants to imagine themselves as royalty or at least wealthy merchants. I guess it's the same as wanting to think you were reincarnated from Thomas Jefferson or Cleopatra. Everyone wants to be someone special.

"My ladies." I bowed to the customers. "Good day and welcome to our shop. What can I assist you with?"

"We're searching for glass goblets." The first lady (her blush was a little heavy beneath her thin veil) smiled at me. "We're celebrating and would like to have these as a souvenir. Do you engrave?"

I glanced at Roger, who nodded. Henry came in as we were speaking. He looked as though he'd been rolling around in the dirt. There were smudges on his face and his shirt was torn. The two ladies began giggling and blushing even more. I couldn't believe they found him that attractive. But it seemed they'd already been there during the last few days, buying something different each day.

"Sir Henry," Veiled Lady simpered. "We knew you'd be here to help us."

"Of course, dear ladies!" Henry took each of their hands and brought them to his mouth for a brief kiss. "What can I do for you today?"

Feeling a little nauseated, I started to walk away. Henry saw me move, I think, and almost jumped out of my way. *Hah!* I guess that little show of strength was enough to scare Sir Henry. Good. Maybe he'd stay away. "Just watch his hands," I remarked in a whisper to the ladies.

They both giggled and agreed that he was *very* good with his hands.

There's just no helping some people. I went back to my bench. I didn't want to be out there with the public anyway. I relit my torch (without help) and picked up my glass rods again. I looked at all the tools on the workbench and tried to remember what Roger had called everything.

I knew the big scissors were supposed to be used to cut off the warm glass after creating an animal or an angel. The brass pick was used, like the cherry wood oval block, to shape and form the glass. The rake was used in feathering and marbling the glass. Flat mashers were used to flatten the glass; the curved masher made it round.

I heated up two more glass rods and fused their ends together. I wished I could do more, but I supposed I needed to prove myself before Roger would trust me to make an animal. Not that I was entirely sure *how* to make an animal of any kind. That might be where the artistry came in. If so, I might be left out.

"How's it going?" Roger asked.

I glanced up and saw that the shop was empty again, except for Henry at his workbench. I'd been so intent on my thoughts that I hadn't noticed when the visitors left. "Pretty good, I think. I've fused these rods together. Should I keep doing it?"

He looked at my fused rods and almost smiled. "Let's go to the next step. Fuse the rods together, then wait for the glass to get warm but not hot. You'll get to know when that is by looking at it. When it's warm, use your shears to cut them apart. I want you to get the feel of how to do that before you tackle something more delicate than the rods."

I was thrilled to move up. I felt a little nervous with him standing there watching me, but I did it right the first time and he seemed very pleased. "Now just keep practicing that, Jessie."

"Okay. This stuff is really hot. I'm glad it's not summer."

Roger glanced at Henry, then lowered his voice. "So you think there's still a chance for me and Mary?"

My thoughts were so focused on the glass that I barely caught the subject change. "Uh . . . yeah. Sure. I know Mary cares about you. Maybe we can set something up."

Another group of visitors entered the shop. Roger patted my shoulder. "I'll let you think about that. Let me know what you come up with."

No pressure. I looked at the two pieces of glass I held and considered that they were like Roger and Mary in some way. Maybe if both of them were heated to the right temperature, they'd fuse together again, too.

I concentrated on my task, fusing the two rods together when they started glowing orange in the heat from the torch, then cutting them apart. I began to imagine faces and shapes in the glass where it became molten. Maybe this was how the first Venetian glassmakers started. I couldn't even imagine how to shape what I saw, but I hoped that would come later.

"Busy?" Henry asked from a safe distance. Unfortunately, I couldn't blindfold him. His eyes kept wandering to my bodice.

"Yes. Go away."

"I know you don't really want that. I know you're embarrassed by your attraction to me. I understand. Everyone here knows you and Chase are a couple. You don't want Chase to find out about me. I'm cool with that. We can meet secretly. No one has to know."

I glared at him. "What part of *go away* makes you think I want to meet you somewhere?"

He smiled in that supercilious way men have when they

think you really mean yes. "Everything about you tells me you want me. Your eyes. Your lips. Your body is singing every time I come near."

I wondered what song he'd hear if I set the blow torch to him. *Just kidding.* For good measure, I put down the glass I was working on. It probably wouldn't be a good thing to hit him with it either. "There's one thing I'd like to know."

He dared to lean a little closer. "What's that, baby?"

"Do you enjoy pain?"

Clearly surprised, he answered hesitantly, "I suppose, within certain guidelines. A little pain could be okay."

"If you *ever* hit on me again like you just did, you're going to experience pain outside of *any* guidelines. Do I make myself clear?" I picked up my pieces of glass again for good measure. I hoped it was enough to scare him away.

He shrugged. "If you can deny yourself, that's fine with me. There are plenty of eggs in the old chicken coop."

I watched him saunter away. *Old chicken coop?* The man was impossible.

Roger came back after a few minutes and smiled at me. "You're doing so much better, Jessie. Have you come up with any ideas about me and Mary yet?"

A huge sigh of frustration escaped my lips. Both of these men were insane. But I wasn't going to let it bother me. I was dedicated to learning this craft. I was also dedicated to getting Roger and Mary back together again. And what else had I told Chase that morning? Oh yeah, finding out who was trying to kill me or Roger.

"Not yet." I smiled brilliantly for his benefit. "But I'm working on it. What do I do after I get used to holding the hot glass?"

"I can show you better than I can tell you," he said. "Come over here with me."

He told Henry to take all the visitors who came in, and

then sat down at his workbench. "I get a picture in my head sometimes. It might be something I see in a magazine or something I imagine. When I first started making dragons, nobody else was making them. I saw some pictures of them in my niece's fairy-tale book. I came to the shop and started imagining them."

As he spoke, he worked with his hands. "I decide on a color and a form. I'm using precolored soda lime glass. It's a soft glass. Today I think we'll use red for the dragon. You take your hollow red glass tube and heat it, then use the tools to begin forming the dragon with the glass."

I watched him perform what appeared to be magic by gently blowing into the hollow tube, creating the body of the dragon. I was amazed at how quickly it began to resemble the beast. The long, slender neck, large head, and bigger body.

"We'll use the stump shaper to sculpt the dragon's body, give it some form. These holding fingers close around the glass when you work with a figure and need to hold it while you're torching."

Watching him work was fascinating. I almost didn't notice that two visitors in really bad ghost costumes (Renaissance-patterned sheets with eye holes) had joined me. I didn't see Henry right away either, but I soon realized he was standing behind me. Did the man have a death wish? I could totally understand if someone was trying to kill *him*—and I wished they'd hurry so he'd stop bothering me.

Roger was adding some gold to the ridges on the dragon's wings and body. The hot glass was smoking in the dim shop light. It was a masterpiece, as usual. I had missed some of it worrying about Henry, but I was beginning to understand how the glasswork came together. I knew I wouldn't be able to do anything so skillful, but I wanted to create something.

"You see?" Roger cut the dragon free from the last piece of glass. "Do you have a picture of something in *your* mind, Jessie?"

At that moment, Henry goosed me, and the only picture I could see was my fist connecting with his eye. Fortunately, I was saved from that violence by the sound of trumpets from the street outside. A page dressed in scarlet livery entered the shop and held out a proclamation.

"Good sirs and ladies," the page announced, "I beg thee take heed of my words. On this evening, my master Sir Reginald will challenge Henry of the Glass Gryphon to a duel on the Field of Honor within Their Majesties' Great Hall. Tickets for the duel are still available at the castle entrance. I bid thee good day."

Roger shook his head. "What have you done *now*, Henry?"

Eleven

"Nothing. I'm as surprised about this as you are, Uncle Roger." Henry looked around the room at the visitors and the page, who still waited. "Really. I don't know what this is all about. You know what a crazy place this is."

Roger groaned. "I saw you outside with Princess Isabel yesterday. I thought you had enough sense not to try any of your crap with her. I guess I was wrong."

Henry laughed in that nervous way people have when they *know* they've been caught. "You know, you people take this place way too seriously. So I had a little fun with Princess Isabel, who by the way is neither a princess nor named Isabel. I'm not fighting anyone. Sir Reginald can take a flying leap as far as I'm concerned."

The visitors in the shop were amazed, torn between wondering if there would be a real duel of honor or if the whole thing was a joke. Roger shook his head. "You have so little regard for tradition. I'm surprised you want to open the shop for me at all. Something like this tells on a man, Henry. You just don't get it."

"You're darn right I don't get it," Henry yelled. "And I don't want to. I don't know why you stay here when you could do just as well outside the wall in the real world. If this were my business, I'd close it down and move it to Charleston."

"Good thing it's not," Roger said. "When I'm dead and you inherit everything, you can do whatever you want. But I'm still here and I'm telling you that you have to face Sir Reginald."

"The hell I do!" Henry stormed from the shop, his short cape flying out behind him.

There was a stunned silence as everyone wondered what would happen next. It was customary for the challenged party to accept the challenge through the page. I wasn't sure what the fallout would be if no one accepted the challenge. I supposed Princess Isabel's honor would have to survive and Sir Reginald wouldn't have anyone to duel. It was a break in protocol for the Village. I hoped the Craft Guild would find a way to save face.

"I'll accept the challenge for my nephew and bring honor to my house and my guild." Roger's voice was firm and ringing in the shop.

I thought the ladies were going to swoon with delight at his pronouncement. It gave me an idea.

When the page and heralds were gone and the ladies had purchased their trinkets, promising to be at the duel that evening, they left. I took Roger aside and told him my idea. His eyes lit up and he grinned. "That's a great idea, Jessie. But she won't believe you now. Who's going to carry the message?"

I still had the two-way radio, and this seemed like an emergency to me. I knew better than to randomly call for help, but I thought about calling Merlin. "He might not come," I warned Roger, "but if he does, he'd be a great advocate."

"I don't think you can just call Merlin," Roger said. "Chase is going to hear you and come running."

"Yeah." I sighed. "There's that."

We sat in the shop for a few minutes trying to decide what to do. The problem was that Merlin could be anywhere in the Village, and that was a lot of territory to cover. There wasn't a lot of time before the feast at the castle. The duel would commence as soon as the visitors were seated in front of their food. Nothing like a sword fight and some jousting to make someone hungry.

"What about if I call and say the message is for Merlin?" I suggested.

"Chase monitors all the calls," Roger said. "I used to do the same thing when I was bailiff. It's the only way to keep up with everything that's going on."

I was worried about losing my newly acquired radio, but the course of true love never ran smooth. If I could get this information to Mary before the duel, it could make things much easier for me.

With that settled in my mind, I took out the radio and pressed the button. "Hello. We need a little help down here at the Glass Gryphon."

There was some static before Chase's voice answered back. "Is that you, Jessie? What's wrong? Did something else happen?"

"In a way. I want to talk to Merlin, but I'm not sure where he is."

"Jessie, this is for emergency use only. Is this an emergency?"

"Sort of. Merlin could take care of it, though. No need for you to bother, Chase."

I could tell from his voice that he wasn't happy with my decision to use the radio. "You'll have to go and find him like you would if you didn't have the radio. I'm sorry, sweetie, but I don't use the radio like this and you can't either. Get off the line."

Before I was thrown off of the only communication that didn't involve a page or the Black Dwarf, I tried one last urgent plea. "Merlin! If you're out there, we need you here ASAP."

"Jessie, get off the line *now*," Chase growled.

I shut off the radio and looked at Roger. "What do you think?"

"I think Chase will stop by the next time he makes rounds and confiscate your radio."

"He wouldn't! He's afraid Death might kill me."

Roger went back to his workbench and shrugged as he sat down. "It was a good idea, Jessie. Thanks for thinking of it. I just don't know what's wrong with Henry. The boy doesn't seem to have a brain in his head. I guess he takes after my brother, his father. He could never think his way out of a paper bag either."

Roger and I spent the next hour practicing with the hot glass. I waited on the visitors who came into the shop and handled their transactions with Lady Visa or Sir MasterCard. Then I hurried back to my creation, which didn't seem to want to take form as Roger's dragon had. It kind of sat like a lump on my workbench.

"Just be patient," Roger advised. "Nobody gets this right away. I think your choice of a dog was a good idea."

"Yeah. But his head keeps falling off. And I can't tell if he has four legs or five."

"I thought that other leg was his tail." He scrutinized my work.

As it happened, Chase showed up at the same time as Merlin. It was a happy little coincidence. Chase was sort of angry, but Merlin was happy to the point of lunacy. They kind of balanced each other out.

"You can't use the radio for nonemergency problems," Chase told me. "I thought I made that clear."

"Of course she can," Merlin disagreed. "She's almost been killed, and Livy wanted to sleep with her. Cut her some slack."

"We have to keep order, sir," Chase said defensively. "The whole spirit of the Village could be lost if everyone starts running around with cell phones calling each other."

Merlin waved his hand dismissively. "Pissh! Chase, you do an excellent job, but you have to learn how to lighten up, boy. Jessie, tell me what your emergency is. I have a friendly little witch waiting back at the apothecary for me. And this better be good."

I explained what had happened with Henry and how it could be used to bring Roger and Mary back together. Then I waited for Merlin's response.

"It's devious and underhanded. I like it! What do you want me to do?"

"Hail to thee, fair lady!" Merlin greeted Mary where she sat making baskets on the back stairs at Wicked Weaves. I watched from around the corner (behind her back) as the sorcerer worked his magic.

"Hail to you, too. You'll keep that robe down if you know what's good for you. There's nothing I want to see under there." Mary was her usual self, not mincing any words. She never even looked up from her basket. This was going to be hard even *with* Merlin's help.

"I wonder if you plan to attend the feast at the castle this evening." He leaned on his staff, carefully not looking my way.

"I wonder if you can keep your nose out of other people's business," she shot back. "Why are you here?"

"I'm here because of sad tidings this day. I thought you should know."

"Know what? I'm kind of busy here. Spit it out."

"Sir Roger of the Glass Gryphon will do battle on the Field of Honor this eve. He will battle Sir Reginald, mayhap to the *death*." Merlin paused dramatically to let his words sink in.

"And?"

"And I thought you might like to know."

"Why?" She finally looked up and paused in her basket making.

"Sir Roger is your chosen one. I thought perhaps you would want him to wear your favor into battle."

Mary's dark eyes narrowed. "Seems to me he should be wearing that little hussy Jessie's favor. She was all over him right out there in the street. Whatever Roger and I had is over."

"Yet it was *your* favor Sir Roger thought of, yet dared not ask for, when he was challenged."

"Roger was *challenged*?" She humphed. "I'll bet that stupid nephew of his was challenged and Roger was crazy enough to take his place. Like I said, you'd best be talking to Jessie."

Merlin shook his head, his long white hair and beard moving slowly so as not to disturb the tall pointed hat. "It is a sad day, dear lady, when two who love such as you and Sir Roger are forced asunder by circumstance. He asked for you. None other. What is your reply?"

"My reply is to tell him he'd better find someone else. Jessie, why don't you give that man your favor, whatever that is? Or was that what you were doing out in the street today?"

It took me a minute (and Merlin staring at me after studiously ignoring my hiding place) to realize she was speaking to me. That little woman has eyes in the back of her head.

I stepped out of my spot at the corner of the building and walked into the backyard. Merlin shrugged when he saw me. "I tried. She's not buying. Maybe you should've tried this yourself before you called me."

"Thanks anyway." I leaned against the plum tree. "Why are you being so stubborn? You know Roger loves you. I know you love Roger. What's the big deal?"

Mary said a mouthful in Gullah that I couldn't understand. I guessed that was her venting. She finally took a deep breath and reverted to English. "The big deal? Just last week, Roger was accusing me of messing around with Damian. Then I see him out in the street with you on top of him and his lips trying to suck the breath out of you. *That's* what's wrong."

"You totally misunderstood." I related the whole story about the sign falling and Roger and I pushing each other out of the way. "The rest was just . . . gratitude."

She laughed. It wasn't a pleasant sound. "If that's all it was, why send this crazy man to talk to me? Why not come yourself?"

Maybe it was a good question. I looked at the almost naked branches of the plum tree. The autumn breezes had already taken most of the little leaves that were so pretty over the summer. "I don't know. It seemed like a good idea. I didn't think you'd listen to me."

"But you thought I'd listen to *him*?" She pointed to Merlin by nodding her head his way. "Jessie, child, sometimes I wonder if you ain't a little *tetched*."

I wasn't sure what that meant, but it didn't sound good. Merlin bowed to both of us and took his leave. I heard one of the wraiths in the street shriek as he passed her. He might be the head of Adventure Land, but he's a dirty old man, too.

"Okay. I'm sorry I didn't come to you myself. I didn't think you'd listen to me. Really. What you saw out there was just stupid. Do you really think I'd give up *Chase* for Roger? I might be *tetched*, but I'm not crazy!"

She checked the blue scarf on her head. "And Roger is going to fight Sir Reginald?"

I told her about Henry and Princess Isabel. "You know he has to show up or the whole Craft Guild will lose face."

"Men are just plain stupid," she declared. "I won't be party to this. Roger should let Henry fight his own battles. The boy needs some growing up. He thinks Roger's work should be handed to him on a silver platter. He's a lazy snake in the grass."

"I totally agree. But I think it's brave of Roger to defend his family and the Guild. Maybe it's not real, but it has meaning to everyone in the Village. What would happen to the Craft Guild if they lost face with the monks? There might be a bread embargo. And the Artist Guild might stop trading with the craftspeople. You know this place is crazy, but it has certain rules."

She seemed to consider it, then waved her hand. "I won't be part of it. Tell Roger I'm sorry. But I don't have any favor to give him. He's on his own if he goes out there tonight."

I thanked her and left her alone. The street was busy with visitors scurrying to get a good seat at the Great Hall and residents trying to close their shops and make their way to the castle. Sunday evening was always a busy time in Renaissance Village.

Roger was waiting at the door to the Glass Gryphon with Chase. "Well? How'd it go?"

"Not well." I told him what she'd said. The light went out of his eyes. "I'm sorry. I guess I wasted my radio time getting in touch with Merlin."

"I'd say so," Chase chimed in. He reached into my pocket and confiscated my radio. "You know we have strict rules for using the radio or any other modern device in the Village. I'm sorry, but you violated that rule."

"What if someone is really trying to kill her?" Roger asked.

It seemed like a valid question to me. Chase shrugged it off. "No one's tried to kill her in the past six hours. I figure it was a temporary thing. Definitely not worth violating the radio rule."

"Maybe not to you," I replied, "but it was worth it to me."

"Oh? How'd the whole thing go with Merlin and Mary?" Chase raised his left brow at me.

"Not so well. But I thought there was a chance it would solve everything. It just didn't happen that way."

"That's why we have the emergency radio use rule or ERU." Chase *dared* to use an acronym at me. "If this had been a real emergency, we wouldn't be having this conversation."

"Don't even talk to me." I looked away from him and turned to Roger. "I'll see you later. Good luck tonight."

"What?" Chase followed me across the cobblestones toward the King's Highway. "You knew when you used the radio for that stuff it wasn't legal. You couldn't resist using it. I understand. Modern devices are addictive."

"Is there an acronym for that?" I demanded as I walked faster away from him.

"You're not mad, are you?"

"Of course not. Why would I be mad?"

My friend Da Vinci looked up from his drawing of a pretty young maid. "Don't answer that question, Sir Bailiff.

Trust me, you do not want to engage in that conversation. Buy flowers and apologize. It will be far less painful."

I wished my costume for this evening hadn't been delivered to the dungeon, but it was too late. Besides, I was angry, not stupid. Chase and I were bound to have disagreements. I just couldn't believe he'd yank my radio like that.

"If you're mad," he continued, coming up behind me as I reached the dungeon door, "we can talk about it. I'm sure we can come to some understanding."

"Like you'll give me the radio back again?"

"That's not going to happen, Jessie."

"Then there's nothing to talk about." I opened the dungeon door and the terrible banshee wailed again. "Chase, what's wrong with you? Why can't you fix that thing?"

He swore softly and started inside. "Don't go up by yourself."

I stopped with my foot on the bottom stair. "Why? Don't you think it's safe?"

"I don't know anymore. I don't know what's happening. Someone keeps coming in here and turning this banshee back on."

"Just give me my radio and I'll call you if something's wrong."

"Hang on while I get rid of this again and we'll go up together."

"You don't even trust me to go *upstairs* with the radio?"

He gritted his teeth but finally took out the radio and handed it to me. "Fine. Take the radio. But don't use it again unless there's an emergency. A *real* emergency, like death and destruction. Can you understand that?"

I took the radio and tucked it into my belt. "I believe I'm capable of making that decision."

"Yeah right," he muttered.

"What did you say?"

"Nothing. I'll meet you upstairs."

The door to the apartment was locked, as it should've been. Nothing unusual was inside. I glanced at the bed and thought about the scythe and the message again. It wasn't really there; all of it had been cleaned up. There was even a new comforter on the bed with my costume and a dozen red roses from Chase.

How could I stay angry at the man? He was so good, most of the time. Besides, I had the radio back, and my costume, meant to appease and provoke the king, was exactly as I'd ordered. Beth—the Village seamstress—and Portia could do miracles if you paid them enough.

By the time Chase came upstairs, I was ready. He took one look at me and sat down hard on the bed. "Where did you get that?"

"I found it during my break while you were busy. I felt like King Harold was issuing a challenge to me after I bested the Devil yesterday. I couldn't let it go unanswered."

Chase got up and walked around me, looking at me from all angles. "It must be Joan of Arc."

"You got it." I smoothed down the miniscule white skirt that began at the armored bodice and ended up high on my thighs. The breastplate jutted out (I've always admired those large bosoms) but managed to be very low cut around a white ruffle that revealed more than it concealed. Part of the armor extended down my arms over the white sleeves that also ended in a ruffle at the wrist above the dainty gauntlets. "What do you think?"

He took off my shiny silver helmet and threaded his fingers through my hair. "I think we have time for you to conquer me before we go to the feast."

I raised my long sword. "On your knees, knave!"

* * *

We didn't quite have enough time for all that much conquering to take place, but we held hands and ran to the Great Hall when we were finished. The Village was empty since everyone was at the castle. There was heavy fog on the ground and rising from Mirror Lake, courtesy of the fog-making machine.

At that moment, the spookiness didn't bother me. Of course, I was wearing armor, carrying a large sword, and had a six-foot-eight, two-hundred-fifty-pound man running beside me. Even I'd be hard-pressed not to feel safe.

Gus Fletcher, master at arms, passed us through the gate. He was a big man, an ex–professional wrestler. He whistled as I ran by, my white skirt flying. "Looking good tonight, Jessie. Stop by my place if you're looking for a *real* Renaissance man."

"Hey!" Chase glanced back at him. "You could at least wait until I'm not standing right next to her!"

Gus shrugged. "Sorry, man."

We kept running, past the serving wenches and the jugglers practicing with plastic skulls for the king and queen. There was music playing, and I could hear the sounds of laughter as the visitors to the court were entertained by the ten different performances going on while they ate dinner.

There were huge cobwebs all over the castle. Some we had to walk through, which was kind of creepy. Mirrors on the wall reflected faces that weren't there, and a soundtrack whispered ghostly voices as we walked by. The effect was pretty chilling. I couldn't wait to see what was happening on the field that separated the tiered dining areas that rose around it.

Chase took us up to the dais where the royal family with their courtiers and hangers-on (including sycophants and fools) sat during dinner. He was probably right in assuming we should make our bow to them before going anywhere else.

The king's guard passed us through, and we came out of the narrow corridor to emerge in sight of Their Majesties. They were dressed in their finest, as always, but with one large change. "They're skeletons," I murmured to Chase. "How did they convince Livy to do *that*?"

Before he could answer, a trumpet fanfare sounded. The king looked our way (at least his empty eye sockets did) and held out a bony hand and arm to me. "We believe one of our champions has joined us. Welcome, Craftsman! You shall best evil again here tonight for us."

Twelve

I glanced at Chase. He shrugged. I didn't like the way this was going. I knew anything could happen at the feast. Residents understood the rule of absolute monarchy at the event. The king and queen were the final word.

Chase bowed to Their Majesties. He looked awesome in his midnight blue velvet doublet and matching blue hose. He'd bought a nice blue and silver cape that complimented the outfit. He was one man who could wear tights and not look silly. A fact Princess Isabel seemed to notice right away.

"King Harold, your bailiff greets you this evening. Command me in your needs."

Harry didn't seem to notice him. His eyes behind the skull mask were fixed on me. "We are at a loss this eventide, Sir Craftsman. The queen's champion, Sir Reginald, has taken ill. He will not be able to exact justice from an evildoer who dared disgrace Princess Isabel as she took her daily stroll through the Village."

I *definitely* didn't like where this was going. Sure, all of it was staged. But for the residents, it was serious stuff. The king obviously wanted me to fight Henry, who I knew was being replaced by Roger. That couldn't happen. I mean, which of us would lie down and lose?

Livy trilled her peculiar laugh. "Harold, we have noticed something odd about your champion. The craftsman appears to be a *craftswoman*."

The crowd of visitors laughed hysterically as they put roast beef and potatoes into their mouths. I didn't see anything funny about what she'd said. But maybe Harry would decide he didn't want a woman facing someone as the royal champion. That would kind of be uncharacteristic. And like my namesake at the moment, I'd probably be burned at the proverbial stake for even daring the task.

"We acknowledge our mistake in supposing the craftsman was a man and not this womanly vision in silver armor." King Harold quaffed something from his large, royal cup. "But we ask if this woman will indeed fight to defend Princess Isabel's honor."

If you ask me, I'd say the king had quaffed a little too much for one night. What was he thinking? So Sir Reginald didn't feel good. He probably ate too much for dinner. There were plenty of other knights who could take on the responsibility.

"Your Majesty." Chase tried to get Harry's attention again. "I would be delighted to fight on behalf of Princess Isabel and vanquish the evil one who disturbed her."

Queen Olivia giggled and held her hand out to him. "Approach, Sir Bailiff. You shall sit at my right for the match as Sir Reginald would have done could he be here.

We feel certain there will be all manner of things for us to discuss."

The crowd laughed again. No doubt there'd been too much ale poured by that time. But I was still in a fix. It was my own fault for daring to pique Harry's interest. I could've dressed in a simple craftsman's outfit. But oh no, I had to show him that it was a woman who beat the Devil. That's what I get for being prideful.

"Now, good craftswoman," King Harold instructed, "you shall go down on yon field and address the evildoer. Whose favor shall you carry with you?"

I bowed my head to the inevitable. "I shall carry Sir Bailiff's favor, sire, if he will give it."

I didn't think before I spoke. The women of the court all carried handkerchiefs to give out as favors. What would Chase give me?

He got to his feet, tall and handsome, his long brown braid over one shoulder. The light glinted on the silver earring he'd exchanged for his usual gold hoop to match his outfit. I apologized mentally for putting him on the spot. I hoped he didn't feel obligated to do anything weird or embarrassing to live up to my request. I mean, if he had to take off his hose or something, that would be bad. Interesting, but bad.

But Chase didn't seem phased by my request. He walked back to me and removed his silver earring, hooking it carefully on my breastplate. He bent his head and kissed me. The crowd went wild. "For luck." He smiled and winked at me. "Keep your sword up."

By this time the crowd was clapping their hands and stamping their feet. The roar was almost too loud to hear the beginning of the challenge as the trumpets sounded and Lord Dunstable came to the microphone.

"Good ladies and gentlemen," he addressed the crowd.

"We have a grievous assault on a royal personage. This slight shall not go unpunished. Fighting for the princess's honor is Mistress Jessie Morton. Fighting for the offender, Henry Trent, is Roger Trent of the Craft Guild."

Roger came out into the arena in full dress garb. His doublet was made of red velvet, embroidered with threads of gold. He didn't wear tights, thank goodness. His black breeches ended in tall, black boots. His short sword hung from his waist in a black scabbard. The light from the ceiling gleamed from his shaven head. It might've been better if he'd worn a hat.

But he cut a good, strong figure on the sawdust-covered floor of the Great Hall. He raised his sword and turned in all directions to face the crowd. As was customary, half of the crowd booed and the other half cheered. They knew which to do by the cheerleaders who held up signs and encouraged their sides to yell the loudest.

Roger knelt before the king and queen. "Your Majesties, I am here to honor my guild and my family for the dishonor caused by my nephew, Henry. I pray you will grant us favor after this match, whatever the outcome."

The king and queen both agreed to forgive the debt after the match. I made my way down to the arena floor, feeling hundreds of eyes on my short, white skirt and silver armor. It was kind of exciting and a little strange. I wasn't sure what exactly was required of me in the match. Obviously we never really fight, just give a good show. Like Tony and I had done.

Lord Dunstable stood between us as I reached Roger's side. He took his finger off the microphone and addressed us. "Decide now which of you is falling down."

"I'm not falling down," Roger said.

"I'm not falling down either."

Lord Dunstable glared at both of us. "You have ten

minutes to decide this while you fight. I'll give you the signal to start and the signal to stop. One of you has to lay down your arms or otherwise surrender. Got it?"

Roger looked at me mutinously. All the good rapport we'd gained that day was obviously gone. I glared back before setting my visor down on my face and raising my sword.

I thought about the two-week training everyone who works in the Village receives. It covers events like this one, jousting, being put in the stocks, all the strange, physical things that can happen to a resident. My sword wasn't sharp like a real sword, but I supposed it could hurt if it hit Roger the wrong way. The same thing could be said for his. At least I *hoped* his wasn't real.

"Let's get this over with," Roger growled, taking out his sword.

"I thought you wanted my favor to have during the duel." Mary's voice was like an angel stopping by to make this whole battle thing better. Roger and I both looked at her.

He fell to his knees at her feet, tears flowing down his face. "Mary! You came! I can't tell you what this means to me."

She resembled an angel, too, dressed in a long, flowing white gown. She looked beautiful and ethereal. I don't know whether the white was supposed to be corpselike, but it worked for her. She put her hand out and touched Roger's head. "Baby, we've been apart too long. It was pride, I know. We won't let it happen again."

He sniffed and wiped his tears from her shoes. "Let's get married. We've been together a long time. You're a widow now. There's no reason for either of us to be alone anymore."

Mary glanced at me. "We'll talk about it after you rough Jessie up some. Right now, I think the crowd is getting restless."

She was right. Without the bones from the little chickens that are normally served (the menu calls them Cornish hens), the audience was looking around for things to throw to show their displeasure—and they found some. A rain of various forms of potatoes and tomatoes flew through the air at us. It was only a matter of time before my silver armor would be marred by a vegetable.

"Yes." Roger sniffed and got to his feet. He wiped his nose and eyes on his sleeve (*yuck!*), then advanced on me with his sword raised. "Make it look good, then yield."

"You make it look good, then yield," I said back. "I'm not surrendering."

As his sword hit mine, I realized it might've been a mistake to disagree. Even though I wasn't in any immediate danger, the clash of the blades tore at my arm and shoulder muscles. I was going to feel this for a while.

Roger hit his sword against mine a few more times while the crowd alternately booed and cheered, depending on their cheerleaders. I hit back, even though it was hard. Roger took a step back, and I pushed my advantage by taking a step forward and hitting his sword again.

"Jessie," he said with gritted teeth. "I have bad shoulders. You have to yield."

"No! This isn't any fun for me either. *You* yield."

"It won't look right for a man to yield to a woman. We'll be pelted by vegetables. We might both end up in the kitchen for the rest of the night. Yield!"

I hit his sword again and he dropped to his knees. "You yield, Roger! I don't care how it looks. I'm not giving up."

Lord Dunstable was giving us the cut sign, which meant, *End it before the audience loses interest.* I glanced up at the king and queen. Chase seemed to be the only one sitting with the royal court who was even watching.

Roger hit my sword again and dragged himself off the

floor. "Jessie, if nothing else, think about me and Mary. How will it look for Mary's future husband to lose to a mere wench in armor?"

That was it. "I can't believe you called me a wench!" I hit his sword hard with mine. He staggered back on the floor again, heavy beads of sweat on his face. "You know, this is so typical. Why do you think all those bishops killed Joan of Arc? They couldn't handle a woman being better than them. But sometimes, we just are."

I didn't think about my apprenticeship with Roger or anything else this duel would affect. I just kept hitting his sword until he dropped it on the floor and shouted, "Yield! I yield."

Then I sat down on the sawdust myself, exhausted. My arm felt like a rubber noodle. I could barely move it. But I'd won. I wasn't sure what I'd won. At the time it was enough that I'd won.

Chase jumped over the guardrail and into the arena to help me up. Mary was at Roger's side right away, darting angry glances at me. Lord Dunstable declared me the winner of the bout. We all stood (or came close to it) and faced the king and queen.

"This has been most entertaining!" King Harold pronounced, and the crowd roared their approval. "We are satisfied that justice has been served. No man will accost Princess Isabel again without facing our wrath."

"Your Majesty!" Roger addressed the king. "I ask that you bless my union with this good woman, Mary of Wicked Weaves. Our two houses would like to be joined."

"What, ho! This is good news for the Village. Of course, Sir Roger of the Glass Gryphon. We would be happy to declare your vows at this time."

Queen Olivia trilled, "It's for the best, Sir Roger. Who else would want a man beaten by a maid? Your Mary is indeed a treasure. Stand before us now and declare your vows."

Chase stood with me (good thing, I don't think I could've stood by myself) while Mary and Roger pronounced their vows. The funny thing was that it was all legal. Mary and Roger would have to get a license from the state, but Harry had taken his test to be a justice of the peace a few years back. There were a lot of weddings at the Village. Once the vows were spoken, they were as good as married.

I carefully glanced at Chase so he wouldn't see me. He was looking at Roger and Mary kissing. What was *he* thinking? Had he ever thought about getting married? Not to *me* or anything. Just in general.

When it was over, the minstrels in the gallery played several songs while the rest of us left the field to make room for the jousts. Tony waved to me from the stands. He wasn't wearing his devil outfit. There was no wraith wrapped around him. No dancing girl either, come to think of it. What was he up to?

I tried to pick up my sword. There was just no way. Chase snatched it up for me. "I think you need to work those arms some if you're going to play with swords," he said.

"This is the last time," I promised him. "No wonder Joan of Arc got roasted. She was probably too tired from fighting. That's how the bishops got her."

Mary and Roger walked arm in arm off the field in front of us. I noticed with a smirk that Mary had to put Roger's sword back in its scabbard. I guess I wasn't the only one who was tired.

"Have you ever thought about getting married, Jessie?" Chase asked.

"No. Not really." I smiled at him, my heart beating fast. "You?"

"No. Not really. My parents think about it for me all the time." He shrugged. "I guess I just don't see any reason for it."

"Me either."

This conversation was charged with unspoken thoughts and terrors that lurked in the night. Did this mean each of us was destined to be alone when we were old and gray? Or did it mean we just weren't right for each other, not the spend-the-rest-of-your-life serious? Who could say? I wanted to bite my nails—my usual response when I'm stressed—but my arms were too tired to lift that high.

As soon as we left the field, Lonnie met us to tell Chase he was needed in the Village. It should've been empty during the feast. Security guards herd everyone who doesn't partake of the King's Feast out the main gate before the event starts. What problem could there be now?

Chase didn't even ask. "I'll take your sword with me, Jessie. I guess I'll meet you back at the dungeon."

I was depressed he didn't even ask me if I wanted to go with him. Back over the summer when our relationship was new, he would've asked.

I stood around after he and Lonnie left, worried about losing Chase to some unnamed woman he might want to marry someday and wishing I could bite my fingernails. It wasn't good or sane. There was nowhere to hide from my own stupid thoughts.

One of the king's pages came up and tugged at my armor. "His Majesty would enjoy your company for the feast as his champion. If you will follow me."

Another time, I would've said no. But depression and anxiety don't make for good eating partners, so I went back with the page to the royal dais overlooking the jousting area. Princess Isabel giggled and told me how much she appreciated my help, then invited me to sit at her side. That was a novelty. She'd always had eyes for Chase and treated me like a third wheel.

The page put a plate in front of me, and Princess Isabel scooted closer at the long table. "We have to do something about Henry. I wanted to see him humiliated tonight. That didn't work out. Any suggestions?"

I sipped my iced tea and contemplated what to say. I didn't trust her. She could just as easily take anything I said back to Henry in hope of having a chance with him. "What did you have in mind?"

Princess Isabel daintily stabbed her steak knife over and over into her slab of roast beef. "Something like that. I wish I could've been there when you took him out. I've heard it was great. There's not a single good-looking woman in this Village who doesn't admire you for that, Jessie."

Okay. I was flattered. She actually put me in the good-looking-woman class. Who knew she'd ever noticed? "It wasn't much. Just a few moves I learned in self-defense at the university."

"Wow! That must be nice. Marian and I might go to the Y and take some classes. She hasn't said anything to Robin or the Merry Men. You *know* how they are. We don't want a war between the Craft Guild and the Forest Guild." I saw her fist tighten on her steak knife, but she took a deep breath and put it down on her plate. "God, it would be good to feel Henry's bones crack under my heel!"

I was a little scared by Princess Isabel's bloodthirsty look. I finished my meal, then excused myself from the Royal Court. I had *thought* it would be better being with people. I was wrong. Or at least not that kind of people.

Tired after the long workday and duel-filled evening, I decided to head for home. Hopefully I'd be able to work on my glass art tomorrow, and I wanted to be fresh. I refused to think that Roger would kick me out again because of the duel.

The moon was still big and round over the castle. The *Queen's Revenge* was sailing back toward the tavern on the other side of the lake. I wanted to shake my fist at Rafe and promise vengeance, but I had no idea what I could possibly do to get back at him. The weird, fake fog had a greenish tint to it tonight. It made the ghostly images look even worse. The bats screeched and the werewolf wailed. I yawned, too tired to be scared.

Then I saw him. The figure of Death was skulking around the privies next to Polo's Pasta. He carried his scythe, the moon glinting eerily off the metal.

I started to cross the King's Highway as fast as I could. He didn't seem to have seen me yet. Maybe I still had time to get inside before he noticed me. But the closest place was the tavern by the lake, and I didn't want to go through anything with the pirates again. My other option, Peter's Pub, was a long sprint from there.

I stepped into the shadows of the Hanging Tree and watched as Death moved in and out of the spaces between buildings. He looked as though he were searching for something. *Probably me.* He didn't get enough of a laugh from scaring the crap out of me before. I certainly didn't want to volunteer for another fun time with him. But besides cowering where I was, I couldn't see any way out of my predicament.

Then I remembered something I'd heard when I was a child. I think it was a story my grandmother read to me and Tony. It was about a kid who was afraid of what was in his closet. We're talking afraid like he wouldn't go anywhere near it. He had good reason because there were colored lights under the door and the closet made a scary noise.

When he'd tell his parents, they'd look and nothing was in there, of course. But as soon as they were gone, it came back. Finally (and this was the moral of the story) he had to get up, in the dark, all alone and open the closet. He somehow managed this (Tony and I never understood how, since we were scared just hearing about it). He yelled out to the closet to stop. After that, nothing scary ever happened to him again. At least not from the closet.

As I watched Death pass Galileo's place and swerve toward the Village Square, I made up my mind to be that little boy in the story. I was going to have to confront Death and demand that he leave me alone. That was the only thing to do.

My arms had recovered a little. They were just shaky now. I clenched my hands into fists and yelled as loudly as I could, "Leave me alone!"

The Village lay sleeping, quiet between us. Death turned to face me and held his scythe high with his bony hand. It was a challenge. I reached for my sword. *Chase had it!* Heart pounding, knees knocking, I grabbed a branch that had fallen from the Hanging Tree. With a victory cry that hopefully curdled his blood, I held my stick up and ran at him as hard as I could.

Thirteen

Death stood his ground. I kept hoping he'd run away. But how many times does the monster run away in horror movies? I don't remember ever seeing Dracula run when the peasants came after him.

The closer I got to the hooded figure, the larger he seemed. The green-tinted fog swirled around him like some ghostly creature of the night.

I clutched my tree branch a little tighter as I reminded myself that this was only a man. Maybe a large man, but still only a man. I'd taken Henry out fairly easily, enough so that the women of the Village were looking up to me. All I had to do was stay cool and remember my moves. How hard could it be? The bigger they are, the harder they fall. That's what they always say.

I was pumped up, psyched for the encounter. I ran faster as I passed the Good Luck Fountain and started yelling even louder. I'd read once that the idea of screaming at your opponent came from the earliest tribal instinct to instill fear in your enemy. I could only hope I was instilling a lot of fear.

When he was finally standing within arm's reach, I hurled my whole body at him, prepared to jump up as soon as he crashed to the ground. I wasn't going to be afraid of this myth anymore, skeletal hand or not.

Unfortunately, nothing happened. Well, not so much nothing happened as nothing happened to *him*. I hit him hard (and I'm no lightweight), but it didn't phase him. I don't think he even moved. I hit his chest and midsection and bounced off to the ground. It happened so fast that I thought for a moment someone else had broadsided me.

But no. It was just me and Death out in the middle of the King's Highway. I fell hard on the cobblestones. *This is going to cause some bruising.* The tree limb flew from my hands. My arm and head ached from smashing into him full force.

I lay on the ground groaning, hoping he wasn't coming to kill me with his giant scythe. I couldn't have used my two-way radio if I had it with me. It didn't work with my costume so I'd left it at dungeon. Still, I hoped my death (or serious dismemberment) would teach him a lesson. I hoped he'd never be able to love anyone again after letting me die in such a tragic, yet heroic, way.

Death stood over me. I couldn't move. He looked down into my face, his hood blacking out whatever lurked inside his robe. I closed my eyes, ready for my final scene in Renaissance Village. Who knew it would end this way?

"Hello, lady." Death had a kind of wimpy voice for someone so big.

I opened my eyes a little and he waved at me. It was a pinky wave where you just move your fingers.

"Are you hurt?"

"Am I hurt?" I mimicked, obviously too terrified to think.

"Did you hurt your head? You sound kind of funny. Do you need me to get help?"

Of all things, this was not what I expected. The words to answer him wouldn't come out of my mouth. I just stared at him until he moved closer and his form blocked out everything but his black robe. He picked me up like I was a toothpick, weighed no more than a small child, holding me across his arms with them extended from his chest so I didn't lie against him.

"I'll take you to get help," he promised in that same little-boy voice.

"Are you sure you're Death?"

"Yeah. I was working here as an ogre. I took my brother Ross's place when he was killed to try and figure out about what happened to him."

His brother? My brain hurt, but I knew that couldn't be right. "Ross's last name was DeMilo. Chase said your last name is Van Imp."

He shrugged. "A stage name. I wouldn't want all my fans finding out I was working here."

I looked up into his large face as we walked by a street-light. He had black curly hair and a large nose that looked like a piece of flesh-colored Play-Doh plastered to his face. His hands were huge, too. He probably could've crushed me with them.

"Do you know anything about my brother's death?" he asked me.

"Not really. Probably not more than you know. No one really seems to know anything. The police think it wasn't an accident, but they're not sure. Sorry I can't be more help."

"That's okay. I've been watching everyone the last few days. There are a lot of crazy people here. I think maybe one of them, the one who killed Ross, will make a mistake and I'll have him."

It sounded like a plan to me. "Why were you following me yesterday? Why did you put your scythe on my bed?"

"I was following you because I thought you might know something. Then I realized you didn't know anything. Then I was following you because you seemed to be the next target for the killer."

"And the scythe?"

"I didn't do that. Why would I?"

"I thought you did it to scare me. Like the skeleton hand."

He finally put me down on my feet as we reached the first aid station behind Merlin's Apothecary. He pulled out the plastic skeleton hand and waved it. "And did it scare you?"

"Yeah. I guess. What about all those warnings, *Death shall find thee*?"

"I don't know. What does it mean? Wasn't that what they said was on my brother's robe when he died?"

I tried to judge him by looking into his homely but amiable face. Was he telling the truth? He didn't seem like the kind of person who'd bother lying. I mean, the man was a tank. He sure wouldn't be afraid to tell me anything he wanted me to hear. "Well, that's just great."

"Why?"

"Because I thought *you* were the killer. Now, I don't know."

"Thank you. I don't like people to think I'm a killer." He smiled at me and shook his big head.

"But you're Death. How much more of a killer could that be?"

"Maybe. But that's only the character I'm playing. Inside, I'm a lover, not a fighter. I like poetry and those little boxes full of sand that come with tiny rakes."

Before I could answer (just as well, what would I say to that?) the door to the first aid station opened and Wanda LeFay, the only registered nurse in the Village, looked out at us. "Jessie? Is something wrong?"

"No!" I started to hobble away from her. I must have twisted one of my ankles when I fell. Every step was agony. No wonder movie heroines always fall to the ground and scream when they turn their ankles. "I'm going back to the dungeon now. Good night."

"But you're hurt," Death argued. "See? You can't even walk straight. You need help."

"Not from her," I mumbled. I sure didn't want Wanda's cold, blue, fish eyes looking me over and finding something else she could hurt. "No," I said louder. "I'm fine. I'll deal with it."

Wanda glanced at Death. "Bring her inside, will you? Let's just have a little look-see."

Wanting to help, Death scooped me up again and deposited me in Wanda's infirmary, otherwise known as her house of horrors. No doubt she didn't have to do much of anything for Halloween. She'd once given me a tetanus shot after an injury and the needle had broken off in my arm. We're talking serious, life-threatening terror dispensed with a pleasant, real-life British accent, one of the few real ones in the Village.

"I'm fine, Wanda. Really." I struggled to escape, but Death held me in place with one hand. Maybe he really *was* destined to kill me.

"Stop fussing!" Wanda commanded. "I believe you've got a small sprain. Nothing to get upset about. I'll just wrap it nice and *tight*. That's all it needs."

Death's colossal figure blocked my view of what Wanda was doing, but I could feel her nice-and-tight bandage technique cutting off the circulation to my foot. All I could do was wince in pain and hope it would be over soon. As soon as I escaped from Wanda's evil clutches, I'd take off the bandage—hopefully before I needed an amputation.

"There we are! Good as new. You take it easy for a few days and you'll never even know it happened." She stood back to admire her handiwork.

When Death moved aside, I knew I had to get out of there before she decided to fix something else. I also knew I couldn't hobble away fast enough. I needed a diversion.

"Maybe I should take your temp, Jessie," Wanda said thoughtfully. "Don't want you to run a fever with your sprain, do we? I only have a rectal thermometer, but that should do."

"What's that?" I pointed out the back window that gave a view of the small patch of ground between the first aid station and the wall around the Village. "I think I saw someone spray painting the wall. I'll bet it's the same person who's been going around the Village putting graffiti on everything."

It was a strategic maneuver: I knew Death would be interested and Wanda, Queen of the Rules, would rise to the bait. And I was right. Both of them hurried into the back after Wanda picked up her extremely large stun gun. I mean, what did she plan on bringing down with that thing, an ox?

I didn't care. I hobbled out the front door and hid in the shadows against the apothecary wall. I could hear Wanda swearing in her native tongue, which sounded nothing like American swearing, and Death lumbering around looking for me. My ankle was killing me, but that was only a metaphor; I feared Wanda was capable of the real thing if given the chance.

After a while, their noise died out and I heard the crowds begin leaving the castle after the feast. I wished I knew where Chase was, but I was going to have to make it back to the dungeon on my own.

I scooted out into the light and another large shadow fell across me. Death had found me again.

"That wasn't very nice," he said. "She was trying to help you."

"Yeah. But the Inquisition was trying to help, too."

"She made your foot better. See? You're walking good now."

"There you are!" Chase crept up on us. "Are you okay, Jessie?"

"I'm fine." I made a fast move to his side and wrapped my arms around him. I was really glad to see him and was surprised by how small he looked compared to Ross's brother. "Chase, this is Death. Death, Chase."

"You know that it hurts for someone to call you names," Death said. "You could use my real name."

I couldn't remember his real name and looked at Chase, hoping he could. Lucky for me, he picked up on my distress and held his hand out to the giant. "Hi. I'm Chase Manhattan, the Village bailiff. You must be Bart. It's nice to meet you."

Bart smiled hugely and reached his hand out to Chase. "Thank you. It's nice to meet you, too. Do you know who killed my brother?"

We sat around a wooden table at the Lady of the Lake Tavern discussing what happened to Death's (I mean, Bart's) brother. Bart was actually a very nice man who was fiercely loyal to his brother and determined to figure out who killed Ross.

"I thought if I took this job, whoever killed Ross would come after me. No such luck." He wrapped his huge hand around a tankard, making it look like a toy.

"At least not yet," Chase said. "This could be dangerous, Bart. I don't think your brother was singled out, unless it was because of the irony."

Bart stared at him, apparently not taking his meaning.

"He means somebody got a kick out of killing Death. You know?" I hoped that explained it. "If that's the case, you could be next in line."

Bart finished his drink and wiped the foam from his mouth with the back of his hand. "That's why I'm here. I want them to come at me. The police don't know who did it. They don't even have a suspect."

Chase shrugged. "There were more than two thousand people here at the time Ross was killed. Unless you have someone in mind who had it in for him, I'm afraid it's gonna be like getting those people off Gilligan's Island."

"I know." The giant smiled. "But I think they got home in that last movie."

"Really?" Chase asked. "I don't think I saw that one. I always thought the professor would die before he made it back. Again, the irony."

I didn't think Bart understood *that* irony either. I leaned forward and put my hand on his. My God! It was huge. "Did your brother have any enemies?"

"No! He was lovable and helpful, just like me. He trusted people. Maybe too much. No one would want to kill him, lady."

"Jessie," I corrected. "You can call me Jessie."

He nodded. "I saw you fight. You're a good fighter."

"Thanks."

Chase looked at me, then looked back at Bart. "I'm sorry

I don't have better answers for you. I wish I knew what happened to him. The honest answer is, it could've been any of those two thousand visitors here that day or any of the five hundred or so residents. I don't like thinking it could be someone who works here, but I don't know for sure."

The tavern was quiet and empty around us as the owner, Ginny Stuart (no relation to Mary Stuart, as far as I know), and her workers cleaned up for the next day. The smell of pine was very strong. I looked out the window and saw the *Queen's Revenge* sitting at anchor close by. Not much worry about marauding pirates after the Village was closed.

"How will we ever find out who killed Ross if he didn't have any enemies and we don't have any suspects?" I asked over the swish of the mop on the wood floor.

"Maybe it's whoever's writing on the walls." Bart shrugged his massive shoulders. "Since that same thing was on Ross's robe, maybe the killer has something else to say."

"I've thought about that, too," Chase agreed. "But again, all those people saw it and it was on TV, so another hundred thousand or so people saw it. Detective Almond thinks it's probably a copycat. I kind of agree with him."

"I don't think so," Bart said. "I think whoever killed my brother is still here. Maybe he plans to kill me, too. For the irony, right, Jessie?"

Neither one of us could disagree with him. It was a complete mystery. I could see Chase's point about someone targeting Death to die. But what would be the point if no one had a grudge against him? If it was someone who had something to say, it seemed like they would've taken responsibility.

Figuring out what happened and why was on my to-do list now that Mary and Roger were back together. I wasn't sure where to start, but looking at Bart's plain but sweet face, I knew he needed closure. He needed to know what happened. Myrtle Beach PD would probably never know. It was up to me and Chase.

But right now, I was exhausted. Too exhausted to think anymore. I wanted to lay my head down on the wooden table and fall asleep like a drunken sailor. My ankle throbbed when I thought of the long walk back across the Village. The ale helped some, but most of me didn't want to move.

"Ye scurvy slugs better be gettin' on outta here," Ginny said in her usual colorful language. Obviously she'd spent too much time with Rafe and the other pirates.

She was a rough-looking, white-haired woman who always wore the same green dress with her large bosom nearly pushed out of the neckline. She'd owned the Lady of the Lake for as long as I'd been coming to the Village. Believe me, no one ever argued with her.

"We're on our way out," Chase told her with a smile guaranteed to melt the hardest heart.

Ginny grinned, showing her gold-capped teeth (another pirate necessity). "Lord love ye, Sir Bailiff. Ye could charm the ravens out of the Hanging Tree."

Chase shook her hand as he walked by, but apparently that wasn't enough for Ginny. She goosed him before he could get out of the tavern.

I wasn't stupid enough to question it. Ginny could split my gizzard (her words a long time ago) without breaking a sweat. Besides, I wasn't worried about *her*. Not like Princess Isabel or the sex-crazy fairies/wraiths. There were way more dangers in the Village than Ginny. At least as far as Chase's body was concerned.

We walked outside and stopped dead in the shadow of the old Hanging Tree. In the hour or so while we were inside talking about Bart's brother, Village decorators had come up with another brilliant Halloween idea.

The entire Village was covered in fake spiderweb. It glistened in the streetlights and moved with the breeze. In some spots, it was too heavy to walk through. Visitors and residents would need scissors to get around in the morning.

"This is spooky." Bart pulled up his hood. He tested the spiderweb against his scythe. "It's good and strong," he added when it didn't pull down.

"Looks like a giant spider from hell or Mars visited," I remarked.

"It would have to be hell," Chase said. "Mars would be sci-fi. We don't do that here."

We said good night to Bart and started across the King's Highway. "This is gonna be a mess for maintenance," Chase said. "It sucks to be them."

I agreed. "Who do you think is making all these choices?"

Merlin ran by us (at least as far as the spiderwebs would let him). His robe flashed in the breeze. "Isn't it wonderful? Don't you love it?"

We watched him continue skipping and running through the webbing. I didn't have to wonder for long who'd decided we needed giant spiderwebs all over the Village. Now that I knew about Merlin being Adventure Land's founder, I knew who to blame for everything.

"Any ideas yet on what you plan to do to get even with Rafe?" Chase asked as we walked past Eve's Garden at the far end of Mirror Lake.

"Not yet. I've kind of been busy thinking about Mary and Roger, and now finding out who killed Ross."

"I have an idea."

"Does it involve pain and suffering?"

"Not really. I thought about emptying his wine casks and filling them with vinegar."

"Too easy." I walked beside him, dodging webbing. "You know, this looks like a trailer for a bad Spiderman movie."

"You think so?" He looked around us at the spiderwebs, which connected every stationary object inside the Village wall. "I like the spider-from-hell scenario best."

"Maybe. I suppose visitors will love it."

"And want to have their pictures taken wrapped in it."

I slipped my arm through his. "Maybe we should just get up late tomorrow."

"That works for me." He grinned. "You are really *hot* in that outfit."

"You already told me that, remember? When you took it off right after I put it on the first time." I smiled, thoroughly enjoying the way he was looking at me.

"That was before I saw you fight Roger. Believe me, there wasn't a knave or king in that room who didn't want you. You have great legs, Jessie."

"Yeah. You probably say that to all the armor-wearing babes in the Village."

We'd reached the dungeon and Chase had his hand on the door. "Besides you, that only leaves Daisy. I don't think that's happening."

"But maybe not because you don't *want* it to."

We both laughed and he opened the door. Laughter turned quickly to groaning when the stupid banshee started wailing again. Chase swore and hit the sturdy dungeon door with his fist. "I don't understand this. I ripped everything out of here *twice*. Who keeps putting it back?"

I glanced at the inside of the dungeon door as Chase stalked into the darkness to remove the banshee again. One of the stuffed scarecrows from the hatchet-throwing booth was pinned to the door with the same blood red words scribbled across its chest: *Death shall find thee.*

"Chase." I swallowed hard on my fear. "If Bart is right, his brother's killer just paid us a visit. Again."

Fourteen

Chase and I both slept at Debby's that night. We had very little with us, but Chase had managed to take back my two-way radio before we left the dungeon. It wasn't much fun, but at least it felt safe. I got up sometime during the long night and went to check on Chase, who was sleeping in the living room. Debby's sofa (really a love seat) was big enough for only part of him. Most of him was either sticking out in the air or on the floor. It didn't look very comfortable. I felt guilty for taking the soft bed. But considering Debby was in the bed, too, I guess I didn't feel *too* bad.

I went back to sleep, and when I woke up at eight, he was gone. No note. No two-way radio. I felt a little less kindly toward him. He could've left me something. My ankle felt better though. I was glad for that.

"Where's Chase?" Debby asked, coming out of the bathroom.

"He had to go to work," I made up. "He's really busy."

She nodded. "I know. With all this stuff going on in the Village, I'm surprised he gets to sleep at all. It must be superexciting to be with him, huh?"

I assured her it was more superexciting than she could imagine, then went to take a shower. The hot water was gone (big surprise) so it was a really quick, cold shower. I put on the bustier and the black leather pants. The blouse made the outfit look decent enough, but I couldn't wear it again. Later, maybe at lunch, I'd wander down to see Portia and return my Joan of Arc costume. If I was lucky she'd have something else for me.

The Village was a mess after the giant spiderweb fiasco of last night. The webbing was damp from the morning's drizzly weather, and much of it had fallen down on the ground like big white strings of polyester taffy. Everyone was jumping over it or ducking under it. Twice I saw some of it slide from a shop roof into the street. It was going to be a huge cleanup job for maintenance, as Chase had predicted.

I stopped at Sir Latte's and listened to the endless speculation by residents about what was happening. Most people thought the red lettering was a joke or something the Village was doing as a Halloween promotion. A few were scared because of the phrase's connection to Ross's death. Many were completely unaware anything had happened.

I ate my muffin and drank my mocha without adding to the speculation. I might have been in the middle of what was going on, but I had no idea why it was happening, and what little I knew seemed better kept to myself.

I finished my breakfast and headed out into the damp day. Hopefully the early morning drizzle would give way to sunshine. The weather at the coast often starts out rainy but clears up by noon. Of course, this time of year was serious hurricane season. Maybe by lunch, none of us would be here.

I didn't realize until I was standing outside of the Glass Gryphon that I was dreading seeing Roger again. Oh yeah, I'd been flip about it last night when I was beating him at fake swordplay. And maybe he wouldn't be upset because I *had* reunited him with Mary in a big way. He might even be grateful. Or he might tell me to get lost.

I opened the shop door just before the main gate was due to open on the other side of the Village. Roger was not at his workbench. Henry looked up from whatever he was creating but didn't say anything. Did that bode well for my return to glass art?

"Good morning." Roger came down the stairs from his apartment. He was dressed in his usual white shirt and brown leather jerkin. "Are you ready to get started?"

My heart jumped a little. I was really looking forward to continuing my apprenticeship. At least I didn't have to beg to have my workbench back. "You bet. My little dog wants a body."

He laughed. I stared at him. It was a *real* laugh, not some snide precursor to a remark that was going to irritate me. I couldn't believe it. Then Mary came downstairs, twisting her red scarf around her head. Suddenly, I understood.

I walked over to my workbench and lit up the torch. At least I remembered how to do that much. I could feel everyone watching me. I put on my glasses and looked up at them. "What?"

Mary shook her head. "Putting that girl next to fire is *not* a good idea. Be careful, Jessie. That thing can give you a lot more than a cut on the finger." She kissed Roger good-bye and sailed out the front door toward Wicked Weaves across the street.

"So you're working on a dog?" Roger looked at my project from several different angles. "Good job! I'm sure it'll take shape. Don't forget, it's all about controlling the heat. You need part of the glass to move into shape, but you want the other part to be stationary."

I was holding my nine-mil glass tube in the flame from the torch as he was speaking. It was the perfect size for my dog's body. Unfortunately, it drooped over on the bench like a big blob of marshmallow in a camp fire. We both stood there staring at it.

"Don't worry," he cheered me on. "You'll get it. Henry did, and he's not as bright as you."

I glanced at Henry and could see he wasn't loving that remark. I wondered if the two had argued about the duel last night. Had Roger tried to coerce Henry into going to save face? I wasn't really worried about it. I could've taken Henry more easily than I had Roger. At least Roger had learned how to fake sword fight like the rest of us. Henry didn't even have that knowledge.

After the main gate opened, the Village quickly filled with visitors. In fact, it was a lot busier than a typical Monday should've been. I was wondering why when the door to the shop opened and Lilly Hamilton entered, complete with camera-toting assistant.

"And this is one of the many shops located here in Renaissance Faire Village that will be affected by a police shutdown of the popular tourist attraction." Lilly spoke directly to the camera, her normally squinty brown eyes wide open. "After yesterday's remarks by the Myrtle Beach Town Council and chief of police, it seems the trendy Village may not last as long as its Renaissance namesake."

Lilly cued her cameraman, a thin, young man who looked a lot like Peter Parker before he became Spiderman. He was barely able to hold up the camera. After making sure her adoring public wasn't watching anymore, Lilly turned to Roger.

"I remember you from yesterday. You and that girl were

almost hit by the sign, right? Would you like to say a few words? Everyone wants to know what's going on here."

Roger couldn't seem to muster one word much less a few, so I jumped in. "What's going on is you not being here while visitors are coming in," I told her. "You're not exactly in costume and you're carrying modern-day devices."

"I checked with Adventure Land," she replied with way too much confidence and perkiness. "They said it would be fine for me to be here just as I am, complete with camera."

"Kind of like TV-Reporter Barbie, right?" I imitated her princess voice the best I could. Only part of my brain that allows me to speak worked with me on that one.

Lilly stared hard at me. "Oh! You're that girl that almost died yesterday. I could talk to *you*."

"Did you forget your contacts?" I squinted at her, then smiled. "You could talk to me, but I probably wouldn't answer."

"Now, ladies." Henry stepped in and slipped an arm around Lilly's waist. "I can see this interview won't get you anywhere. I'll be glad to give you the whole story. Would you like to step out back?"

Lilly giggled (obviously good fairy/wraith material) and went outside with Henry. Her cameraman heaved a huge sigh and followed them out the back door.

"What just happened?" Roger asked.

"Lilly Hamilton said Myrtle Beach might close down the Village," I explained. "I guess we're too much trouble for the police."

"I'm going to kill Henry," he vowed.

I picked up a thick, sage green glass rod, but it was too big. Nice color, though. I grabbed a six-mil red rod (my dog needed eyes) and stuck it in the torch. "Just don't do it on Village property. I wonder if Chase has heard anything about this."

* * *

I had to wonder only until lunchtime when Chase stopped by the shop. Lilly was long gone, probably interviewing and annoying dozens of other people in the Village. Henry had come back inside with a satisfied smile on his face and showed me a slip of paper that supposedly had her phone number on it.

Like I care. Anyway, Chase caught me at the right time. I'd just killed my fifth glass dog. Pretty soon we'd have to open a glass pet cemetery just to keep up with me. I'd managed to burn my hand as well, but it wasn't bad enough to go see Wanda.

"How's your ankle this morning?" Chase asked after Roger told me it was fine to take lunch.

I glanced up at him, hoping the disdain I felt was apparent on my face. "I'm *sure* it really matters to you since you didn't leave me a note or anything before you left this morning. What was so important that I had to wake up to the invisible man?"

"Detective Almond asked me to come into town and talk to the chief of police about the Village. They have some concerns."

"So *that's* what Lilly was talking about this morning." A burly woman dressed like a Viking brushed by me, almost knocking me into the tent set up for a traveling palm reader. "And that's why there are so many people here today. We've gotten lots of bad publicity."

"That's right. And that's why I had to leave, my dear Watson." He smiled at me and pulled me to the side before another visitor, this one dressed like Frankenstein's monster, could mow me down. "Am I forgiven?"

"Are you buying lunch?"

"You're a cheap date, Jessie Morton. I might've sprung for more than lunch if you'd played it right."

I stood up close to him in the shade of Bawdy Betty's Bagels and kissed him slowly and carefully. It is one of the many things I excel at.

When I was through, we were both breathless and crushed up against the side of the building. People were smiling in that way they do when they see other people kissing. It's a combination of *I'd never do that in public* and *I wish I was doing that.*

"How was that for playing it the right way?" I asked him.

"Forget lunch. We're not that far away from Debby's place. I wouldn't mind being hungry for a while."

I laughed. He always makes me laugh. "I'd like to oblige you, but I need food and a change of clothes. I have to accomplish both these tasks in one hour. You'll have to wait your turn since you skipped out on me this morning."

He glanced up at Bawdy Betty's sign. "I guess this place is as good as any then."

We sat down to a lunch of bagels, pickles, and cheese, along with some warm beer (Betty's fridge was on the fritz). There was a light crowd in the shop, but outside, the visitors were going by the window in droves. I guess they weren't hungry, just looking for dead people.

"None of this makes any sense," Chase said around his bagel. "What's someone hoping to achieve?"

"Maybe they wanted to bring in a hundred thousand more people this year," I suggested. "If so, they're doing a good job."

"But you and Roger could've been seriously hurt when that sign fell."

"That might've meant an extra-extra hundred thousand." I put my bagel down. "You know, Chase, not everyone sees things in terms of right or wrong. People do things emotionally without thinking about the consequences."

He considered what I'd said. "I know you're right. But would someone go so far as to kill Ross to bring in more customers? I don't think so. There has to be something else."

"You talked to the police. What do they think?"

"They think the Village was always doomed to become the hotbed of crime in Myrtle Beach. I think they have too much empty space between their ears."

"Don't they have any ideas about Ross? Have they checked out his background to see if he had any enemies?"

"I don't know. When I try to get specifics from Detective Almond, he goes all Jack Webb on me, quoting the rules and regulations. I don't know what they're doing, Jessie. I feel like we're alone out here on this one."

"And all the other ones." I slumped in my chair, unable to eat the rest of my bagel. It was depressing that all of this was going on in my beloved Village and no one, except us, would lift a finger to help.

We sat there together totally depressed for a few minutes as we watched the crowds go by. Eventually Lilly Hamilton walked past with her human camera in tow. She was definitely someone I didn't want to see. The woman was completely obnoxious.

"I have to go take my costume back to Portia and see if she'll give me something else to wear that won't catch on fire."

"I'd like to go with you, but I have vegetable justice again in a few minutes."

"Why don't you let Lonnie take care of it like Jeff did last summer?"

"Lonnie isn't quite as handy as Jeff. I wish he was. The poor little guy has two left thumbs. He's always hurting himself. I've never seen so many bruises on a person.

Except for you." He smiled at me and played with my fingers on the tabletop. "So, dinner and a movie tonight?"

"Like we're leaving the Village for that long right now." I stood up and stretched. Sitting in one place can be exhausting. "I'll settle for dinner sans pirates throwing me overboard and no marshmallow cream heaped on the Village. Maybe we can make our own entertainment."

"Maybe you shouldn't take back that Joan of Arc costume yet," Chase suggested. "I love a woman in armor."

"Too expensive!" I kissed his cheek and whispered in his ear, "But I was recently seen shopping at Cupid's Arrow. I might have something amusing for you."

Of course just then his radio went off (stupid radio) and he answered quickly, telling someone he'd be there right away. "Someone ate too many brats over at Baron's. I wonder if there's any way to incorporate the word *barf* into that name. It happens all the time over there. Maintenance is always complaining."

We kissed briefly, then went our separate ways through the crowd. I crossed past Galileo's place, where he was talking to a group of kids about the stars. The King's Highway was packed. Two carriages pulled by black horses came through, making the congestion worse. In one of them was the ghost of Good Queen Bess. Personally, I think her appearance is more effective at night. In the daylight she just looks kind of gray, and not so scary.

I walked past the entrance to Sherwood Forest as any sane person would. I'd known residents who'd disappeared in there for days, coming out like they were drugged, clutching toaster ovens. Not a pretty picture.

This took me past Our Lady's Gemstones, very near the lake. Between Sherwood Forest and the gemstone store was a large group of privies. Imagine my amazement when I saw my good friend Rafe step into one of those privies.

But, I thought, *You don't have time for this.* True, it was a perfect setup for revenge. I'd seen many different privy pranks through the years. Any of them would be perfect for him. All of them were guaranteed to be bad news for the prankee (Rafe), leaving the prankster (in this case, me) laughing hysterically.

I had *almost* convinced myself not to lock the door and make him yell for help. My nobler self had *almost* talked me out of doing anything to avenge myself (at least right now).

Then the second thing happened; it was time to clean the privies.

This doesn't usually happen during the day while the Village is open. I had to assume it was due to someone thinking ahead after seeing the huge crowd. Either that or the privy company wasn't on schedule. Either way, it was too much for me to resist.

Usually, the company emptied and then cleaned the privies on site. But once in a while, one of them had to be taken back to be serviced. It took only a moment for me to realize that's what had to happen to the privy Rafe had entered.

Now I just had to convince the driver.

It helped that I was wearing the leather bustier and my pants were tight in all the right places. I'd probably blush if I ever saw a video of me working this poor privy dude into a frenzy over taking this one privy back to their shop.

But I didn't let that stop me. Privy Dude was on his first run ever to the Village. He was already overwhelmed by all the half-dressed wraiths and low-cut bosoms surrounding him. I convinced him to pack up the privy (with my help, of course), and he got in the truck, prepared to lift it with the winch.

I couldn't let Rafe think this was an honest mistake. I

jammed a stick in the lock so he couldn't get out, then gave the all clear to the driver.

"Hey! What's going on out there? Someone's in here. Find another can."

"No problem, sir," I said loud enough so he'd recognize my voice. "Have a good trip!"

"Jessie? Is that you? Open the door. Don't be stupid. This is juvenile and beneath you."

I saluted as his bellows were drowned out by the sounds of a squeeze box being played by a wandering group of pirates (loved that irony). He was on his way to a better place, and he certainly deserved everything he got.

The driver smiled and waved, then pulled carefully out of the Village through the special gate set up for large deliveries. Without so much as a blip of remorse, I continued on my way to see Portia. It was a grand and glorious day in Renaissance Faire Village.

But that was before I had to argue with Portia and Beth about my costume. Beth said it was inappropriate for a craftswoman to wear pants and a bustier, even if the leather could keep me from catching on fire. I argued about the yards of linen just waiting for an accident to happen with the torch at my workbench. Portia leaned heavily on one arm and interjected useless information at every available opportunity.

"Not everything here is done exactly as it would've been done during the Renaissance," I told Beth. "They're selling pizza, for goodness sake! What's up with that? And Lady Visa has to be used with a computer. Cut me some slack, huh?"

"It's important to stay as realistic as we can," Beth argued with that tone in her voice that said she couldn't believe she had to explain this to me. "Maybe it would've been a better choice for Master Trent to choose a male apprentice where the leather pants would've been more appropriate."

"He didn't have many volunteers. And I'm already filling that position. I need something safe to wear."

Portia shrugged. "I already offered her a demon costume and she turned it down."

"Talk about inappropriate for a shop apprentice." I couldn't believe we were having this discussion either. I mean, how many times did we have to go through the same thing? Why not just give me the clothes?

"All right." Beth finally gave in. "But I should tell you Queen Olivia herself complained about your attire last night at the feast."

"No!" I hoped my face registered as much mock shock as my voice. "If she has something better that's safe for me to wear, she can send it on over. Now, do you have something or not?"

I went away with my new costume after plenty of dirty looks from the other people waiting in line behind me. At least it was simple: plain white shirt and black cotton pants. It looked like something one of the varlets or the Village Idiot (they like the simple stuff) would wear, but that was okay. At least I'd managed to keep the leather bustier. Since Chase liked it so much, I didn't want to part with it.

I was on my way back to the Glass Gryphon (only twenty minutes late) cutting through Squire's Lane where the three large manor houses sat when I heard a low, moaning sound. Had it not been for the brick walls on either side of me, which reduced some of the noise from the Village, I would've missed it completely.

I followed the sound through the shadowed corridor, which was marked by No Entrance signs at either end. It made a good shortcut for residents. Visitors weren't allowed to use it because they might be tempted to hide out there after closing time.

I saw a person leaning against one of the walls as I came out toward the Village Square. He collapsed on the ground as I reached him.

I knelt down, wishing for that darn two-way radio, and tried to comfort the poor man. I put my nice, clean costume under his head and looked into his bloody face. It was Roger.

Fifteen

"Roger?" He seemed to be unconscious, even though he was moaning. Someone had beaten him badly. It looked to me like the marks had been made by some kind of stick. They were long red welts about an inch wide.

I spit on the clean white blouse sleeve and tried to wipe some of the blood off his face (hey, it worked for my grandma). He still didn't come around and I wasn't sure what to do. I knew I needed to go find help but didn't want to leave him alone like this. What if whoever attacked him came back? And if he was going to die, I didn't want him to die alone.

Of course this wouldn't be one of those times when these side alleyways were filled with resident traffic. I waited for a few minutes hoping someone else would show up and they could go for help. No luck. I was about to give up and go find security or some vendor who could help me, and I was just telling Roger I'd be back when the Black Dwarf (aka Marcus Fleck) came racing around the corner, his lantern jiggling on its stick. He glanced my way but didn't slow down.

"Hey!" I tried to hail him. "I need you to go for help."

"Can't stop," he said. "I'm late. The king will have my head."

And he left us there. I couldn't believe it. I was shocked and outraged. How single-minded could someone be?

Then I heard voices and walked down into the flirty sunlight that was creating threatening shadows across the Village. It was two monks. I didn't recognize them, but when I told them the situation, they ran for help. I stayed with Roger, trying to soothe him somehow. He was a crotchety glassmaker, but no one deserved this. Who would do such a thing?

As I waited, Roger finally came around. He grimaced but seemed to know who I was. "Jessie? What happened?"

"I was hoping you could tell me. I think someone hit you with something, Roger. I sent for help. Someone should be here soon."

He groaned much louder than he moaned. "I feel like somebody hit me with a two-by-four. I didn't see anyone. I was walking through the shortcut on my way to the bakery for lunch, and whatever it was hit me hard across the back of the head. I didn't feel anything after that."

"I can't believe something like this could happen here. I wish you'd seen who did it."

"Me, too." He half smiled (a kind of yucky sight because of the blood all over his face). Then his already messed-up face contorted with fear. He held out one bloody hand and started yelling, "No! No!"

All I could think of was that his attacker had returned and was standing right behind me. I pushed back hard with my legs, hoping to throw whoever it was off balance. My effort met a hard wall of human flesh. "Bart?" I craned my head around to see him standing there.

He wiggled his fingers. "Hello, lady."

"Keep him away from me!" Roger yelled. "I'm not ready to die!"

"He's not really Death," I tried to explain, but Roger was too frantic to listen. All he could see was the large figure with the scythe. Maybe he thought he was dying.

Anyway, it was just as well when he passed out again. Bart offered to lift him, but I didn't think that was a good idea. "He could have internal injuries. We have to leave him here until the paramedics come."

He nodded. "You think the same person who hurt him might have killed Ross?"

"I don't know. I wish I did."

It only took a few more minutes for two security guards to arrive with paramedics. I was grateful to Bart for waiting. Being between the Squire's Lane houses had never made me nervous before. Now I wasn't sure if I'd ever cut through here again.

Bart and I followed Roger's stretcher into the spotty sunlight after I picked up my pile of clothes. A few drops of rain were coming down. The whole day seemed to be in bad shape. Maybe it would have been better if it rained and everyone went home. Maybe the Myrtle Beach police were right and the Village wasn't safe anymore.

"What's that on your hands?" Bart looked at them. "Did you cut yourself?"

I looked at the red all over my hands and arms. It was paint. "Wait!" I called out to the paramedics.

They stopped for me, and I approached the stretcher and saw the red lettering on Roger's chest. I hadn't noticed it earlier because of the shadows between the houses. Now it was smudged from my efforts to make him comfortable, but it was still legible.

"It says the same thing as all the rest of them," Bart noticed. "*Death shall find thee.* But why is Roger alive? Ross is dead."

"I don't know. I'm sorry. I just don't know."

After that, Lilly Hamilton and her cameraman showed up and turned the whole thing into a media circus. Detective Almond appeared with two uniformed officers at his side. They questioned Bart and me separately while the rain began falling in earnest on the cobblestones. Visitors ran through the main gate or holed up in eating areas, hoping the downpour would pass. Residents watched as Roger was put in an ambulance, muttering to themselves about what was happening to the Village.

"What about this black elf?" Detective Almond scratched his head as he read from his notes. "Where did he go?"

"Black Dwarf," I corrected. "I don't know. I don't think he could see Roger in the shadows."

"So you don't think he was involved?"

"Not really. He's not even three feet tall. I don't think he could do this much damage."

"You never know." He checked his notes again. "You said he was going to see the king. Where would that be?"

"The castle, of course. On a day like this, Livy and Harry aren't going to promenade."

"Of course. How silly of me." He shrugged and frowned. "If you people would just make sense out here, it would help a lot."

I didn't feel like arguing with him about that. "Can I go now?"

"Go on. If you see that boyfriend of yours, tell him I want to talk to him."

I didn't have to, because just then Chase arrived with Lonnie and a few other security guards. Detective Almond beckoned and Chase followed him, with a worried backward glance at me.

I tried to mouth that I was okay, but Chase isn't a great lip-reader. I was already soaking wet and cold. The Monastery Bakery was packed with visitors, so I walked over to the Honey and Herb Shoppe next door.

"My dear, come and sit down," Mrs. Potts, the owner, said by way of welcome. "You look dreadful! Let me make you a nice cup of tea. I believe I have some borage here, maybe with a touch of chamomile. That will make you feel much better."

I always forget how nice Mrs. Potts is. She's been here forever but isn't as temperamental as some of the other shop owners. Today, she looked very grandmother-like in her white mobcap and starched white apron over a sky blue dress. She was fussing a little too much over me, but it made me feel safe and I welcomed it.

"What happened out there?" She seated me at a little table by the window that looked out into her neat garden. I could see a real pumpkin growing there.

I explained a little, not going into detail. Everyone would know everything soon enough. "I just can't believe this could happen here."

"No, indeed." She shook her head and put a few of her delicious honey cookies in front of me on a pretty lace napkin. "This is a respectable place. I think it's time the bailiff makes sure everyone else realizes that as well."

"Not so respectable," a woman dressed in non-Renaissance fashion stated. "My brother disappeared here two months ago. But no one seems to know what happened to him."

"This is Jeff Porter's sister, Jennifer," Mrs. Potts told me. "Jeff used to work with Chase."

"I remember." I held my hand out to Jennifer. "I'm Jessie Morton. We've all wondered what happened to him."

My casual inquiry brought on a long bout of tears and the story of Jeff's disappearance and everything she'd done to look for him. It sounded like a case for the police, but she scoffed at the notion.

"I've tried everything. Police. Private detective. I'm reduced to hanging flyers all over the Grand Strand." Jennifer handed me a flyer with a bad photo of Jeff on it. "He's got to be somewhere."

"If I hear or see anything, I'll let you know," I promised, carefully folding the flyer and putting it into my belt pouch. "I have a brother, too. Jeff probably just forgot to call."

I asked Jennifer to join me for tea, but she was in a hurry to walk through the rest of the Village. Mrs. Potts sat beside me knitting as I drank my tea. Her marmalade cat, Jasper, sat at her feet. It was all so homey and sweet. Maybe that's why I never spend much time here. I've always been a little darker than homey and sweet. But after the day's events, it was comforting to be here.

When Chase appeared in the street again, I tapped at the window and waved to him. The rain was still coursing down and he was as soaked as me. He didn't waste any time coming inside where he enfolded me in his arms and lifted me right out of the chair.

"Oh my!" Mrs. Potts exclaimed, leaving her chair and bustling into the kitchen. "I'd better put on more tea."

"I didn't know what to think when I saw you," Chase whispered. "Detective Almond told me what happened. Are you okay?"

"I was fine until you squished me." I buried my nose

in his chest and realized that I was crying. "But that's okay. Bones are overrated. Just hold me like this for a lot longer."

He obliged until we both felt better, and then he took a seat opposite me at the little table. "This can't go on. If anything else happens, they're going to shut us down. There has to be someway to find out who's behind it."

The door to the shop opened and closed, but I didn't pay attention until the floor creaked and groaned under Bart's weight.

Mrs. Potts came back in from the kitchen, kettle in hand, and said, "Oh dear! I never expected to see *you* here!"

"Hello, lady. Can I sit down?"

Handling it like the trooper she was, Mrs. Potts smiled. "Why, of course! I'm sure I have a chair here somewhere that will fit you. I think we'll need more honey cookies, don't you?"

So the three of us sat at the little table by the window. We were like big, dirty giants relaxing in a neat dollhouse with Mrs. Potts scurrying around trying to make us comfortable.

"These are good." Bart ate the last six cookies. "But too small."

"I think I have an idea," Chase said after a few minutes of brooding into his cup of tea. "I should've thought of it sooner, but I was hoping it would take care of itself."

"Whatever it is," Bart said, "I want to help. You know that, don't you?"

Chase gulped down the rest of his tea and ate his honey cookies. "I do. And I'll need all the help I can get. Come on. Let's go."

"Could I get some of these cookies to go?" Bart asked Mrs. Potts.

She blushed prettily. "I'm afraid you've eaten all I had. But I'll be baking later if you want to come by in the morning for more."

Bart agreed, and I picked up what had been my clean, dry costume. "Portia and Beth are going to kill me. I'll never get another costume again."

Chase summoned the heads of the guilds to meet at the castle that evening when the Village closed. It was almost unprecedented in the history of the Village to have all the guilds in one place at one time. For the most part, the guilds don't really get along. Each one is sure it is better than the others and they all have secrets they jealously guard.

But Chase said come and so they came. Master Archer Simmons, head of the Weapons Guild, walked into the castle joking with Da Vinci, the head of the Artist Guild. Harpist Susan Halifax, head of the Musician Guild, kept a wide berth between her and Da Vinci. Robin Hood, head of the Forest Guild, walked in with several of his Merry Men, but the extras were turned away at the door by Gus Fletcher. After all, the meeting was for the heads of the guilds only.

When the room was full with members from all of the guilds, the Brotherhood of the Sheaf, the pirates, and the nobility, Chase got their attention and settled them down fairly quickly. "I brought you all together because we have one last chance to keep Renaissance Village open. As of today and the attack on Roger Trent, the Myrtle Beach police have said that any additional incident will cause the town council to shut us down."

Immediately, worried conversation broke out among

guild members who usually never spoke to those outside
their own groups. Many of them didn't even know Roger
had been assaulted. As the story buzzed around the room,
tempers rose and words became heated.

"If you let the Weapons Guild members patrol the
streets, ready to do battle, we can take care of this," Master
Archer Simmons promised.

"If we let *you* patrol the streets, we might as well all live
somewhere else," Little Bo Peep, head of the Entertainment Guild, retorted.

A lot of people agreed with her. Robin Hood laughed
at the idea. "If they patrol, then so do my Merry Men. It's
only fair."

Everyone seemed to agree with that statement. I stood
in the midst of the crowd, not my rightful place since I
didn't head any guild and wasn't even a permanent resident. I guessed everyone knew Chase and I were together
and just accepted me there.

Still, I wouldn't have been there at all except that Chase
had placed me and Lonnie in the crowd to hear what was
being said. I wasn't sure whether he suspected someone
from the Village of the attacks or if he just wanted to hear
the crowd gossip.

"Exactly!" Chase yelled out over the bickering crowd.
They all grew silent at the sound of his voice. "We're going
to have to work together to keep the Village open. I need
everyone's eyes and ears open in the next few days. I don't
care if all of the guilds patrol the streets so long as com-
merce continues and our visitors keep coming."

Lord Dunstable came up to stand beside Chase. "As duly
appointed representative of the nobility, including their
Royal Highnesses King Harold and Queen Olivia, I am here
to say that we back the bailiff's plan to keep the Village
open. We offer our assistance with the help of our knights

and lords and ladies. They will do what they can to flush out the knave who is responsible for these acts of atrocity."

"Hey!" the head of the Knave, Varlet, and Madman Guild protested. "It wasn't one of *us*!"

Lord Dunstable cleared his throat and apologized. "I did not mean to imply anything by that, my good sir. Perhaps a rephrasing of my words is in order."

"Don't go through all that again, please!" Merlin, head of the Magical Creature Guild, implored him. "I think we've got the idea."

The crowd turned to him, a bony old man in his sorcerer's robes.

"Why doesn't the Village hire more security?" Hans Von Rupp (Debby's blacksmith boyfriend) of the Craft Guild asked. "Why do we have to protect ourselves?"

Merlin started to answer, but Chase took over again. "Because we need people who know the Village. Detective Almond is already planning to send in several plainclothes police officers. The problem, besides them not knowing what to wear, is that they don't know their way around. We need each other to make this work."

Everyone laughed, recalling other times the police had tried to dress officers to blend in with the Renaissance theme. Their efforts had ranged from 1920s gangsters to Roman soldiers and everything in between. What Chase said was true and we all knew it.

"We'll do our part," Robin promised.

"Without lifting all the toaster ovens in the Village, I trust?" Brother John, head of the Brotherhood of the Sheaf, interjected.

Robin grinned (not a good start). "Of course not! You can trust us, Brother Monk."

"We'll all help, Chase," the head of the Musician Guild vowed.

It was a remarkable moment, something that would live in history. All the guilds agreeing on something was unbelievable. I guessed with their livelihood on the line, they could all find something they had in common. The Village made money for these people. No one wanted to be out in the cold on the Strand plying their wares alone again.

"All right! That's what I wanted to hear!" Chase pushed his fist into the air in that time-honored salute of triumph. "We'll start tonight with the biggest guilds who can spare a few members to patrol while the Village is closed. There won't be any visitors to work around, so a few should do."

"But no one has been hurt at night," Hephaestus of the Food Guild remarked. "Why not wait until tomorrow?"

"Because that person is out there. Writing on the walls is just part of the problem. It seems to be part of a larger pattern. Maybe if we can stop it, we can stop the violence, too," Chase explained.

"What about that snoopy reporter, Lilly Hamilton?" Little Bo Peep demanded.

"I'd be glad to take care of that problem," Grigg said with a grin.

"Who are you representing?" Lord Dunstable asked him.

"I'm representing the pirates," Grigg told him with a glance at me. "Our Pirate King had an unfortunate accident this afternoon. He was unable to attend."

"No one needs to do anything with Lilly Hamilton," Chase said to a chorus of guffaws that implied most of the men thought Chase wanted to do what *they* wanted to do.

"Yeah, Bailiff," the head of the Knave, Varlet, and Madman Guild said. "Like we aren't all thinking what you're thinking."

Chase glanced at me, a little red spot on each of his

cheeks. He settled the crowd down again and got everyone in line with the plan to protect the Village.

Was he really thinking about hitting on Lilly Hamilton? I couldn't believe it, but I also couldn't explain that guilty look or that unusual flush. Of all people! Lilly Hamilton! What could he possibly see in her? The fairies threw themselves at him all the time. Lady Godiva actually removed her bodysuit and rode naked to the dungeon to impress him two years ago. But no! Chase wanted that stupid ex-weathergirl turned Myrtle Beach Katie Couric wannabe. I missed the tail end of the meeting dwelling on it.

"So did you guys hear anything besides what everyone was yelling?" Chase asked me and Lonnie after the guild heads were gone.

Lonnie shrugged and scratched his little rat face. "No, boss. I didn't hear anything except what you heard."

I couldn't say what I'd seen and heard. I mumbled something similar to what Lonnie had said, all the while looking at Chase's handsome face and wondering where I went wrong. My grandma always said to be careful of the pretty boys. Chase qualified for that. Certainly all the women in the Village wanted him. He could've swatted them away as they were thick as flies.

But instead, he wanted Lilly Hamilton.

I was almost too depressed to care about what happened to the Village. Lonnie picked up some plastic-wrapped food and headed back toward the dungeon. Chase and I took the long way around, past Baron's, Lady Cathy's Crochet, and Bawdy Betty's.

"I was thinking maybe I should stay at the dungeon tonight and you stay with Debby just to be safe," he said to me.

"Yeah. Sure."

"Is something wrong?"

The moonlight gilded the Village around us. Crews had cleaned up the spiderwebs (big mistake), leaving the buildings looking mostly normal. The lights in the pumpkins still burned at the entrances to each house and shop, but someone had apparently turned off the bats and werewolf soundtrack. It would be easy to believe we had been transported into a real Renaissance village.

"Wrong? What gives you that idea?" I sure wasn't going to talk about it. If Chase wanted Lilly Hamilton, she was welcome to him.

There was something going on between Fractured Fairy Tales and the Romeo and Juliet Pavilion. Two men were digging what looked like several holes. Beside them were tombstones. That was just what we needed right now. A graveyard would make everyone feel so much better.

"You're upset about Roger," Chase guessed.

Hit the buzzer! Could he be any more wrong? "Yeah. That's it."

We stopped walking only a short distance from the new cemetery. Chase stood in front of me and refused to budge. Every time I tried to walk around him, he got in my way. He's not exactly a mountain (or even as big as Bart), but I couldn't get around him. "What?"

"What?" he demanded back. "What's up with you?"

I could hear footsteps running up from behind us in the quiet street long before a breathless Grigg reached us. "Chase! You have to see this!"

"I'm kind of busy fighting with Jessie right now. I'll get to it later," Chase answered.

"Oh, so this is fighting?" I asked. "I suppose you wouldn't be fighting if you were seeing Lilly Hamilton, star reporter."

"What are you talking about?" Chase asked.

"I'm talking about you blushing when everyone was razzing you about her at the meeting. What was up with that?"

"Will the two of you please shut up?" Grigg interrupted again. "There's another dead man swinging from the Hanging Tree."

Sixteen

" At least it's not a *real* dead man." I finally stated the obvious after a group of us had been standing for several minutes at the base of the Hanging Tree. "I mean, it's just a scarecrow kind of thing with those stupid words on it again."

"Death shall find thee." Chase said it out loud. Not like any of us needed to hear it again.

"What do you think?" Grigg asked.

"I think we at least have some idea of what's going on now," Chase responded. "This isn't one particular man. The figure represents the whole Village. Whoever's doing this wants to shut Renaissance Village down."

Master at Arms Gus Fletcher and Death, really Bart, had joined us as we reached the tree. Everyone seemed to agree with Chase's assessment. Even I thought the figure represented the Village since it was wearing a Village T-shirt. It didn't take a lot of brainpower to figure that out.

"Why would someone want to shut the place down?" I hoped the dismay and horror of the idea didn't color my voice. "I can't believe anyone here could be that unhappy. Why wouldn't they just leave?"

"People are strange." Bart shrugged. "Who knows what anyone is thinking?"

Wasn't that the truth? I would've never guessed Chase could be interested in that skinny-legged, know-nothing Lilly Hamilton either. Bart was obviously a very wise man.

"This person could be anyone in the Village," Grigg said. "I think it has to be a resident. Who else would have this kind of access?"

Chase lowered the figure from the tree branch. Grigg caught it in a plastic bag he'd snagged from a nearby trash can. "I wish you were wrong. But I agree with you. It has to be a resident."

"Wait a minute! What about those times when visitors managed to sneak in and out? You don't know that isn't what's happening now. After all, you can't be everywhere." I knew I was again pointing out the obvious, but it had to be said. I didn't want to think any of the people I saw every day on the cobblestone streets could be responsible for killing Death—Ross—and hurting Roger.

"We'll need to look at everyone's past-history profile," Grigg said in police language. "The chances are we could find the answer right there. I suppose Adventure Land must have that."

"And that would work if anyone here had ever given a past-history profile," Chase replied. "We have hundreds of high school and college drama students who have never even voted or held a job other than here. There are probably another few hundred semi-adults who have also never worked anywhere but here. The only thing we really require for employment is a Social Security number and a valid ID."

"No background check?" Grigg said it as though the very idea violated his thoughts of how the world should be.

"Nope." Chase shook his head.

"That has to change," Grigg replied. "You can't just let anyone run around crazy in here. You have to know if they're really crazy or not."

I laughed. I knew this was a serious subject and I was looking at my home away from home falling victim to *real* thieves and scoundrels, but I couldn't help myself. "I'm sorry. But most of the people here are hiding out from one thing or another. Haven't you noticed? They tend to duck and cover whenever a police officer shows his face. Except for you, Grigg, because you fit right in."

"I'm afraid Jessie's right." Chase agreed with me, which perversely made me angry. "If we get rid of all the crazies, the Village will be empty."

Grigg took that statement personally. "I'm not crazy."

If he was waiting for one of us to rush in and assure him that he was right, he was disappointed. He was a middle-aged ex–police officer who spent his time pretending he was a pirate. Nope. Not crazy at all.

"But I think you're onto something, Grigg." Chase changed the subject. "We've needed to upgrade our system for keeping track of employees for the last two years. I think this might be the push we need to get Adventure Land to take some responsibility."

Bart agreed by punching one large hand into the other. "Yes. We need a better database on all the people who work here. Or have ever worked here. Systems get so outdated."

We all kind of stared at him. I wondered where all that tech talk came from. He hardly seemed the type.

"What?" He looked around at us. "Don't we have a database? I wasn't always Death, you know. I like computers."

"I don't know if we even have a computer," I said.

"Okay, Bart, you're my go-to guy on this since I can't stand computers," Chase said. "I'll call the main office in the morning and see if we can get some names to work with. There must be someone who knows who's being hired around here."

Someone screeched not too far away from where we were standing. I was fairly sure it wasn't a soundtrack. There were sounds of scuffling and one of the trash cans getting knocked over at the Lady of the Lake Tavern.

Chase ran that way and the rest of us followed. Sure enough, a group of Robin's Merry Men seemed to be roughing up one of the minstrels. The odds were not in the minstrel's favor.

"What's going on?" Chase demanded when he reached the group.

"We found this knave out here alone, probably looking for someone else to kill," one of the Merry Men accused. "We were patrolling the area, as you requested, Sir Bailiff."

"I was out here getting my mandolin from the Merry Mynstrel Stage." The young man in blue velvet held up his instrument as proof. "They took my hat and tried to shove me in the trash can. I think they broke my mandolin."

As soon as he finished speaking, he started crying. My heart went out to him. He was very young. Maybe one of those high school drama students Chase was talking about.

"Don't worry," Bart told him. "I'll take care of it for you."

A moment later he had two of the Merry Men hanging upside down by their feet. Who knew someone so big could move so fast?

"That won't help my mandolin." The young musician grabbed his blue velvet hat, whose large peacock feather had been crushed in the fight.

"You want me to shake them until all their money falls out?" Bart asked in the most polite of voices. None of us had any doubt that he could and would do exactly what he offered.

"No." Chase stepped in. "Put them down, Bart. They meant well. I'm sure they just got carried away. And I don't think it will happen again, right, Merry Men?"

The Merry Men were all too happy to agree with him. Anything to have the giant figure of Death let them go. Of course, he dropped them all on their heads (hopefully it knocked some sense into a few of them). They lay around on the ground, whimpering and complaining. Chase was certainly going to hear about this from Robin.

"I'll see to it that you get a new mandolin," Chase offered the musician. "I'm sorry this happened."

The musician seemed satisfied with that. He sniffed, wiped his nose on his hat (*yuck*), and went on his way.

"The rest of you, use some common sense, huh? Did he really look like a threat to the Village or was he a convenient punching bag?" Chase yelled at the Merry Men. "If anything like this happens again, the Forest Guild won't continue their patrols."

"Methinks you are too harsh, Sir Bailiff," said the Merry Man who seemed to be in charge of the group. "Forsooth, we were but challenging the lad to protect everyone."

"You heard me." Chase was obviously not impressed with his Village speak. "Don't let it happen again unless you only want to see the monks and weapons makers out here."

The Merry Men didn't say another *forsooth* or *methinks*. They started off toward Sherwood Forest to lick their wounds, no doubt.

Grigg said good night (he was already close to where the *Queen's Revenge* was docked) but added a personal word of warning. "That was an evil stunt you pulled this afternoon, Jessie. Rafe has declared there must be vengeance."

I shrugged and bowed. "I await his Royal Smelliness whenever he can drag himself out of the shower."

"What did you do?" Bart asked me after Grigg left.

I explained what happened and why I did it. "It seemed like a perfect opportunity. And he so deserved it for throwing me overboard."

"I agree. But you better watch yourself. I hear those pirates can be dangerous." He smiled at me. "You want me to watch your back?"

He was really the nicest figure of Death I had ever known. Not that I've known many, but I'm sure they weren't as nice as him. I thought about flirting with him a little to make Chase jealous, but I was too tired and I wasn't sure it would do any good. Bart was nice but not exactly the male version of Lilly Hamilton.

"Thanks. I'll manage. Rafe and I go back a long way. I know the inside of that pirate ship better than my apartment back home. But it was sweet of you to offer. It's nice to have *someone* that cares."

Bart said good night and melted into the darkness between Sarah's Scarves and Brewster's.

I counted to four after we passed the Good Luck Fountain before Chase spoke. "What was that all about?"

I started to answer, but Chase cut me off before I could get a word out.

"And what was all that stuff about me and Lilly Hamilton before Grigg met us by the cemetery?"

"I know you, Chase. When all those guild people were giving you a hard time about Lilly at the meeting, you were blushing."

"I was not blushing."

"You were, too. You were super red in the face, and that's saying a lot with your skin tone."

"If I was red, it was exertion."

"You looked guilty to me."

He stopped walking as we neared Harriet's Hat House. "I didn't look guilty. I haven't done anything to look guilty about. Lilly Hamilton is so *not* my type."

"Right. Whatever."

"What makes you think she is?"

"I've seen her looking at you like you're a six-foot-eight, two-hundred-fifty-pound ice cream cone she wants to lick. Then there was the red face and the guilt. Need any more proof?"

We were standing near the Romeo and Juliet Pavilion. The irony of having this discussion at that spot wasn't lost on me. Maybe we were star-crossed lovers who were never destined to be together. Our time was sweet but fleeting.

"Proof?" Chase demanded (truly red in the face now). "I'll give you proof that there is only one woman for me. She's completely crazy and messed up, but I love her anyway. Any idea who that could be?"

"Lilly Hamilton?" I whispered. He was looming over me with an expression on his face that boded no good. At least not for me.

"No, you idiot. I really think they miscast you in the Village. You should be in the Knave, Varlet, and Madman Guild."

With that, he kissed me and lifted me off the ground, as he was so fond of doing. Okay, I didn't really mind all that much. Besides, I was assuming he meant that I was the crazy person he loved, and I could live with that. I wrapped my arms around him and let him carry me into the night.

Then he dropped me into the fountain.

"Chase!" I screeched, coming up out of the cold water with something besides unspeakable passion on my mind. "I'm going to get you!"

The next morning, we were up early and headed to the hospital to visit Roger. Mary was already there but left as we arrived. "Don't upset him," she warned. "He's been through enough."

"We just want to ask him a few questions," Chase told her. "If he gets too tired, we'll leave."

She nodded and smiled at her new husband before leaving us alone with him.

If I'd thought Roger was a mess the night before, it was nothing compared to what he looked like now. His whole body (at least the part I could see) was black-and-blue with angry red welts. The marks were rounded on his skin. I got down closer to the arm that seemed to have borne the brunt of the attack. I could almost envision the exact tube-shaped weapon that had hit him.

I stood up quickly when I noticed Roger looking at me. He could barely see out of one eye, and his nose was crooked on his face. No casts though, so it appeared as though nothing was broken.

"Roger." Chase sat down in a chair beside the bed. "If this is too much, just say so."

"No way," he kind of slurred. "I want whoever did this, Chase. I can't get him for a while. Maybe you can. Fire away."

"Okay. I know the police probably asked you these questions, but I don't know if they plan to share that information with me. Did you notice anything before you were attacked?"

"No. I was walking through the shortcut when something hit me in the back of the head. Next thing I knew, I was on the ground and Jessie was with me." He lifted his head a little and tried to smile at me. It was pitiful enough to make me want to cry. "Thank you for helping me."

"Sure." I mean, what do you say in the face of life-saving gratitude? "Any time."

"Was there a smell or a sound that could help us?" Chase persisted. "I know you have experience with this. Whatever you can tell me might help."

Roger closed his eyes for a long time. I glanced at Chase, afraid Roger had fallen asleep. But eventually he looked at us again. "There was one thing. A faint burned smell, you know? Like something on fire."

Chase wrote down Roger's response, then asked, "Can you think of anyone who might want to hurt you?"

"Whoever the crazy SOB was who did this to me."

"You know what I mean."

"Yeah. I know. I've been lying here all night trying to figure it out myself. Honest to God, Chase, I know I've had a few run-ins with people in the Village but nothing that would warrant something like this. I can't imagine who'd do this, or why."

Having known Roger for a few years, I could imagine some people who might be willing to beat him up. "Remember that guy with the funny brown hat two years ago? He seemed like someone who might come back for revenge."

"You mean that pervert I threw out of the Village?" Roger gritted his teeth. "People like that don't belong here."

Chase and I exchanged meaningful glances. "That's

kind of what I mean," I explained. "You were the bailiff here for a long time. One or more of those people you tossed out could've come back."

Roger seemed to consider the possibilities. "In that case, the list of men waiting to kick my ass could be pretty long."

"Are you sure it wasn't a woman?" I asked with logical authority in my voice.

"Maybe." He tried to smile again (I had to look away). "You think Mary got fed up with me again?"

This was all well and good, but where was the serious Roger who'd been such a pain in the butt the last few days? He had the crap beaten out of him and suddenly he's funny Roger. Go figure.

Chase asked him a few more questions, but it was obvious Roger had reached the limit of his strength. A nurse came in and we left with Roger asking Chase to catch the person who'd hurt him.

"Well that wasn't much," Chase lamented as we climbed into his silver BMW parked in the no-parking zone. "I was hoping for more than a strange burning smell."

"But that might be important. Maybe the person who hit him works at one of the shops that have charcoal-broiled food."

"Or maybe," Chase said as he started the car, "whoever did it didn't smell like burning at all and Roger was smelling a campfire from Sherwood Forest. As clues go, I don't think this is the big one."

"We need DNA and access to hair and tissue fibers from his clothes." I smiled at him. "My misspent youth craves *CSI* deduction."

"That would be nice but again probably not going to happen. Unlike *CSI*, it could take weeks for the police to have any answers like that."

"Yeah. And that's saying they'd share them." I sighed, depressed. "How are we ever going to catch this guy and save the Village?"

"We have a large force of people at our disposal. Sure, some of them might be IQ challenged, but something should turn up."

"Maybe we could put out a sign-up sheet for people ticked off at Roger. I wonder if any of them are still around."

"I know a few that have been here for a while. We might be able to get them to talk."

I didn't share his optimism, but I didn't say so. We'd made up during the night, and I was still in the afterglow where I didn't want to see him unhappy. We drove back to the Village tossing lots of lame ideas around that really didn't make any sense.

We talked about Marcus, the Black Dwarf, being a possible suspect. Chase said the little man had a giant-sized temper when he was crossed. Was it possible he was a new convert to the I-Hate-Roger Society? I liked Marcus, but a suspect was a suspect. We had to consider all the possibilities.

Chase had a hundred people waiting to report to him on their Village patrols. Bart was waiting to get a look at the new employee files Adventure Land had promised to send to the brand new computer in the castle.

I kissed him good-bye (Chase, not Bart) and went on to the Glass Gryphon. I'd managed to get my clothes fairly clean and dry. They were at least wearable until I could tackle the gorgon dressmakers again.

I wasn't sure how Henry would be with Roger out of the picture. But he was in good spirits and fixed on a little demon he'd met that morning, so he kept his hands to himself.

Everything on my workbench was just as I'd left it yesterday. I sat down and turned on my burner, then picked up my pathetic excuse for a glass dog, which looked more like a mutant than anything else. Filled with sorrow, I dropped him in the trash and started over.

Business was brisk as the gates opened. No doubt the publicity from Ross's death and now the attack on Roger were bringing them in. Their money spent the same, though, so I was sure no one minded the extra visitors, whatever their motivation for coming.

I waited on the first customers, who bought several hundred dollars worth of glasses Roger had made. Henry told them about his uncle getting hurt. The nice lord and lady (sporting expensive Renaissance garb they didn't get in the Village) bought a few bowls to go along with the glasses. I wrapped all of them up and wondered at Henry's lack of discretion.

When they'd gone, he burst out laughing. "Can you believe those idiots? Like it matters that Uncle Roger got hurt. At least it shouldn't matter to *them*."

"But you knew it would." I sat down at my workbench again and took up a clear tube to resurrect my little doggy.

"Yeah. So what? The idea is to make money. You can't eat art glass, Jessie." He walked close to where I was working. "It's all about controlling the heat," he directed. "Start at the tip of the tube and work your way back. You have to get it hot enough to move but not too hot. Then heat your colored rod and lay it down on the tube."

He went to his own bench, and I watched him, fascinated. He was a jerk but he was gifted. He slowly blew into the mouthpiece attached to the heated tube, shaping it with the graphite paddles to move the way he wanted it to move. It took only a few minutes before the figure was taking form. He was making a horse, probably a unicorn since there were more than a few of those on display in the shop.

Determined to make something recognizable, I heated my glass tube until it began to glow, then used my mouthpiece to blow ever so gently into the glass to expand it. I had already chosen my shape. A dog was beneath my talents, I decided; I would make something beautiful and ethereal instead. Maybe a fairy or a butterfly.

Everything was moving exactly as it should. I picked up a sapphire blue rod and began applying the colored glass to the tube. I planned to use pale green with it as my fairy/butterfly began to take shape. Unfortunately, the four-foot glass rod of the sage green color I'd noticed yesterday was nowhere to be found. I looked everywhere in the shop, but all I could find was an emerald green.

"Have you seen that lighter green rod?" I asked Henry. "It was like a sage color. One of the long rods."

He looked up at me with a two-foot blue rod that he hadn't begun using yet in his hand. He held it in his fist like a weapon. Visions of the terrible welts formed in exactly the same shape on Roger's body flew in front of my eyes.

Wham!

I was suddenly pretty sure what had happened to Roger.

Seventeen

I'd seen enough horror movies and murder mysteries to know better than to fall apart at this moment. You know what I mean. The girl finally figures out who the bad guy/vampire/werewolf is and she stands there by herself and accuses him. Of course, he kills her (and sometimes eats her) without a second thought. It's the logical choice to getting caught.

So I played it cool. I sauntered over to my workbench as though I hadn't just realized what and who had made those red welts all over Roger. I spent the next thirty minutes working on my fairy/butterfly. It was really starting to look like something when a few customers came into the shop.

"Will you see to them, Jessie?" Henry glanced up at me and smiled.

It turned my stomach imagining him bludgeoning

Roger with a solid glass rod, but I managed to smile back. "Of course."

I forced myself to speak normally to the king and queen of the werewolves out for a stroll through the Village. Their little gold crowns fit between their pointed wolf ears on their gray furry heads while their elaborate blue satin robes rustled in the quiet shop.

They finally decided to watch Henry as he completed his unicorn with touches of gold glitter to the horn and hooves. When he was finished, they applauded with their wolf paws and purchased it.

"That was amazing!" Queen Werewolf remarked. "You're quite a craftsman."

Henry bowed handsomely. I could already see that look of lust glazing his eyes. "Thank you, Your Majesty. And may I say your choice of gown looks particularly lovely on you today."

King Werewolf was not so pleased by the way Henry was looking at his mate. He growled (obviously into the part) and took the queen by her arm (or is that leg?) and led her out of the shop.

"Well that was a good morning's work." Henry was pleased with himself. "Why don't we break for lunch, Jessie. We'll close the shop until two since it's only me and you here."

That sounded like an escape plan to me. "Great! I'm certainly going to enjoy working for you while Roger is out of commission."

I guess that was too much to say. He sidled closer and put his hands on my waist. "I can think of lots of things we could do together instead of eating. You know, Uncle Roger might not come back at all. I might take over the shop."

"What makes you say that?" I wanted to move away

from him, but I was attracted to the sometimes fatal task of trying to get more information from the suspect.

"Psychology." He shrugged. "I majored in it at college. Sometimes after a traumatic episode, people have to cut their ties to past associations. Uncle Roger might have to cut his ties to the Glass Gryphon. He might not be able to handle the memories."

Is that why you attacked him? I didn't dare go that far. Henry could stuff me in a closet somewhere and it could be days before anyone found me. My heart was pounding in my chest in a mixture of excitement and fear. I couldn't wait to tell Chase what I'd discovered, but first I wanted to get out of the shop alive.

"I don't know." I casually turned away from his loose embrace. "Roger doesn't strike me as the emotional kind. I'll bet he'll be right back on the job as soon as he can get up."

"I guess we'll see." He smiled lazily at me, and I would've continued being the target of his lust, but that cute little demon from earlier in the day chose that moment to stroll into the shop. After that, he only had eyes for her. *Thank God.*

As soon as my feet hit the cobblestones, I ran to the dungeon to look for Chase. He was in the middle of settling a dispute between two shopkeepers while a crowd of visitors watched the proceedings.

"Bailiff, this man promised to marry my daughter. He took her dowry, then decided against marriage." The complainant was Lucas McCoy of the Three Pigs Barbecue. The defendant was Diego Tornado of the Tornado Twins. Not really a shopkeeper at all, more an obnoxious pest. Of course, it was all just a performance, designed to give the audience an idea of what justice was like back in the Renaissance. I guessed Diego was the only one they could find to play the errant lover.

"It was not that way," he declared. "She no longer wanted me. I keep her dowry because she abandoned me."

The crowd of fifty or so visitors, eager for someone to get put in the stocks and have vegetables thrown at them, booed at his words.

Before Lucas could speak again, a Renaissance lady joined the group. Her lovely pink gown and veil couldn't hide her masculine shoulders and chest, or her hairy face. "Sir Bailiff," Lorenzo Tornado (this was too snarky), Diego's brother, addressed Chase. "I am the innocent maid Lorenza who has been wronged by this devil."

Lorenzo slapped at Diego with his fan and tried to kick his ex-lover, but he/she couldn't get her leg up high enough.

"And you see now, Sir Bailiff," Diego protested, "what I have had to endure for this lady? I deserve her dowry, and more."

After one look at Lorenza, the crowd shifted its favor to the defendant. Their boos filled the area around the stocks. "Put the father in the stocks for trying to marry off such an ugly girl!" Everyone roared with laughter.

Chase pounded his large mallet on the side of the dungeon. "Silence! I shall deliver my verdict."

As usual, the crowd grew quiet. Lonnie passed out the very overripe fruit and vegetables for the coming assault.

"I pronounce the lover guilty in this case and demand that he give back the dowry, after he goes through vegetable justice." Chase's mallet on the wall was final. There were no reprieves or appeals.

Lonnie took the protesting Diego to the stocks, where he was locked in place with his head and arms through the holes of the wooden device. Lorenza laughed and slapped him with his/her fan while the wronged father stood to the side, watching justice take its course.

The crowd took their best shots with squishy tomatoes, half-rotten balls of lettuce, and massively molded kiwis. It took only a few minutes for Diego to be covered in vegetable matter.

The crowd was satisfied and moved on to other Village attractions. Lorenza slid a piece of lettuce from Diego's nose and laughed. "Better you than me, brother!"

"It will be *you* next time, brother," Diego said. "Get me out of here."

"I rather like you in that position." Lorenzo swept up his veil and grinned. "You look so good, I could eat you up."

"If only you were a real woman," Diego quipped. "Jessie, come over here and follow up on my brother's suggestion."

Lorenzo turned around suddenly and slid his arm through mine. "Oh, we have so much to talk about, my dear. Why don't we go and take our clothes off and look at each other's breasts like all women do."

I slapped his hand away even as I felt him goose my butt. "Get away from me!"

"Don't make her hurt you," Diego warned as Lonnie got him out of the stocks. "You saw what she did to Henry. Just imagine being alone with her and a sword."

Lorenzo shivered dramatically. "I must go and change my panties now before the next act. Coming, lover?"

Diego took his arm, and the two comedians wandered away toward their act at the Dutchman's Stage.

"That was ridiculous," Lucas McCoy complained. "We're all supposed to take turns at this. Where is everyone?"

"I think they're all out patrolling the Village." Chase took off his black judge's robe and white wig. "I've noticed a few places are shorthanded."

"I guess I can sympathize with that. My brother Danny has been out since this morning. I don't know if he has any idea what he's looking for, but I guess it's better than no one looking for anything."

He invited me and Chase over for barbecue that evening, then started walking back toward his shop on the far side of the Village. Lonnie was cleaning up the mess as I followed Chase into the dungeon.

"Going to lunch?" he asked as the now familiar banshee wailed through the dungeon. "Let me put stuff away and I'll go with you."

"I didn't come over here for food. I think I know who attacked Roger." It was such a relief to finally be able to say it. I felt as though I'd been holding it in forever.

"What do you mean?"

"I mean I think I know who attacked Roger. It was Henry, on the shortcut, with a solid glass rod. Probably sage green."

"And you have proof of this?"

"Not exactly." I explained my theory and why I was so sure I was right. "I'm sure if we take one of those rods and put it on one of Roger's welts, it will be the same size. Think about it, Chase. A person could do some serious wailing with one of those rods."

"Why would Henry hurt Roger?"

"I don't know yet. At least not for sure. I think it might be to get his hands on the Glass Gryphon. He's counting on Roger not coming back to the Village."

"But I thought he was getting the spin-off store at the beach. Why wouldn't he be happy with that? And how does it tie into Ross's murder?"

"I don't have all the answers yet. I might have to do some more sleuthing to find out."

Chase took my arm and spun me toward him. "The only place Henry is going to let you sleuth anything is in his bedroom. We both know that, Jessie. Let's give this info to Detective Almond and let him run with it."

"I can handle myself. You don't have to worry about me."

"Too late. At least let's have some lunch and talk about it. I think there has to be a better way."

So during lunch, we agreed that I should take another shot at finding out if Henry attacked Roger. This was after Chase called Detective Almond and couldn't get in touch with him because he was out on another case.

"I still don't think this is a great idea, Jessie." Chase refused to see the rightness of my plan. "If he has any idea that you know what's going on, you could end up like Roger, or worse. Besides, I have some interesting news about Marcus that might take Henry off the suspect list."

"What? No way. What news?"

"I found out that Marcus was accused of hitting one of the other residents with his staff—the one the dwarfs have to carry. He denies it, and the man he hit wouldn't go any further with it. But I'm thinking his staff could leave the kind of impression we saw on Roger."

He sat back with a triumphant look on his face while I digested his information. "You're right. That *is* interesting. And it is possible. Marcus might have gotten riled up over something stupid Roger said and attacked him. What about the other long-term residents? Any other incriminating events among the employees?"

"Nothing on that yet." He shrugged. "So who do we go after first?"

"I'm not exactly sure now. But since I already have this plan for Henry, what about you tackling Marcus? In the intellectual sense, of course."

"I'd like it better the other way around. You take Marcus and I'll take Henry."

"Don't be silly. It's my plan. He'll never know that I know. I'm supersmooth when it comes to getting people's secrets out of them. Ask Tony. He confesses everything when he sees me because he knows I'll get it out of him one way or another."

"It's the *another* that I'm worried about." Chase finished his Coke. We both got up and rinsed our cups out. You can always tell the residents from the visitors by the cups hanging from their belts. As long as you have your own cup, you drink for free. A sweet deal!

"You're just jealous," I told him.

"Maybe. I think you might feel the same way if I told you I was willing to do whatever it takes to get something out of Princess Isabel."

"That's totally different. Nothing at all the same."

He laughed. "I *knew* you'd say that. Maybe I'm better at getting information out of people than you are."

His face was close to mine and I kissed him, loving him for worrying about me even though I knew it would be okay. "You could give me another radio if you're really worried about me."

"That might not be such a bad idea." He started to take his from the pouch that hung at his waist, then stopped. "But you won't abuse it, right? No more calls about anything except an emergency. Right?"

I crossed my heart with my finger. "Absolutely. No calls unless it's an emergency. I swear on my love for Renaissance Village."

That seemed to appease him and he took out the radio. "I'm adjusting it so you're only on my channel, not broadcasting to the whole park."

I took it from him like Lancelot accepting the Holy

Grail. "You won't hear from me unless I absolutely have to tell you something."

We kissed and separated, Chase heading back toward the dungeon and me walking toward the Glass Gryphon. I had some time to kill since it was only a little after one, so I decided to pop into Pope's Pots.

I walked past the petting zoo, where a long line of kids were trying to get their hands on the poor little animals. I wasn't surprised to see the goats and pigs running toward the back of the enclosure. Sticky, sweaty, grabby hands probably didn't look like much fun to them.

There was a long line waiting for a ride on a camel or elephant. I waved to one of my former students who'd spent one summer here then dropped out of school to be here full-time. I lose more students that way. The stench from the large droppings was intensified by the damp weather, so I breathed through my mouth as I walked by. I'd spent one summer helping visitors on and off the large animals. I wouldn't volunteer to do it again.

I watched the performance at the Hawk Stage, hoping to see the fake-hawk-snatching-someone's-eye-out routine, but no such luck. Lady Lindsey was up with her trained songbirds. Her little bluebirds and robins performed their tricks in response to her whistled commands. Lucky for them the hawks weren't out or one of them might've been lunch.

I sighed and started past the privies, noticing the crowds gathering down the street, where Arthur was due to pull the sword from the stone. The privies were busy, of course. There seemed to be an unusually large number of pirates at this end of the Village. Other than for the occasional stroll (usually accomplished by one or two of the brigands) they never gathered in large groups except near the lake.

I smiled at Grigg when I saw him standing with his arms folded across his chest, the tattoo on his forearm telling the world (in case someone didn't guess) that he was a pirate from the *Queen's Revenge*.

He nodded, and I walked past him. I had almost reached the Sword Spotte, where they sell those really huge Scottish claymores, when all the pirates moved suddenly. It was like being enveloped by a sea of leather and tattoos. I looked up, wondering what was going on, and one of them threw a smelly old blanket over my head.

Next thing I knew, I was being rolled up in it and lifted off my feet. I could only assume that was why they'd been hanging out by Arthur's stone. Apparently I had taken Rafe's vow of revenge too lightly. And it was cheating to use his whole pirate clan against me. It's not like I used the whole Craft Guild to get him taken away in the privy. This seemed totally unfair.

But I had something they didn't know about: Chase's two-way radio. I sighed at their ignorance (and my good fortune) and pressed the button to call Chase.

There was no response.

Surely he was back at the dungeon by then and had picked up another radio. I tried again.

Still no response.

What was the good of having a radio if I couldn't use it? I screwed around with the settings, hoping to raise someone else, maybe Merlin. I couldn't see anything with the blanket around me, but I hoped to find someone listening to one of the channels.

No response.

I put the radio away. It was best that the pirates didn't know I had it. I had no idea what they planned to do with me. Probably put me somewhere on the smelly old ship until I begged Rafe to forgive me. It would be a celebration of the 1950s in Renaissance Village before that happened, especially since I had my secret weapon. Though it certainly wasn't as reliable as I had expected it would be. Thank God Henry wasn't trying to kill me. At least the pirates just wanted revenge.

They walked with me hoisted above their shoulders for a long time. I felt sorry for them because I'm not exactly lightweight. I'm not Tiny Tina, world's largest woman, or anything, but one of the fairies/wraiths would've been an easier load to carry. Of course, none of them would have a feud going on with the erstwhile Pirate King either.

I decided to try the radio again. I was pretty sure they were taking me across the Village to the lake, and that would take a while with the day's crowd. I adjusted the radio again and tried calling out. "Mayday, mayday. This is Jessie Morton of the Craft Guild. I'm being abducted by pirates. Can anyone hear me?"

"Jessie? This is Mrs. Potts. Where are you, child?"

Thank goodness! At least someone heard me. Who would've thought Mrs. Potts had a two-way? It made me wonder if I was the *only* one in the Village without one after all. Me and Fred the Red Dragon. "I'm being carried in a really smelly blanket by a group of ten pirates. Probably to the lake or the ship. Can you help me?"

"You had to expect some retribution from them after trapping their king in a privy and having it hauled away to be repaired. What were you thinking?"

"Rafe threw me overboard and I had to swim to shore. What was *he* thinking?"

"You kids and your feuds." She sighed. "I'll see what I can do. You're with the Craft Guild, right?"

"Yes, but Chase will come for me. I just can't get his frequency on the radio."

"That's right. You two make a lovely couple. I was just saying to Daisy Reynolds the other day about how striking you are together."

"I appreciate that, Mrs. Potts. But if you know Chase's frequency, please give him a call for me." The pirates dropped me suddenly. We'd reached our destination, it seemed.

I stopped talking and hid the radio again. I would still need it to call for help if my would-be rescuers couldn't find me. I wasn't terrified, exactly, because I knew the pirates wouldn't really hurt me. But they were impeding my investigation into Roger's beating. Henry could decide to leave the Village and then he might never be caught.

I lay on the ground for a long time, so long that I fell asleep waiting for Rafe's retribution. When I awoke, I could hear voices, but they were muffled, as were the sounds of footsteps, which seemed to come from every direction. It was dark, darker than it would've been if I were still outside, even on this cloudy day.

I moved my arms and legs experimentally. Escape could certainly be an option. But I struck something hard on either side of me. Maybe the idea of being put in a wooden cask wasn't too far off. This felt square like a box, though, rather than round like a barrel. It was barely long enough to hold me. I thought about the hiding places under the floor in the Lady of the Lake Tavern. That could explain the footsteps and muted voices above me.

I kicked at the top, hoping it might move and surprise some visitor into exploring and finding me. No such luck. I supposed the pirates were waiting for dark to move me to the ship. They'd probably realized Chase was looking for me and didn't dare continue their parade through the Village.

It seemed like I was in there forever. I was hungry, hot, and getting a little irritated with the whole abduction scenario. I knew I had it coming, but so had Rafe for tossing me overboard like some extra cargo. I had thought we were

even. I was wrong. Of course, this would mean further retribution from me once I got out of this situation. I focused
my thoughts on all the awful things I could do to him once
this was over.

Finally, I heard a squeaking noise and felt a rush of
cooler air. Hands lifted me in the blanket again, and my
abductors started walking.

"This is way beyond funny, guys," I yelled out. "Let me
go. Or at least feed me and give me a privy break."

"Quiet!" I heard one of them yell back. "The king will
decide what to do with you."

I was about to take out my two-way again when the
pirates dropped me and decided to take off the blanket.
Thank goodness! I didn't know if I could stand that musty
smell much longer. I was going to need a long shower to get
it off of me.

I looked around. The room was dark. I was fairly sure
it was the pirate's stash room under the tavern. I'd visited
here once with Rafe before taking part in a raid on the tavern. They kept their ropes and other supplies down here.

Someone scraped a match and lit a single lantern. I
could see Rafe's darkly handsome face in the dim light.
This whole thing was getting a little weird, even for the
Village.

"We formally convene the pirate court to sentence Jessie Morton of the Craft Guild for her crimes." Rafe's voice
echoed in the room that had been dug out in the hill under
the tavern. "How do ye vote, my brethren?"

Eighteen

"Walk the plank!" someone yelled.

"Tar and feather 'er! Argh!"

"Hang her from the yardarm!"

I was surprised no one yelled, "Draw and quarter." That would've been my addition. Nothing like drawing out someone's intestines, then cutting them into pieces. That really gets the rabble roused.

I still wasn't worried. I knew most of the pirates by name or face. We all worked here. Just that some of us got a little carried away with our jobs.

It was nighttime already. I looked out of the open door from the basementlike hideaway and saw the lights from the castle shining across Mirror Lake. I could appreciate how pretty it was because I knew I wasn't really going to die. I'd be uncomfortable for a while until Chase found me, but that was about it. With that in mind, I decided to rile the pirates even more.

"What are the charges against me?" I yelled through the pirates shouting out what they should do with me. The last one was "Make her wear a pirate tattoo." Kind of lame and silly when you thought about it.

"The charges are assaulting and abducting the Pirate King," Rafe yelled back at me. "You went too far, Jessie. I had to burn my clothes. Do you know what that vest cost me? And those boots were handmade."

"But you didn't stop to wonder what would happen to *my* clothes and boots when you tossed me over the side of the *Queen's Revenge*," I baited him. "Where's the jury to hear *my* side of what happened?"

"There is no *your* side," Rafe argued. "You disobeyed a command from me on the ship. You had to be punished. Every dog here understands that order must be maintained."

"What about you, King Rafe?"

I recognized that last voice, although I hadn't heard it for a while. Queen Crystal had been absent from the village since she'd had her baby sometime last year. The tall, cloaked woman stepped into the dim light and threw back her hood. Her hair was silver and she looked like the Elf Queen from *The Lord of the Rings*. She held a long bow instead of a sword and was flanked by two big men.

"Queen Crystal!" Rafe was surprised to see her, too. His voice got all girly sounding when he realized who she was. "We thought you were gone. Like gone forever. You didn't say you were coming back."

She glanced slowly around the room. Only a handful of the Village's twenty or so pirates were there. "I never said I wasn't coming back. You've usurped my position by false words, Rafe. What's the punishment for usurping the pirate crown?"

"Hang him from the yardarm!" someone yelled. I think it was the same person who'd yelled it the first time. There's no loyalty among pirates.

"Tar and feather him!"

"Make him walk the plank! Argh!"

"I demand my right to challenge!" Rafe drew his sword from its scabbard.

The pirates drew in their breath at his challenge. According to the pirate code, no one was supposed to challenge the king or queen. Rafe knew that meant combat between the two. Of course, he had a big sword. I wasn't going to make odds on Crystal surviving with her long bow. Bad choice of weapons at close range.

"I accept your challenge," Crystal agreed. "And as queen, I appoint my two champions to battle for my honor."

The two really big guys stepped out from behind her. They were not massive like Bart, but they were both well built and strong like Chase. Rafe was tall but kind of slender. They'd make mashed potatoes out of him.

Rafe obviously made the same assessment and sheathed his blade. "That's not fair. I don't have two champions to fight for me."

Crystal smiled. "That's why I'm queen."

"Your Majesty." Rafe got down on one knee and bowed his head. "Please forgive me. I never intended to usurp your throne. It was the furthest thing from my mind. I was merely trying to keep the pirates going until your return. Now that you're back, of course you're still the queen."

There were loud "Huzzahs" from all the men. I was wondering if that would be it and we could all go home, but it wasn't going to be that easy.

"I forgive you, Rafe," Crystal said. "But I must still punish you. This evening, as my ship plies the water, you will follow behind in a dingy, rowing until we reach our berth on the other side of the lake."

"Yes, my queen." He accepted his punishment with humility. "But what about *her*?" He pointed at me.

"Hang her from the yardarm!" someone yelled.

"Okay, this was fun the first time around." I stopped the litany of possible punishments. "I've been wrapped up in a smelly blanket most of the day. I'm tired, hungry, and I want to go home. I enjoy a good pirate rally as much as the next person—"

"Argh!" one of the pirates agreed.

"But this is it for me. Don't worry. No one has to show me the way home. I can find it by myself."

But as I walked toward the door, all of them jumped in front of it. Crystal said, "I'm sorry, but you can't just leave. You attacked one of our brethren and you must pay the price."

"I'll jump overboard before I spend another night in a dingy with Rafe on the lake," I assured her.

She smiled. "*Another* night? I believe you and my usurper have been close, is that right?"

"At one time," I admitted with a glance at Rafe.

"Then your punishment shall fit the crime." She turned her head toward the door, the dim light shimmering on her long, silver hair. "I give you to the Village bailiff for punishment in the stocks or the dungeon as he sees fit. This is my judgment."

Chase, dressed in his blue cloak, stepped into the light where everyone could see him. I was relieved and happy he was here, although my finger had already been poised on the two-way for several minutes. "Let's go," he said in a rough voice reserved for evildoers in the Village. "You may face our fine justice tomorrow."

"That's no justice," Rafe disagreed. "That's her boy-friend. Why is that justice?"

Crystal glared at him. "Because you and Jessie were once close and I'm handing her over to whom she's close to now. And because *I* say it's justice. Do you have a problem with that, that you need to discuss with Sven and Bjorn?" The two bodyguards stepped forward, arms crossed over their large chests.

"No. That's okay. I'll get her later." Rafe hung his head.

"No, you won't," Chase demanded. "The feud is over. You both did terrible things to each other. You're even."

"That's right," Crystal agreed. "This is it."

"Fine," Rafe said.

"Okay," I agreed.

Crystal inclined her head toward Chase. "I give you thanks for your help this eventide, Sir Bailiff. Perhaps a latte in the morning to talk over old times?"

Chase bowed handsomely. "It would give me great pleasure, Your Majesty. Seven at Sir Latte's?"

"I look forward to it."

Chase took my arm and ushered me out of the pirates' lair. The harvest moon was coming up over the castle, a deep golden yellow with orange highlights. The were-wolves were howling, and there was some kind of groaning going on in the streets. "It's the zombies," he told me before I asked. "I guess that's why they were putting in the cemetery yesterday. They needed zombies."

"So what's with you and Crystal?"

"No *Thanks for saving my butt*, or *Glad to see you after spending all day with the pirates*?" He sighed. "This is getting to be a thankless job."

"No, I was really glad to see you." I kissed him, then looked into his dark eyes. "Really, what's with you and Crystal?"

"It's old stuff, Jessie. Like you and Rafe. We had some-thing together for a while, but she met another guy and they got married. She was off having a baby when Rafe took over. Now she's back with a baby daughter. I suppose she'll groom the girl to say *Argh* at an early age."

"Okay. I can live with that." I jumped on him and wrapped my legs around his waist. I started the difficult process of kissing every inch of his face when two zombies walked past. They were super yucky with great makeup and missing body parts. It was a little past closing time and they were chasing scared visitors toward the main gate. "You know, I don't think the Village will ever be the same again after Halloween."

"Never mind them." Chase shifted me in his arms and started walking toward the large Swan Swing usually reserved for children during the day. But sometimes, resi-dents used it after hours for other things. "I was worried to death about you all day."

I glanced at the Swan Swing and smiled at him. "Didn't you hurt your back the last time we tried this?"

He kissed me again and laid me down in the bottom of the swing. "I've been working out. Let's try it again."

W e spent the rest of the night in the dungeon (after getting past the banshee). Of course, that was after getting past the zombies. This Halloween thing was too complicated. I like my Village time simple. All these zom-bies, witches, and ghosts sounded like a good idea, but in practice, having them wandering around was kind of like letting the guilds patrol the Village. Things tended to get out of hand.

Anyway, we were both tired of sleeping somewhere other than together; me with Debby and Chase on her sofa. We watched the moon go down, talking about everything that had happened, before we finally fell asleep in each other's arms. There were no late-night shrieks or mad bombers so we slept through the alarm going off and had to scurry to visit Roger.

Before we left the Village, Chase used his master key to get into the Glass Gryphon so we could pick up a solid glass rod to bring with us. Detective Almond and the assistant medical examiner were meeting us at the hospital to decide if my idea had any merit.

Chase told me he'd tried his best to find anyone else with a complaint against Marcus (in between looking for me) but had come up empty-handed. Short of irritating the Black Dwarf and trying to get him to hit someone, Chase wasn't sure what else to do.

The Village was quiet and sleeping for the most part when we left. A few shopkeepers were up and around (thankfully not Henry). One or two fools or madmen were already practicing their new routines for the day. Adventure Land had decreed that all fools, varlets, and madmen were to become zombies after five P.M. each day. I guessed they didn't think zombies came out in the daylight. (Zombies aren't vampires. They don't have to wait until the sun goes down. Everyone knows that.)

Detective Almond was waiting for us at the hospital. I handed the glass rod over to the assistant medical examiner. He examined it, then looked at the welts still plenty visible on Roger's body. He held the rod against one or two of the welts, measured it, and mumbled something.

In the meantime, Roger looked extremely uncomfortable. Who could blame him? "So you think Henry was the one who attacked me? I can't believe he'd do it."

Detective Almond finished cleaning out under his fingernails, then put his pocketknife away. "Why not? Maybe the girl is right. Maybe it isn't enough that you're letting him take over the other shop."

"Jessie," I added. There's something about being called *the girl* that's worse than being wrapped in a smelly blanket.

"Yeah. Whatever."

"I can't believe that little weasel would dare do such a thing," Roger growled, visibly agitated. "And I'm not letting him take over the other shop. Just run it for me, that's all. He's flesh and blood, for God's sake. When I tell his mother, she's gonna have a heart attack."

"If you could hold off on that until we get some real proof, Mr. Trent." Detective Almond gestured in my direction. "Maybe the girl can get back in and find the rod he used to beat you. Otherwise, it's just conjecture unless he admits it. Frankly, I wouldn't confess if I were him."

"Jessie," I corrected again. "He probably already melted that rod. I don't know what good I can do."

"I agree." Chase stepped in. "I don't think it's a good idea to send her in to spy on him anyway. If he catches on, she could be in a lot of trouble."

"No worries, mate." Detective Almond laughed at his little (very little) Australian humor. His smile faded when he saw none of us were laughing. "Look, there's the hard way and the easy way. If we find something with Mr. Trent's blood on it and his nephew's fingerprints, that's the easy way."

"What's the hard way?" Chase asked.

"I guess hoping he'll do the right thing and turn himself in." Detective Almond looked at me. "You work with him. Does he seem like the honorable type?"

"I'll rip him from limb to limb," Roger continued raving. "There won't be a scrap of his stupid hide left when I get done with him. No woman will even look at him again."

Obviously we were not only upsetting Roger but also

provoking him into acts he probably wasn't capable of doing. It seemed we all realized this at the same time that Mary showed up for a visit. Without much explanation as to why we were all in Roger's hospital room, the four of us went into the hall and left her with him.

"He won't turn himself in," I said without any hint of doubt in my voice.

"Then whatever you can get for us will be better than nothing." Detective Almond took his assistant medical examiner and left the hospital.

"In other words, it's all up to us, as usual," Chase said. "I'm glad I had those sixteen hours of training to be a police officer. This way I know *exactly* how to run a murder investigation."

"Murder?" I looked at him. "Roger's not dead. A little feeble maybe, and kind of slow on the uptake, but not dead."

"I'm talking about Ross," he explained as we left the hospital.

"Whoa, Perry Mason! How do you ever get anywhere? This is like a road map going from one place to another. But it doesn't lead to Ross. It may have happened at the same time, but Henry isn't a killer."

"No?" He asked. We had reached the car, and he climbed in behind the steering wheel before continuing. "You know so much about him because he groped you a few times?"

"That and because I can knock him down," I replied with confidence as I sat down in the passenger seat. "Henry is weasel enough to sneak up behind Roger and whack him a few times. No doubt. But whoever killed Ross wasn't as sneaky. Two different people."

"Care to make a wager on it? Because my Spidey sense is tingling and it's telling me Henry has done all of this leading up to what he *really* wants to do. Note the words in red on his uncle."

"No way. It was the other way around. Henry took advantage of what happened to Ross and everything else to get Roger. And yeah, I'll put my money where my mouth is."

"Not money. Let's be creative." Chase started the engine in the BMW and pulled into traffic. "If I win, I want a full body massage by Joan of Arc."

I'm sure my face mirrored my disbelief in his wager. "I can't believe you with that suit of armor. I never knew you had a metal fetish, Chase. But if that's what you want, fine. I'll have a very large hot fudge sundae with whipped cream, cherries, the works, served by a naked bailiff."

"Anyone I know?" He grinned at me. "Don't you think you should make it something unpleasant for me?"

"You didn't make it something bad for me." I smiled and leaned back in the seat. "Why should I be evil to you just because you're wrong?"

"Done!"

We agreed on the bet, which started my brain working overtime to prove I was right. I'm nothing if not competitive. I always have been. Competing with Chase isn't too bad. Either way, I seem to win.

"Don't take any stupid chances." He pulled the Beamer into the Village parking area for residents. "Take the two-way with you and make sure you keep it on my channel this time. I'll have all the other security guys set up to come running in case something happens."

"I won't take any chances at all if I can help it," I promised. "Although I don't think Henry would hurt anyone, except Roger. I think he'd be afraid to take me on again."

He shut off the car and turned to me, putting his hands on my arms. His eyes were so sincere. I loved him so much

at that moment. "A little bit of self-defense can be a dangerous thing. Let the professionals handle it."

"You mean after I find the evidence the professionals
are worried they can't find." I played with the end of his
dark braid, painting pretend mustaches on his face. "Don't
worry. I won't take any chances. I'll wait until Henry goes
out for something, probably to chase some woman, then I'll
spring into action. There's only the two of us there now. He
can't be everywhere."

"Okay. I don't like this, but I guess we're going to do
it anyway." He kissed me for such a long time, I thought
we were going to have to climb into the backseat for a few
minutes. Finally he let me go and gave me the radio. "I love
you, Jessie. Take care. If anything happens to you, I'll kill
Henry, then end up in a cell with a guy named Bubba for the
rest of my life. You don't want that to happen, do you?"

"Would we get conjugal visits?"

"No. You'd be dead, remember? Don't let that happen."

"You worry too much. Henry isn't a killer."

We parted at the gate. Several security guards met
Chase there. There was always something he needed to do.
It was a demanding job.

I stopped for a snack at the Monastery Bakery. Things
were about the same there. Brother Carl was still playing the subservient role. He was scrubbing an oven when
I ordered brioche and mocha. I smiled at him, but there
wasn't much I could do since he didn't want to upset the
applecart. Brother John was still lording it over him. You
know, the more I saw Brother John, the less I liked him.

I walked with my snack through the street toward the
Glass Gryphon thinking about how I was going to prove
that Henry hadn't killed Ross. Bart (always in his Death
robe) dropped in beside me with a little wave of his huge
hand. "Hello, lady."

"Hi there. Brioche?" I held out the bread to him.

"No thanks."

"I thought you were overhauling the employee files on the computer?"

"I was." He made a face beneath his hood. "I am. What a mess! I shouldn't have volunteered. People don't think when they set up databases. Something like this can be important. No one cares. Just give them a few zombies after dark and they're happy."

"I know. I mean, what's up with zombies after dark, right? They can come out whenever they want to. I'm surprised the Knave, Varlet, and Madman Guild hasn't complained."

"You're funny." He giggled. No joke. The giant giggled.

"I'm on my way to burn some glass," I explained, keeping my secret assignment a secret. "Are you looking for victims to claim?"

He held out his scythe. "Yeah. They want me to haul in some dead souls a few times a day. Don't ask me why. I'm a frightening mythological figure, don't you think?"

"Definitely. Maybe that's why they want you out when they think the zombies can't be out."

"That's probably it."

We'd reached the glass shop. I could see Henry inside with two Renaissance ladies visiting for the day. "I guess I better go. Good luck finding your victims."

"Good luck to you, too, lady." He smiled at me and waved. "There might be more frightening figures than me stalking the streets. Be careful where you walk."

Nineteen

I thought about what Bart had said to me as I walked into the Glass Gryphon, maybe for the last time. My glass-making skills were subpar, but if I could prove Henry had attacked Roger, that would be sweet.

Of course there was that bet with Chase to win. He was so wrong about Henry killing Ross. I had no idea who did the deed, but I knew it wasn't Henry.

"There you are, Jessie." Henry hailed me as soon as I stepped through the doorway. "I'm taking these two lovely ladies out for coffee. Think you can hold down the fort?"

One of the ladies giggled and adjusted her pearl head-piece. "Oh, Henry, you say the smartest things! You're a genius, really."

I agreed generously to take care of the shop for him. What would be a better opportunity to snoop around some? "Go ahead. I'll hang out here."

"Thanks, sweetie." He chucked my chin as he went by.

To think I found him even remotely attractive made my stomach turn. I was glad to see him and his two ladies hit the cobblestones.

I figured I could keep the shop open and still look around for the sage green glass rod. Not that many people were wandering in and out yet. It was still early.

I left the back door open and checked in the shed first. If Henry hadn't burned the rod, he might've stuck it behind something until he could get to it. If he had burned it, there might still be some trace of it. I didn't know whether that would help the police or not. For all of my years watching crime shows on TV, I couldn't recall a case where a glass rod was the murder weapon. This might be a first, even though Roger wasn't technically dead.

But there wasn't a sign of green glass inside or outside the furnace in the storage building. I had barely finished looking when the front door opened for two witches with warts covering their faces. I was pretty sure the warts were real.

"We're looking for a glass image of the devil," the first witch told me. "Do you have anything like that here?"

I showed them the tortured demon/creature aisle, but that's not what they were looking for. "Were these forged in the fires of hell?" the second witch asked.

"Not exactly, unless you call this hell," I answered.

"I suppose it could do." She glanced around, then kind of fluttered away to look at the aisle of mystical creatures.

"I don't think we're interested," First Witch said.

"Maybe we are," Second Witch disagreed. "Look at these centaurs!"

The two went on about how realistic they were until I thought I might toss both of them out of the shop. But they finally each bought one. I wrapped them up, processed Lady Visa, and shipped them out.

When I was alone again, I searched through Roger's work area looking for the green glass. There was still no sign of it. It was depressing. Henry could have hid it anywhere. He could've heaved it out into the ocean or dropped it on a rock somewhere and smashed it into a gazillion pieces. I might never find it.

There was still no sign of him coming back from coffee. I drummed my fingers on my workbench and glanced toward the stairs going up to Roger's apartment. *Hmm.* That was one place I hadn't checked. Would Henry have been daring enough to hide the weapon he'd used on his uncle right in his own living space?

Because he didn't strike me as being particularly bright, I ran for the stairs. I didn't think he'd recognize the irony of hiding the glass upstairs, but I thought he'd do it without thinking.

Roger's apartment was clean and neat. Everything that could be folded was folded. Not a spoon or cup was out of place in the kitchen. No wonder Mary loved him. Chase is neat but not over-the-top about it. I like that about him.

I checked out the tiny sitting area and kitchen. No luck. I moved into the bedroom, which was reminiscent of military movies. Roger didn't throw his clothes around either. Not even a dirty pair of socks hanging in the bathroom. A paragon.

I climbed under the bed and found only a few old photos of Roger in his heyday as a police officer. He wasn't half-bad-looking. Not that I'm attracted to the law enforcement type (except for Chase, of course, and he's not real law enforcement).

I heard a noise downstairs, and I shoved the photo book back under the bed (no dust bunnies either). I straightened my shirt and tried to think of plausible excuses why I could be upstairs. *I burned myself and was looking for a ban-*

dage. Or I heard a sound upstairs and went to find out if there was a problem.

I heard a footstep on the stairs and my heart beat double time to match the military mode around me. None of those excuses made any sense. I panicked. What if Henry took one look at me like I'd looked at him yesterday and realized why I was really up here? What if the jig, as they say, was up, and I was left standing here with stupid excuses he wouldn't believe?

The footsteps came farther upstairs. I looked around the room like a cornered animal. What was I going to say? What would he do? I'd promised Chase I wouldn't get killed. He was going to be ticked if he thought I'd lied to him.

Why doesn't he call my name? What is his game?

I sneaked into the kitchen and looked for knives or something to defend myself with. The biggest knife I could find was a butter knife. The next possible weapon was a wooden salad tong that looked kind of deadly, if you were a piece of pottery.

The door to the apartment opened into the kitchen. I stood with my back to the sink, wondering if I could still contact Chase in time to make any difference. We might be the whole length of the Village apart. He couldn't get to me in time and would have to listen to my dying screams on the two-way radio. A horrible way to go but worse for the one left behind, consumed with guilt and wracked with despair.

"Jessie?" Henry smiled when he saw me. "I thought you were up here. Had to use the john, right?"

Why didn't I think of that? It was ingenious. "Yeah. That's right. It was either that or I might not have made it to the next privy, if you know what I mean. That breakfast just didn't sit right with me."

"You shouldn't leave the doors open when you have to come up here." He looked around the empty apartment. "It just isn't the same without Uncle Roger here."

Before he had a chance to get truly pretend maudlin, the shop door rang downstairs. *Thank God.* If I'd had to hear how much he cared for Roger, I would've been sick. "Sounds like a customer. Race you down there."

I ran past him and waited on the young couple who'd come in to scope out the place. I could tell they didn't have much money, so I gave them a deal on a little blue dragon. Everyone needs a souvenir and I was feeling particularly generous, being alive and all.

"Have you tried your hand yet this morning on your fairy or whatever you were working on yesterday?" Henry looked around at my workbench when we were alone again. "I know Uncle Roger would've been excited to see how well you've been doing."

"He's not dead, Henry," I reminded him as I switched on my torch. It was fun watching him jump away from the flame. "He'll be back."

"I wouldn't be so sure." He strolled toward his workbench with a demonic smile on his handsome face. "I told you about the psychology of the problem. I don't imagine Uncle Roger will be back, Jessie."

I picked up my work from yesterday, deciding not to argue the point. I looked at my fairy/butterfly. The colors were good, and I could tell it was something with wings. The rest was kind of a blur. I wondered if I could layer eyes on it, maybe a little red for the mouth. If it was going to be a fairy, it would also need legs. Clear legs, I guessed, since there were no flesh-colored glass rods to shape.

"Hey, did you ever find that sage-colored rod?" I decided I could question him without him realizing I was questioning him. "I sure wish I had it for my fairy's dress."

"Nope. Sorry." He was brief, immersed in his own work.

"Whoever attacked Roger didn't even steal his wallet. It doesn't make sense that someone would attack him yet not steal anything, does it?"

"I don't understand the criminal mind," he said finally after a few long moments. "Maybe whoever did it had a motive other than theft."

"Like what?" I glanced up at him. Maybe I could get him to give himself away. Okay, not to the extent that he'd try to kill me. Just enough so I'd understand what *his* motive was.

"I don't know. He's always talking about his past. Maybe one of the people he put in jail found him and wanted to get rid of him."

"But that's just the thing," I argued. "Whoever attacked Roger didn't get rid of him. Ross was killed but not Roger."

Henry looked up at me through his goggles. "Ross?"

"Death. The first figure of Death. Not Bart."

"Just because Uncle Roger was spared doesn't mean his attacker didn't *want* to kill him. Maybe he didn't have time."

"There was no one there when I found him. It's not like I scared the bad guy off or anything. Wouldn't he have still been there when I got there?"

"Maybe he heard you coming."

"And what do you think he used to beat Roger so badly? Whatever it was, it was different than what killed Ross."

"You sound like you know something about it," Henry scoffed. "I know you were there, Jessie, but sleeping with Chase doesn't make you a cop."

He was rattled. I could tell. I wasn't sure where to go from there. If I kept pushing his buttons, he might say something he'd regret. Or he'd chase me around the room with his torch. Either way, I'd have my answer.

A short older man wearing a neat two-button suit came into the shop. He didn't look like the usual visitor (if there is such a thing), but he smiled at Henry, who promptly dropped the glass dancer he'd been creating. The shattering glass broke the silence between them.

"Hello, Henry. How's it going?"

"Lou. I wasn't expecting to see you today. We should talk out back."

"We should." The man nodded politely in my direction as Henry ushered him out the back door while he tried to remove his work apron.

I gave them a minute, then crept to the open door to listen. The sounds of William Shakespeare spouting his newest ode mingled with the cries of the wraiths as they strutted through the Village. The Lovely Laundry Ladies called out to visitors as they passed by. Fred the Red Dragon roared at some kids dressed like vampires.

I listened for the sound of Henry's whining voice as he spoke to Lou behind the glass shop. "Listen, you know I'm good for it."

"I know what you're good for, my friend," Lou said. "It ain't thirty Gs."

"I know it's a lot but things are finally going my way now. I had a horse that came in second place yesterday."

"That won't help you with this here."

"My uncle owns this shop and the one I'm opening over by the Pavilion. I'm sure I could get something out of that." I couldn't see Henry, but I could imagine the weasely look on his face.

"How soon?" Lou came right to the point.

"Tomorrow. I can have it all tomorrow," Henry promised. "My uncle met with an unfortunate accident. Because of our recent partnership, he gave me his power of attorney.

While he's laid up, I have charge of his affairs. I'm sure I can get a loan for the money."

"Spare me the details. Just get it. I'll be back tomorrow. Don't think about skipping off without it."

"You know I'm not skipping, Lou." Henry said it like it was something good. "There's going to be a costume contest. We could meet there. No one would notice."

"Yeah. I'll be sure to come as Death in case you don't have the money."

The conversation sounded like it was over. I ducked back into the shop as the front door opened and several customers came in to browse. I went right along with them so Henry would think I'd been there the whole time. He came in and went to his workbench.

The two ladies were very extravagant. They'd obviously gotten into the spirit of things; they were dressed in beautiful velvet gowns and gauzy headdresses. The men looked bored and hadn't bothered to dress up, though that didn't matter when it came time to take out Sir MasterCard.

The whole time I'd been waiting on them my brain was on fire with this new information. Roger had given Henry his power of attorney. That meant as long as Roger was in the hospital, Henry could do what he wanted with his belongings. Of course, when Roger got out there'd be hell to pay. But, I supposed for Henry, it would be better to owe Roger than Lou.

As soon as the visitors left the shop, Henry put away his tools and turned off his torch. "I have some important matters to take care of, Jessie," he said. "I know I can trust you to watch the shop. I'll be back as soon as I can."

He went upstairs as a Renaissance craftsman and came back down as a twenty-first-century businessman complete with coat, tie, and attaché case. Roger would've been so

proud to see his evil-spawn nephew going out to sell everything out from under him. Ah, the ties of blood.

He kind of saluted me as he walked by. I counted to
ten after he was out the front door, then called Chase. I
explained the basic situation, not wanting to say it all where
we could be overheard. He told me he was on his way, and I
turned off the radio as another group of visitors joined me.

The pace was frantic that morning. Lilly Hamilton had
stirred up a hornet's nest. Everyone wanted to be at the
Village in case something awful happened that they could
relate to family and friends ahead of the six o'clock news.
I'd never seen so many video recorders and cell phones
open to take pictures, just in case.

Chase finally arrived about an hour later. He brought
beer and brats. Good thing, too. I would've pretended not
to know him after he took so long to get to the shop.

"I'm sorry," he said as we sat down to eat. "This place is
like a zoo today. I've had to confiscate more than one hundred cans of red spray paint. I guess the word is out, thanks
to Lilly, and now everyone wants to leave their mark."

"Good thing we just about have this wrapped up." I
scraped the onions off my brat.

"What do you mean? I thought you said Henry didn't
kill anyone."

"He didn't. But as soon as we sort through this mess with
Roger, I can concentrate on finding out who killed Ross."

"I'm not sure I understand how Henry having Roger's
power of attorney makes him Roger's attacker."

"Don't you see?" I squished a package of horseradish
mustard on my brat. "Henry was setting this up all along.
He knew if he injured Roger he could have power over
his belongings. He couldn't kill him or he'd lose that. You
should know all about it since you're a lawyer."

"A patent attorney," he corrected around a mouthful

of brat. "But that's not what I mean anyway. Just because the two incidents coincide doesn't make Henry guilty of attacking Roger. He might just be taking advantage of the situation. That's a long way off from proving he actually hit Roger with a glass rod."

"If the Myrtle Beach cops sweat him for a while, he'll sing," I assured Chase.

"And what would they take him in on? Being a jerk?"

"How about circumstantial evidence? We've already proven Roger's attacker used something the size of a glass rod to beat him. The green glass rod I saw here is gone. Henry desperately needs money. That sounds like enough to bring him in."

Chase raised his left brow. "You've been watching too much cop TV, Jessie. All he'd have to do is ask for a lawyer."

"If they don't charge him, they don't have to give him a lawyer. They can just have a conversation."

"But he wouldn't have to join in if he didn't feel like it and if he didn't have an attorney present. It would be a lot better if we could find some physical proof while Henry is out about his business." He took out his two-way radio. "I can't get my security guys onboard with this. But I can call in a few reserves. Let's take advantage of the time we have and see if we can make that happen."

I agreed that physical evidence was superior, and we ate the rest of our lunch in companionable silence while we waited for the A-Team to arrive.

We were kind of a sorry lot. Bart came in response to Chase's call. Merlin answered and Grigg dragged himself away from the pirates to help out. I saw Tony going by in his Devil costume and volunteered him. I felt in good company with the Devil, a pirate, a sorcerer, and Death on our side. All we needed was a zombie or two.

"So, what are we looking for again?" Tony asked for the third time.

"A sage green solid glass rod about two feet long," I explained as slowly and patiently as I could *for the third time*. That was about it, too. I'm only good for three times before I'm ready to strangle someone.

"What color exactly *is* sage?" Grigg began foraging through the shop.

"It's a soft shade of green, kind of like the underside of tree leaves," Bart explained. "Or the color of sage, which some people call salvia."

"You know your herbs, my boy!" Merlin commended him. "Who'd have thought it of a mythological figure?"

"A little more looking and a lot less talking," I told the group in general. "Henry could be back anytime."

"In that case, we're here purchasing glassware," Merlin said.

"Pirates don't purchase glassware," Grigg growled.

"Pretend," Bart advised.

"Never mind that. Let's just find the glass rod." Chase cut the discussion short.

I found myself looking in the shed again with Grigg beside me. "You know I didn't mean you any harm with that abduction thing, right, Jessie?"

"How is it having a pirate queen instead of a pirate king?"

He shrugged. "Different. She has us do different things."

"Like what?"

"Like babysitting for one thing." He shook his head. "It's not piratelike to change diapers, you know what I mean? I'm not even sure it's manly. I'm thinking about trading guilds and becoming a Merry Man again. At least Robin can't be replaced."

"There's always Maid Marian," I reminded him.

"That wouldn't happen." He picked up a burlap bag he'd found hidden away behind some tools. Glass rods clinked together inside the bag.

"Careful!"

"You think this is it?" He lifted the bag higher, making the rods clink again. "Sorry."

He finally put the bag on the floor, and we searched through it. There were plenty of glass pieces, but none of them were the right color. And most were too short for Henry to have used on Roger.

"That was no help." Grigg covered the odds and ends back up again and stashed the bag in the corner. "This seems like a wild goose hunt to me."

"I know. Henry's stupid but probably not stupid enough to leave the glass rod he used lying around. I just don't know if we're going to get that physical proof Chase wants."

"Maybe there's another way."

"Yeah. I'm for having Detective Almond take Henry in and beat it out of him."

"I meant something legal, Jessie. If you get anything by coercion, it won't do any good in court."

"What did you have in mind?"

Twenty

There were several components to our plan for getting Henry to confess. Since we weren't having any luck finding the glass rod Henry had used on Roger, we had to do something else.

Grigg came up with the basic idea, which included getting Henry to reveal his precarious relationship with Lou (obviously a loan shark). It was my idea to have Lonnie impersonate Lou in the dark, crowded square during the costume contest. We hoped Henry would spill everything to the faux Lou and we'd be there to witness it for Detective Almond. It was a long shot, but it was the only shot we had. Without physical evidence, only a confession would do. Tricks like this work regularly on TV detective shows.

Just as we finished formulating our plan, Henry came

back to the shop and everyone scattered. Except for me, of course. I was left there with him, hoping I was right about him not killing Ross. Henry just didn't strike me as the type who could kill someone. Beat them up pretty badly with a glass rod, yes. But murder took a whole other breed.

I thought about why someone would want to kill Ross and then spend days afterwards advertising it all over the Village. Obviously, the killer wanted everyone to know what he'd done. And he wanted attention for it.

I snapped on my torch between visitors to the glass shop and worked on my fairy's legs. They were difficult to shape, even with the help of the myriad number of graphite objects I was supposed to use. Legs are usually kind of round and narrow. Mine kept breaking off when I tried to shape them. The best I could do was something that looked like a large spaghetti noodle. Not too leglike.

I noticed Henry was unusually quiet even when a group of schoolteachers in cute ghost costumes floated through around five. He barely looked up as they oohed and aahed over his work. That wasn't like him, especially since a couple of them were young and kind of sexy. For teachers anyway, I supposed. I'd had to endure professor jokes for years from Tony and my students.

When the ladies had made their purchases and departed, I shut down my torch and cleaned up some of the fairy legs that had collected on the floor. "Everything okay, Henry?"

"Sure." He looked up. "Why? Was I squinting or something?"

"You hardly even looked up this afternoon. Those young teachers were doing everything they could to get your attention. It's not like you to ignore people that way."

By *people* I really meant *women*, but I didn't want to antagonize him. There was still a small chance he might just confess what he'd done. It was small, very small, but it was worth a shot.

"You know, there are more important things than looking at women." He turned off his torch. "Why don't you get out of here, Jessie? I'll close up."

I *knew* something was dramatically up with him then. "Sure. Are you going to see Roger tonight?"

"Not tonight. It's been a long day, and there's still that costume contest tonight. I said I'd help judge it. There's supposed to be someone there from each guild. I'm taking Uncle Roger's place for the Craft Guild."

The door to the shop opened and the little bell chimed. Roger stumbled in from outside with one arm in a sling and a metal crutch to help him get around.

"Uncle Roger!" Henry's eyes took on the true meaning of *big as saucers* at that moment. I thought he might run out the back door, but he managed to find some measure of calm. "I didn't expect to see you."

"I'm sure you didn't." Roger pushed his way in, then collapsed on one of the chairs near the door. "I wouldn't be here except that my lawyer called. He had a little bit of news for me. Can you imagine what that was, Henry?"

"No. Not really." Henry's voice was almost too soft to hear.

"The hell you can't!" Roger's crutch hit the floor with such force that a teardrop-shaped ornament fell from the ceiling and crashed on the floor. "Did you think I wouldn't notice that you were trying to sell my stores out from under me?"

"Not trying to sell," Henry disagreed. "Just trying to raise some cash. I had a little cash-flow problem at the other store and I didn't want to bother you. You were in the hospital and all. I didn't know if you were up to discussing it."

"Of course not. My own flesh and blood and you were

the only one who didn't come to see me. Then I find out you're trying to take my shops. If I could get up from here, I'd brain you with this crutch."

"You don't understand. I was just trying to keep up with the new store opening. I needed some cash. That's not a crime, is it?"

"How much cash? What for?" Roger confronted his nephew. Mary came in behind him and stood at his side, glaring at Henry.

"There were some problems with the other store. Damages that had to be repaired and supplies that had to be ordered."

"How much?" Roger asked again.

"Thirty thousand, give or take."

"Thirty thousand? Are you deranged? Where's that power of attorney? I'm rescinding it and giving it to my wife."

"That's okay, if that's what you want to do." Henry shrugged as though he really didn't see how thin the ice was beneath his feet. "Now that you're back, I'll just get to work on opening the other shop."

"You think I'm going to trust you with the other shop? After I gave you this time in the Village to prove yourself to me and all you've proven is what an idiot my sister-in-law gave birth to!"

Henry looked seriously confused. "But who'll run the other shop?"

"Someone I can trust!"

"Uncle Roger, you don't understand. I *need* that shop. I need that money. Something really bad will happen if I don't get it."

"*You* don't understand, Henry. I don't care. Just get out of here." Roger leaned his head against Mary. He looked really tired, as though yelling at Henry had taken all the strength he had. Mary put her hand against his face and soothed him.

I didn't know what Henry would do next. He had a wide-eyed, glazed-over expression, kind of like the Tasmanian Devil just before he whirls around on Bugs Bunny. I thought he might spin out of control since there didn't appear to be anything holding him together.

With tears in his eyes, Henry searched for words, finally saying, "You'll regret this, Uncle Roger. I'm your *only* blood relative. You need *me*."

Roger didn't reply. He seemed unable to. Henry swooped out of the glass shop through the back door. It was as if he'd taken all the air with him, leaving a vacuum in his wake. I knew I felt drained, and I hadn't even been involved in the shouting match.

"Was that good enough?" Roger asked me.

"Lord, I hope it was," Mary fretted, "else you'll need more time in the hospital."

"I think that was fine. None of us expected you to get up out of bed and come down here." I turned on the two-way radio to raise Chase and let him know step one was in place.

"You couldn't have kept him there once I told him what you'd said," Mary explained. "Are you sure about all this, Jessie?"

"All of us are. Let's just hope the rest of the plan works as well."

Chase said he understood after I told him what happened. "Meet me over at the Merry Mynstrel Stage for the contest. Watch out for Henry in case he gets a case of retribution and you get in his line of fire."

"Check!"

"I'll see you in a few minutes."

"I wish I could be there tonight, in some ways." Roger shook his head, his face lined with sorrow. "In other ways, I don't want to know. Tell me what happens, Jessie. I hope we're all wrong about Henry."

I really didn't hope I was wrong, but I managed not to tell Roger that. I had that sweet bet with Chase that I didn't want to lose even if it would make Roger feel better. His nephew was a stupid pig who didn't deserve his compassion. I suppose it's a bad thing to realize the only person you thought you could count on would be willing to hurt you to get what he wanted.

"I see him," I heard Bart say to Chase over the two-way. "What should I do?"

"Don't do anything," Chase responded. "Stay in position. We have to get Henry to admit what he did."

I had to give Bart a lot of credit. I don't know how calm I'd be if I thought it was possible Henry had murdered my brother. It wasn't true, of course, but Bart didn't know that. He spent too much time with Chase, who still thought it was possible. And not that Tony didn't have his *duh* moments when I wanted to slap him. But if I thought Henry had killed him, I'd be seriously trying to get my pound of flesh.

The closer I got to the Merry Mynstrel Stage, the denser the crowds became. I guessed all of those flyers had done the job. The contest was only for visitors, and there were three cash prizes. It was going to be fun to see who won.

I didn't try to look for Henry, although *not* looking for him made me kind of nervous. Walking down the street, I felt as if someone was standing over my shoulder. I finally couldn't stand it anymore, and as I passed Cupid's Arrow, I glanced back.

"Hello, lady." Death in all his iconic splendor loomed

over me. Of course this figure of Death came with a boyish
smile and wave that belied his dark shroud.

"That's quite a gleam you have on your scythe this evening, Sir Death."

"The easier to separate your body from your soul." His
tone got deeper as he spoke. His voice had a peculiar reso-
nance to it that was kind of spooky.

"Good. Make it quick. I hope there are plenty of mocha
lattes and chocolate cake where I'm going."

"Of course." He grinned. "Who do you think *invented*
chocolate cake and coffee?"

"Don't forget whipped cream." Tony came up and
wrapped his arm around my shoulder. His devilish contact
lenses glinted in the gathering twilight.

"I know where I want to go," I assured them both.

King Harold and Queen Olivia were onstage, getting
ready to begin the contest. I looked around for Chase or
Henry, but I didn't see either one of them across the sea of
Ren vampires, pretty witches, and mummies (I'm not sure
how they fit in). I asked Bart to look around since he was so
tall, but he couldn't locate either of them.

"Lonnie's moving in," Chase advised us over the two-way.

We'd asked Lonnie to pretend to be Lou, the guy Henry
owed money to. They were about the same height and
weight. I figured with the costumes and the near darkness,
it would be hard for Henry to tell the difference, and hopefully he would spill the beans to Lonnie.

"I don't see anybody." Bart looked back and forth over
the crowd like a human lighthouse. Without the light, of
course. "How do we know they're out there?"

"We just heard Chase say they were out there," I reminded
him. "Somewhere in this Halloween Ren crowd, we have to
hope Henry is nervous enough to talk."

"Has anyone considered that if none of us are around

when Lonnie pretends to be Lou, we won't know what
Henry says?" Tony has a way of getting to the nasty heart
of any problem. I wasn't sure he hadn't picked up on the
black spot in this one.

It didn't make me feel any better and I didn't dare call
Chase. Tony and Bart both offered to go and find Lonnie
and Henry, but that could give the whole thing away, too.

"We'll just have to hope it goes the way we planned," I
told them, crossing my fingers behind my back.

The trumpeters onstage blew their horns, announcing
the king and queen. Applause broke out from the two hundred or more visitors in the street, crowded into the seating
area that was meant to hold only about fifty people.

"Good people of Renaissance Village: Welcome to our
Royal Costume Contest." King Harold's voice echoed a
little with the microphone, but he was easy to understand.
"My queen and I will be judging the contest. Our royal
servants are spreading amongst you now to choose ten
finalists."

"If you are chosen," Livy continued, "come up on the
stage with us. We shall begin judging thereafter. May the
best costume win! Huzzah!"

There was a kind of mass shift toward the front where
the stage was located. Musicians began to play while the
king and queen's minions went among the people. There
were loud calls for different costumes to be chosen and a
certain amount of chaos as visitors tried to get noticed.

I saw Chase's head. At least I *thought* I saw his head.
Maybe it was him. I couldn't be sure. I bit what was left of
my nails as I worried about the plan. What if Henry didn't
fall for it? What if he did but no one except Lonnie heard
him confess? It wasn't like Lonnie was wearing a wire.
Chase had called Detective Almond (who could be in the
crowd as a vampire for all I knew). Maybe he'd be stand-

ing beside Henry when he confessed. Still, there was so much that could go wrong. Maybe this wasn't the best plan after all.

"I'm nervous, too." Bart looked every inch of his seven feet like a nasty incarnation of Death. It was comical to hear him admit something bothered him. "I wish I had some potato chips. They always make me feel better."

I didn't have any potato chips, but I did have some Tic Tacs. He took a handful of those (my hand, not his) and they seemed to calm him. Tony had deserted us for one of the dancers who'd swaggered by. It was just me and Death waiting to see what happened next.

I waited for a few minutes as the stage began to fill up with contestants. I shook the two-way radio a few times, but there was still no word from Chase. Something had to be done.

I looked up at Bart. He nodded. "I have an idea. Do you trust me, lady?"

"I'd trust you a lot more if you'd call me Jessie."

"It's not good for Death to know your name."

"I'll take my chances. What did you have in mind?"

I don't know why I went along with it. It seemed like a crazy idea at the time, but crazy times sometimes demand crazy ideas. At least that was what I told myself. The only thing I can say in my own defense is that it wasn't my idea. Surely that counts for something.

Bart thought it might be useful if we were able to see above the crowds. Then we could spot Chase, see if he was near Henry, and generally scope everything out for our own peace of mind. So he suggested I sit on his shoulders.

When I did, I felt as if I were twenty feet tall. I was afraid of nosebleeds and motion sickness. Everything seemed to be swaying.

"Keep still, lady, or you're going to fall down."

Oh. It was *me* swaying.

"That's better. What can you see?"

"A lot of nothing in particular. It's almost too dark to make out any one person in the crowd. I can't tell Chase from anyone else. I wish they had better lighting during the Renaissance."

"Maybe it would help if we walked through the crowds," he offered.

"I don't know. I'm not exactly a little kid to ride on your shoulders like this." I tried to sound concerned for his welfare, but the truth was that I was nervous enough with him just standing here. I didn't know if I could handle a stroll through the crowd.

"Here." He tossed his black robe up to me. "This will hide all of you and some of me. Then we can go."

"Maybe we should wait until we hear from Chase." I backtracked even as I threw the huge (*huge!*) black robe around us, keeping an opening so I could see. I couldn't even imagine what we must look like. I'm sure it was something I wouldn't want to see coming out of the dark toward me.

"Ready?"

"Like I'll ever be," I mumbled. My next words turned into a gasp as he started walking. He must've had a very low center of gravity to be able to walk like this. At first I thought I was going to fall off, but after a few minutes I got accustomed to his rolling gait. It was kind of like riding a camel.

I concentrated on looking for Chase or anyone I knew besides Livy and Harry, who were still onstage. I could barely make out any faces in the dim light. I saw a few people rear back in fright as we came upon them.

"I can see everything, but I can't tell what I'm seeing," I whispered to my bottom half.

"Keep looking," he advised. "We know they're out here somewhere."

At that moment, I saw Chase standing toward the back of the crowd. Almost immediately beside him, Henry was doing what we were doing: searching faces for the man who should be there to meet him. I wondered what would happen if the *real* Lou got there before Lonnie's fake Lou could lure Henry away. Probably disaster.

"I see them," I told Bart. "They're standing over there close to the side of the apothecary. Can you walk that way?"

"I can't see. Which way is the apothecary?"

"Hands on the clock. It's at two o'clock."

"What? Where's the clock?"

"There is no clock. You have to pretend there's a clock. You're looking at it from where you're standing. Walk toward two o'clock."

"Is that the twelve part of the clock or the two part of the clock?" I felt him shake his head. "I'm confused."

"Just walk straight ahead and then veer a little to the right." I couldn't figure out how else to explain where he needed to go. I looked toward the spot where I'd seen Chase and Henry. They were still there, but there were several people standing around them. I couldn't tell if any of them were short like Lonnie and Lou. When you're twenty feet tall, everyone else looks short.

Bart was starting off in the right direction when two of the Queen's minions waylaid us. "Wow! What a great costume! You belong onstage. Their Royal Majesties will want you in the contest for sure. Come right this way."

I tried to argue. Bart tried to argue. We were drowned out in the sound of the musicians from the stage and Livy talking loudly into the microphone. With the minions helping us toward the stage, it was impossible to get away without falling over. The crowd helped push us toward the rest of the contestants under the lights and we were herded up the stairs.

"I don't know how to get away," Bart said. "Are you okay, lady?"

"Yeah. Maybe this will be for the best. We can't really hear anything, but at least we can see. See over there?" I pointed toward the apothecary. "I think I can still make out Chase and Henry."

"Well, we have a wonderful group of costumes up here, don't we, my dear?" Livy asked Harry. "It will be very difficult to judge which one is best."

King Harold did his Henry VIII belly laugh. "It will indeed, my dear. What have we here?"

The king and queen were standing beside Bart and me, careful not to hide us from the crowd (like that was possible) but making sure that the visitors could see them as well.

"Let us go!" I said it in my sternest professor voice. Usually it had an immediate effect.

"Let us go or *die*." Bart added a dimension to my words that didn't necessarily help our cause, although they were well spoken.

Livy's laughter trilled out. "How very amusing you are, Sir Death! We should not fear you in our chamber at all. Perhaps we shall engage you to be our fool when this is over."

"It's me, Livy," I said, trying to reason with her. "Me and Bart. We're not visitors. Pick someone else."

"Dear me!" She put one hand to her heavily rouged

cheek. "We do believe both halves of this creature are speaking!"

The crowd laughed loudly. I was about to kick her in the face when my two-way radio suddenly decided to start squawking.

"I've been looking for you, Henry. You've been a very bad boy."

Twenty-one

That was Lou. The *real* Lou. Our plan was backfiring right before my eyes.

"We have to do something," I hissed at Bart.

"Something like what?"

"I don't know. I think Chase must've had Lonnie leave his two-way on. He must be close enough to Henry to pick up what's being said. But Lou could kill Henry and we'd never know the truth about what happened. I don't know about anyone else, but I have a huge bet riding on this. Henry can't die until he 'fesses up."

"That's fine, but we're a long way from them. What can we do?"

Our conversation was going on as an overlay to the queen's humorous repartee with the king and the crowd. She was still intent on keeping us in the stupid costume contest even though I'd told her we weren't visitors. Probably wanted to keep the grand prize for the Village—in other words, herself.

I swallowed hard on my fear and closed my eyes. "Jump off the stage."

"What? Did you say jump?"

"That's what I said. We'll create a diversion. Even if we can't get to Henry and Lou fast enough, it will give Chase, Grigg, and Detective Almond a chance to take care of it. I don't dare say anything on the two-way, but if we're hearing Lou and Henry, Chase must be, too. Just jump."

"Okay, lady. Hold on tight."

He grabbed both of my legs, which were resting on his chest. He didn't really need to because I was clinging monkeylike to try and stay on through the whole thing. I felt him take a deep breath, then he bellowed loudly and threw himself off the stage.

Despite my supreme terror, I heard everyone around us start screaming and running. Apparently we were so frightening that it was causing a general panic. I heard Livy yell to Harry that she was getting out of here. I couldn't see what was happening as Bart landed on his feet with a hard thud, then took off running through the scattering crowd.

Death was light on his feet for a seven-foot guy who possibly weighed in at over three hundred pounds. I didn't blame the crowd for running. With Bart continuing to shout terrible, threatening phrases as he ran, we were superscary. If I'd seen us, I'd be running, too.

But the hood from his cloak had dropped over my face and I couldn't see anything. I tried to pull it up, but it kept falling back down. I hoped Bart could see where he was running so we didn't end up crashing into the apothecary or the privies, but I knew there was no guarantee. While it would be some sort of poetic justice to end up in a privy after my stunt with Rafe, I kept hoping karma was asleep.

Please don't let us fall in a privy. Please don't let us fall in a privy.

"Can you see where you're going?" I asked in that unique voice that comes from having your entire body jogged up and down at breakneck speed. "Bart? Can you hear me?"

"It's hard to talk. I can see it."

He sounded breathless. It was probably hard to push that big body so fast. I hoped he didn't have a heart attack or something before we found his brother's killer. I decided not to distract him again and hoped we'd get wherever we were going in two pieces. Once you put yourself on the path of destruction (especially riding on the shoulders of Death), you get whatever comes next.

The people in the crowd rushed in every direction. Lou stood in one place with Henry while Bart and I rushed toward them. Of course, he couldn't have known we were coming for them. I didn't even know. I thought we were a diversion, but we ended up being a cataclysm.

I felt a whack and thud before I flew off of Bart's broad shoulders. I couldn't tell anything since I was totally swamped in the huge, heavy robe. The only thing I was sure of was that I'd lost my ride somewhere. I squeezed my eyes shut and tried to tuck into a fetal position, hoping to minimize the damage from the coming impact.

I was praying, too, as though I hadn't just been consorting with all kinds of demonic creatures and recently said I wouldn't mind going someplace besides heaven if there was plenty of chocolate. Surprising how quickly you can recant when it comes right down to it. Mostly my prayer went something like this: *Not the privies. Not the privies. Oh God, not the privies.*

And someone must've been listening because I didn't crash into the privies headfirst. Instead, I crashed into a

person. I heard the air whoosh out of their body when I hit
them, and whoever it was went down like a stone.

I tried to get to my feet, muttering all kinds of apologies
(and secretly glad not to be in the privies as long as the
person I fell on wasn't dead), but the stupid robe kept swal-
lowing me. I'd pull it one way and a huge glop of it would
fall back on me again. I could hear groaning and moved
my feet off of the person I'd hit. "Sorry," I said louder. "I'm
trying to get out of this. Sorry."

I heard a sound like a sharp click of metal and pulled
hard at the right side of the robe, hoping to finally see some
light. But instead, because the left side of the robe was still
under my foot, I jerked my leg out from under me. I collapsed in a heap of robe and desperate woman on top of the
person I'd just cannonballed.

There was a loud, deafening retort, like a car backfiring
except much closer. *Like directly underneath me.* The person swore and pushed at us (me and the robe), but it didn't
do any good until strong arms lifted me from my predicament and another set of hands pulled the robe straight off
from above my head.

"Are you okay?" Chase's face was very close to mine.

A dozen flashlights were playing over me. I put out
my hand to fend them off. "I'm fine. Turn off the mini-
searchlights. They're blinding me!"

Chase grabbed me up in a tight bear hug. "Jessie, you
scared the crap out of me. What were you doing? You're
lucky you didn't get yourself killed."

I was totally confused. "I know it was taking a chance
when I had Bart jump off the stage, but I thought it might be
a good diversion. I heard Lou out here talking to Henry."

The man standing beside me (dressed like an inquisitor)
pulled back his mask. It was Detective Almond (kudos on

the costume). "We had it in hand, young woman. We didn't need your interference."

I glanced beyond our small circle and saw several zombies (probably plainclothes cops) picking someone who looked like Lou off the ground. One of them had just snatched a gun from him. "Did he try to shoot me? Was that what the noise was?"

Chase put his arm around me. "I think that's exactly what happened. You're not shot, are you?"

"No. Not as far as I can tell. I mean, how do you tell if you've been shot? I didn't feel any pain or gushing blood."

"And don't let Detective Almond kid you. We'd already tried to close in on our real-life thug as soon as Lonnie's radio caught his conversation with Henry. It was a disaster."

"As soon as Lou realized who we were," Grigg continued, "he held the gun on Henry to get out of the Village. He might've shot him or actually escaped if it wasn't for you falling on him. Good work, Jessie."

I glanced around. "Where's Bart?"

"Here I am, lady." He already had his Death robe on again. He was probably the only one who could've pulled that yardage straight off over my head.

I left Chase's side and went over to hug the big guy. "What happened back there? Are you okay?"

"I don't know what happened. I think I tripped over someone."

"You could say that," Tony groaned from somewhere behind Bart. "How much do you weigh, dude?"

Bart laughed. "Not enough sometimes. Sorry I hurt you, Mr. Devil."

Two zombies walked through what was left of the fleeing crowd with Henry held between them. "Now we'll figure out what's going on, right, Mr. Trent?" Detective Almond seemed pleased with himself, although I couldn't see where he'd played much of a part in all this except for being in the right place at the right time. And even that, we'd set up for him.

"I'm not saying anything," Henry decided. "I want a lawyer."

"That's fine with me," Detective Almond told him. "I wonder how long it'll take Lou to make bail. An hour? Maybe less. With someone like him, it's hard to say. But I *guarantee* no one will be around to save your ass next time he comes for you."

Henry started crying. "Okay. Okay. I get the idea. I borrowed some money from him. I spent thirty thousand dollars from the money my uncle gave me to start the new store. I had some bad breaks at the track, but I thought I could win it back before I had to use it. I was wrong."

"So you used the sage green glass rod to beat Roger up so you could use his power of attorney to get the money back while he was in the hospital," I finished for him with a flourish and quite a bit of satisfaction.

"You were listening!" Henry glared at me. "That's rude, you know, even for this place."

"I get that part," Detective Almond said. "What I don't get is why you killed the giant? Was it just for fun?"

"Wait a minute!" Henry looked at all of us as if we'd act as witnesses for him. "I didn't kill anyone. All I did was borrow some money and use Uncle Roger to try to pay it back."

"Is that all?" Chase mocked him.

"That doesn't make me guilty of murder," Henry continued. "I didn't kill that big Death guy. That wasn't me."

"His name was Ross," Bart said quietly. "He was my brother."

Detective Almond looked back and up. I could see his mind working when he saw Bart. He obviously didn't know he was Ross's brother. I suspected he was worried that he wouldn't be able to stop him if he lunged at Henry. "Let's wrap this up at the station. Read him his rights, boys. Let's go."

I could hear Henry's shouting and pleading that he wasn't Ross's killer halfway out of the park. Maybe no one else believed him, but I did. I had an extravagant hot fudge sundae riding on it. But how could I prove the two crimes weren't linked? It wasn't like the real killer was going to rush out and confess to save Henry.

"Don't worry," Detective Almond told Bart, "we'll get him to confess. It's a slam dunk from here."

"Thank you, sir." Bart extended his hand. "I appreciate all you've done for my brother."

"I appreciate your help as well." Detective Almond shook his hand, his fingers disappearing into Bart's. "I'm sorry for your loss, sir."

"That sounds like a job well done, *Sir Bailiff.*" Grigg said it loudly as though trying to make a point.

"Of course." Detective Almond shook Chase's hand, too. "Good job, Manhattan."

"Thanks. I have my Scooby-Doo gang to thank for tonight. Maybe now the Village can get back to normal."

"As normal as that is," Detective Almond muttered as he walked away.

"Huzzah!" Grigg yelled. "I believe this calls for a round or two of ale. What say you, my fine companions?"

There was a general round of "Huzzahs," then everyone started toward Baron's, which was the closest tavern.

"I think we might pass on that, guys." Chase put his arm around me and grinned. "I have a bet to collect on."

* * *

Of course I never believed for one minute that Chase had won the bet. I made him wait two weeks before giving in. He bought the Joan of Arc armor and sword, but it rested on a chair in the bedroom all that time. Finally, I admitted he seemed to be right about Henry.

I mean, everything went from one hundred to zero once the police had him in custody. All of the dire blood (and not blood) *Death shall find thee* messages disappeared from the Village. Everything was as calm and smooth as Mirror Lake. It appeared as though Chase had been right and Henry was a killer as well as an attacker.

We watched on the eight o'clock news one night about two weeks later as Henry, through his attorney, pleaded not guilty to killing Ross DeMilo.

"Is that Henry standing there with him?" I asked Chase. He looked so different. I knew it had to be him, but I didn't trust my eyes.

"That's him. A few weeks of jail can do some bad things to a man." Chase lay beside me in the bed above the dungeon. We'd been back there for a while and nothing weird had happened. Even the banshee had been silent.

I looked at him, enjoying the Monday morning quiet after the relatively uneventful King's Feast the night before. I ran my hand through his long, loose hair. "And you'd know so much about that," I teased him.

He grew strangely serious. "I do, actually. My dad was in prison for almost ten years when I was growing up. He was a stockbroker who went a little off course and did some insider trading. I remember going to visit him one Sunday each month from the time I was eight until I was eighteen. It was a rough time for my family. It's what made me decide to be a lawyer."

I was touched that he had opened up to me that way. I hugged him with tears in my eyes for the little Chase that he had been. "That's awful. What does he do now?"

He shrugged. "He's been retired since then. Lucky for him he married an heiress. Lucky for me, too. We never had to go without because he was gone."

"An heiress, huh? Does that make you an heir?"

"Maybe. I don't know. My mom's family owns a major national distribution company. I haven't exactly been popular for moving away from home and not being involved with the family business."

I sat up and stared at him, not really surprised to find out his family was loaded. I had always kind of suspected as much from little tidbits of information he'd dropped from time to time. "So you became a lawyer, but not the kind that helps people. But you don't want to inherit from your mom either. What do you want?"

He smiled at me and pulled me back down beside him. "You. Everything after that kind of blurs out. Besides, I'd have to be in Scottsdale if I wanted to be part of the business. I couldn't be here."

I kissed him, not able to argue with that logic. I wanted him to be here, too. But it did sort of amaze me that someone who was rich would choose not to live that lifestyle. My brother Tony and I had always been financially challenged as we grew up. From what I can tell, my parents were the same. My grandmother who raised us had received poor packages from the church each week.

I thought about how life could change a lot as I worked with Roger after Henry went to jail. He'd become the perfect teacher after almost having his brain smashed out. I guessed that was what Chase had meant about circumstances changing a person. Roger had certainly benefited from a whack on the head and marriage to Mary.

I got the hang of using the torch enough to create some nice little animals to take home with me. Nothing Roger could sell, but that wasn't my goal in learning glass art. I had lived as a poverty-ridden student for so many years only to find myself an assistant professor barely surviving. It was excellent incentive for me to get my Ph.D. I wondered what Chase used as incentive since he'd never gone without.

Of course, I could've used my education outside of the university and probably made a lot more money. That had never occurred to me even though I'd eaten my fair share (and someone else's) of Ramen Noodles. I guess we all have choices to make.

Roger had chosen that Monday for an outdoor demonstration of glassblowing. He had enlisted my help to give me a taste of what the Venetian glassblowers had brought to its highest art form hundreds of years ago.

The day was warm and sunny, though it had started with a heavy frost that settled on the rooftops and pumpkins between the dungeon and the Glass Gryphon. I kissed Chase good-bye and promised to meet him for lunch. I was in an exceptional mood since he had shared something important about himself and his life with me. It didn't hurt that he'd also surprised me with my wager for winning our bet even though he believed I'd lost. Let me tell you, he makes a mean hot fudge sundae (with all the trimmings).

Mary and Roger were still working out the details for how they'd live together. Neither one of them had much space in their small apartments. The plan seemed to be that they'd use the space upstairs from the glass shop as storage and they'd live in Mary's slightly bigger apartment above her basket shop.

They'd been busy all week moving stuff back and forth. It was kind of like watching two big ants rearranging their anthill. Mary's extra blankets came one way and Roger's favorite chair went another.

Crowds had slimmed down some from the record highs between Ross's death and Henry's arrest, but there were enough visitors that Chase had told me Adventure Land was already planning Halloween II in the Village. I liked it better when it wasn't so busy. The Village wasn't meant to be that crammed full of people.

Bart had stayed on as Death even though he had his answer to what happened to his brother. It was only a few weeks after all, and I supposed management had offered him enough money for the part to make it worthwhile. He'd totally stopped working on the computer program to identify employees in the Village, past and present. Now that the threat was over, what was the point?

Roger had the furnace all ready to go by the time I got to the glass shop. He'd shown me the basic maneuvers of getting the molten glass out and using the long pipe to gently blow into the glass and create a hollow opening. Aside from the extreme heat, the process was fairly easy and a lot like a larger version of working with the torch.

During the two hours we spent outside, I would start each project, then Roger would finish using the graphite shaping tools, in most cases. In others, he created glass balloonlike objects that became vases and artistic glassware.

We attracted a good-size crowd (including a bus of seniors from Surfside Beach). They were very appreciative of our joint efforts and bought more than five thousand dollars worth of merchandise after the show was over.

I enjoyed the process and didn't even mind putting everything into the annealing oven afterward to cool. Sure, I wouldn't see any of those mammoth profits, but I'd picked up a lot of valuable information that would go into my dissertation.

Chase and I had lunch and spent an hour walking around the Village, looking at everything and everyone. I felt thoroughly relaxed, a nice change after the stressful beginning to my stay. He left me at about two P.M. to deal with a problem at the main gate.

I walked back to the glass shop, but Roger was busy moving most of the afternoon (they were calling for rain the next day) and I mostly waited on customers. That gave me some free time to think about the night ahead. I hadn't yet used my guaranteed incense from Cupid's Arrow and decided to make that evening something special for Chase and me. After the shop closed, I made a run down to Polo's Pasta for some takeout Italian and wine in paper cups. Not perfect, maybe, but not bad. I went back to the dungeon and dressed the place up some. I dressed me up, too (or down, depending on how you look at it), lit the incense about eight thirty, and waited for Chase.

He arrived not long after carrying a huge bouquet of flowers he'd bought from one of the undead flower girls in the street. We met each other at the door to the dungeon apartment and Polo's excellent pasta was largely forgotten.

Unfortunately, that was where everything started going wrong. Chase started sneezing (it seems he's allergic to patchouli), and for some reason, the banshee began to wail again.

"I'll be right back," he said between sneezes. "Could you open a window?"

"Of course. I'm really sorry." I apologized for the tenth time, mentally promising to strangle Adora tomorrow. How could she sell me something Chase was allergic to? Not very romantic.

I opened all the windows in the apartment and turned on the fan to help the incense dissipate a little faster. Maybe it would be better to eat first and get romantic later, after

Chase took some Benadryl. Hopefully the whole night wasn't ruined.

I put the pasta into the microwave, then struck what I hoped was a sexy pose and waited.

Fifteen minutes later, I was still waiting. Most of the incense had dissipated. I hoped Chase was okay. Finally I put on his robe and walked downstairs. "Chase? Are you still breathing? I thought maybe food with a side of antihistamine. What do you think?"

No answer.

"Chase?" I opened the front door and set off the banshee again.

Vowing to totally obliterate whatever the mechanism was that was causing that sound, I switched on the inside light and stopped breathing for an instant as my heart pounded in my chest.

On the wall beside the big door was the phrase I'd hoped never to see again: *Death shall find thee.* But there was no sign of Chase.

Twenty-two

I didn't panic at first. I thought maybe someone had called him. It's not like it hadn't happened before. Maybe he didn't want to worry me and thought it would be a short job. I went back upstairs and sat on the bed for a long time (at least five minutes), then I started calling around.

I figured if another security guard or one of the guild members had called him, they'd know where he was. The *Death* message frightened me, especially after having gone so long without seeing it. But that didn't mean someone had broken into the dungeon, hit Chase in the head, and dragged him out by his feet. No, sir. It didn't necessarily mean anything like that.

Thirty minutes later, I'd talked to the three security guards who patrol the Village at night. I'd forgotten that the guilds had stopped their patrols last week after everything seemed to have quieted down. They weren't happy about it either. Chase had told me how hard it was to get the two-way radios back from the pirates and the monks.

Where are you, Chase?

I got on the phone with the Myrtle Beach police as soon as I'd confirmed Chase hadn't been called out by security. The first man I talked to, Sergeant Somebody or Other, told me I couldn't report Chase missing for forty-eight hours. I explained the circumstances. He said it didn't matter.

I hung up the phone and got online. My hands were clammy and cold on the keyboard. Every noise in the dungeon below sounded like someone coming to get me. *Had someone actually come to get Chase?* It wasn't likely that he'd go wandering out in the dark in his boxers. Only an emergency could've tempted him to go out like that. If there was an emergency, I couldn't find anyone else who knew about it.

I looked up Detective Almond in the online phone book. That didn't work, so using his name, I did an Internet search, which produced a long list of hits. Finally, I saw that he and his wife had the yard of the month in May. I knew what subdivision he lived in and his address. I used that information to ferret out his phone number. His wife belonged to every club in Myrtle Beach!

It was after eleven when I called him. Detective Almond was probably asleep, but I didn't care. Something was very wrong. I wasn't sure what else to do. I let the phone ring until someone answered. "Hello?"

"Detective Almond. This is Jessie Morton from Renaissance Village. I think someone kidnapped Chase Manhattan."

"The bailiff?" He yawned into the phone. "Who'd want to do that?"

I told him about the words written on the wall downstairs. "I don't know who it is. But I wish you'd come out here and take a look."

"We can't officially look for a missing adult for forty-eight hours. That's police policy. Maybe he went out for a pack of smokes or a cheeseburger. Sometimes people just need some space, you know? Were you arguing when he left?"

"Not exactly." I didn't elaborate on what we were doing. "Chase isn't the kind of person to just rush out in the night wearing boxers to get a cheeseburger from McDonald's. And he doesn't smoke."

"Let's give him some personal space, okay? Call me tomorrow if he's still not back. Then we'll talk."

"What if he's dead by then? What if whoever wrote those words took him?"

He laughed. "First of all, Manhattan is kind of a big, strapping boy for someone to just come by and pick up if he didn't want to go. You know what I'm saying? And the man who wrote those words is in jail."

"The *other* words," I agreed. "Not the words downstairs. They weren't there yesterday."

"Maybe it's a joke or maybe Manhattan wrote them to buy himself some personal time. Just go to sleep and I'm sure he'll be back in the morning. Good night."

The phone was rudely clunked down on the other end. I stared at it, thinking of all the evil tricks I could do to get Detective Almond's attention. In college, we'd frequently ordered dozens of pizzas for unsuspecting professors who'd done us wrong. Once we'd even ordered a thousand pounds of sand delivered to the president's garden party. That one had come back and bitten us in the butt.

I realized this was no time to reminisce about past fun or worry about getting back at Detective Almond. Chase's life could literally be on the line. I had to act. No way could I lie down again that night not knowing what had happened to him.

Of all the people in Renaissance Village I could think of to help me find him, Grigg came immediately to mind. I might've gone with Roger since he'd been a police officer, too, but he was still having a hard time walking. And he'd been on the job about twenty years ago. Grigg was a recent police officer. If I could convince him to take my concern seriously, I thought he might be the one to help.

I put on some jeans and a sweater, tucked a two-way radio into my waistband, and put my cell phone in my pocket. I found a flashlight and a baseball bat. I wished I had a gun. But the only weaponlike thing in the dungeon was a crossbow.

I looked at my new Joan of Arc sword. It wasn't metal like the one I'd used to fight Roger at the King's Feast. It was silver-painted plastic (Chase didn't want to own the real thing), but maybe it would do in a pinch. I wouldn't be able to kill someone with it, but maybe I could at least frighten them. I hung the sword in the scabbard across my back and sneaked out into the night.

The Village was very quiet. All of the special effects (including the zombies) had been off for a while. I saw a security guard walking past the tree swing and set out in the other direction toward Mirror Lake and the pirates. It wouldn't do much good to tell a security guard I couldn't find Chase, I supposed, after Detective Almond's response.

I stayed purposely in the shadows where the streetlights wouldn't find me. I wanted to talk to Grigg before anyone else. Maybe he could help me make some sense of what had happened.

All the pumpkins were still glowing as I passed the Jolly Pipemaker's Shop, Peter's Pub, the Honey and Herb Shoppe, and the Monastery Bakery. The Village looked serene and otherworldly. A small breeze shivered through the skeletal trees set up and down the street. I glanced into the darkness of Sherwood Forest and thought about going that way for Robin and Alex along with a few dozen Merry Men. I wasn't looking forward to going to visit the pirates, but I kept an image of Chase in my mind for strength. He needed me. I wouldn't let him down.

The *Queen's Revenge* was berthed on the side of the lake closest to the main gate tonight. That would save me some time. Of course, it also meant the pirates were mostly on board the ship. When they spent the night on the other side of the lake, some of them were likely to be at the Lady of the Lake Tavern.

Either way, probably not good news for me. At least Rafe wasn't the Pirate King anymore, and Crystal seemed to have an old-flame thing for Chase that could work in my favor. I just had to get past all the other pirates, who were as likely to throw me in the brig for the rest of the night as they were to take me to see Grigg.

I walked cautiously up the gangplank to the heart of the ship. The pirates slept below deck in a makeshift room filled with hanging berths. Some of them were asleep on deck since it was a nice night. A few looked as though they had gone to sleep where they fell on the rough, wooden planking.

Where to look for Grigg? He could be anywhere. I was about to invade the Pirate Queen's lair when one of the pirates yawned and rolled over in his sleep. I jumped out of the way and kicked another pirate in the side. It took only a few seconds before they'd realized I'd boarded illegally and they raised the alarm.

"I only want to talk to Grigg," I told them. "Something's happened to Chase and I need Grigg's help."

The older pirate gave me a squint-eyed look. "That's why ye came with yer sword and baseball bat? I be thinkin' you be here to cause more mischief. Like what ye did to Rafe wasn't bad enough."

"I say take her below and leave her for the captain in the morning," suggested the second pirate (the one I'd kicked).

The first pirate agreed, but there was no way I was waiting in the bottom of the ship until morning. I wouldn't wait at the dungeon. I sure wasn't waiting here.

I grabbed my sword at the same time that I jumped next to the older pirate, putting the blade against his Adam's apple. "Find Grigg or your friend goes down to Davy Jones's locker."

Like I said, the sword wasn't real enough to cut the pirate, but he didn't seem to know that. The younger pirate could've tried to jump me, but he wasn't that ambitious. He went tearing off toward the captain's quarters, screaming his loudest.

"Ye'll get it now," the old pirate said. "We don't take kindly to scallywags."

"Yeah. Well, I don't take kindly to being threatened. You guys are way too far into this part. I mean, what would you do if you had to go sell insurance or something? Maybe you should take some time off."

"Argh!"

I didn't bother responding to that. Besides, everyone was awake by then. Crystal was dragging herself out of her quarters while the other pirates, including Rafe, were crawling up from the bowels of the ship.

"What's going on?" Crystal demanded. "It's too late at night for this. If you want some kind of revenge on Rafe, Jessie, I suggest you do it during the day."

"That's not why I'm here." I explained the situation to her. "The police won't help me. Grigg is the closest thing we have here to a police officer with Chase gone. I need his help."

She nodded. "Let my man go and we'll talk."

I looked around me at all the angry pirates. "How do I know you won't just throw me in the brig?"

"You don't." She tossed her long silver hair back over her shoulder. "And I might if it wasn't for Chase being in trouble." She glanced around the deck. "Grigg, you and Jessie come into my quarters. The rest of you, go back to sleep."

I let the old pirate go. He rubbed his throat as if my fake sword had hurt him. There was a lot of grumbling and muttering, but no one went against the queen. Grigg and I went into Crystal's private quarters with Rafe coming up behind us. I sheathed my blade warily, keeping a close watch on my one-time lover.

"Tell us all again what happened." Crystal gestured for us to sit down at the heavy wood table. "Make sure you don't try to hide anything. I don't want to have you locked up while we investigate what happened."

Leaving out the more private details, I told them exactly what had happened. When I was finished, Crystal was staring off into the darkness and Rafe seemed to be asleep.

Grigg sat forward in his chair. "The police never look for any adult who doesn't have a medical or some other problem for forty-eight hours. It's the way things work. I don't know what I can do to help."

"You could look over the dungeon and see if there are any clues to what happened," I told him. "Chase didn't just wander away. Someone had to take him against his will."

Rafe seemed to perk up at that idea. "Good luck with that. I wouldn't want to be the man who tried it. We got into a little dustup last year. He's strong and fast."

Crystal sighed. "I know. I did my best to turn him into a pirate. His heart just wasn't in it." She looked at me thoughtfully, then looked away again.

"At least come back with me and take a look around,"

I implored Grigg. "If you think nothing happened, maybe I'll be able to relax until morning."

"Okay," he agreed. "Just for the sake of argument, have you checked the parking lot to see if his car is gone?"

We dutifully checked the parking lot after leaving the *Queen's Revenge*. Chase's car was still parked close to mine. The cars looked so forlorn out there. It made me want to cry.

"Well I guess he's here somewhere," Grigg said. "Let's take a look at the dungeon."

"Thank you. I really appreciate you doing this."

We walked together—me, Grigg, Crystal (she left her baby with one of the pirates), and Rafe. It was a little after midnight according to the street clock on the main gate. There was no ducking in and out of shadows this time. I felt even more empowered surrounded by the pirates. Even Rafe seemed to take Chase's disappearance seriously.

A large shadow loomed up out of Squire's Lane, and I knew that familiar black robe before he spoke. "Hello, lady. Are you out for a stroll? Who are your friends?"

Doesn't anyone sleep around here? "You know the pirates, don't you? Pirates, Death. Death, Pirates."

Rafe laughed. "I've been outwitting you all my life. Welcome!"

"I don't think so," Bart disagreed. "I think you might be older than me. Where are we going?"

"Chase is gone," I told him.

"Gone where?"

"I don't know. That's why we're going to the dungeon. I think something bad has happened to him."

"I want to help," he offered.

"That's kind of funny," Crystal said. "Death wants to

help us find Chase. Does anyone else see the humor in that?"

Rafe yawned. "Not really. But you're the queen, right? Whatever you say."

"That's right," she pointed out. "And don't you forget it."

We walked past a silent Dutchman's Stage and were joined by Brother Carl from the bakery. We told him what had happened, and he fell in line with us. I was beginning to feel like Chicken Little broadcasting to all my friends that the sky is falling. Losing Chase would be about as bad as the sky falling for the Village and for me. I hoped everyone appreciated him as much as I did.

"I'll unlock the door," I said when we arrived at the dungeon. "The banshee will wail, but it stops after a few minutes. I don't know where to turn it off. Not that it ever does much good."

I slid my key in the lock and opened the door, but there was no banshee. Surprised, I pushed the door open all the way. Still nothing. The others crowded in after me, and I switched on the light.

"Tell us again what happened," Grigg instructed as he began looking around.

The fake cells were supposed to be replicas of a real dungeon in England during the Renaissance. They were nothing but some cement and boards painted to look disgusting. There was a little loose straw on the floors as there would have been during those days.

Other than that, there wasn't much to see. With the unearthly red light and groaning from the fake prisoners (scarecrow figures on the floor), that was about it. I followed Grigg as he searched the area, hoping he'd see something I'd missed. It had been almost five hours since Chase had disappeared. I didn't want to imagine what someone could do to him in that amount of time.

Crystal put her hand on my shoulder, obviously guessing what I was feeling. "Like Rafe said, Jessie, Chase is tough. Somebody might've gotten him, but they'll have a hard time keeping him."

I winced at the thought. "That's kind of what I'm worried about. I'd rather him be a live coward than a dead hero."

"Well there's no doubt in my mind that someone kidnapped Chase or at least persuaded him to leave the dungeon." Grigg squatted down and came up with something in his hand. It was a two-way radio. "I don't think he'd leave this behind."

The awful thing was, I couldn't confirm that Chase had the radio with him when he came downstairs. If he had, he must've picked it up on his way out the door without me noticing. Of course, that could've happened. I wasn't really paying attention.

"How can we know if this is Chase's radio?" Rafe asked.

I was relieved not to be on the spot. "It should have the number 01 on it. But to be sure, we can call it with another radio. Chase has his own frequency."

"It says 01 on it." Bart read over Grigg's shoulder.

"I can call his frequency," I said, taking out my radio.

"That's okay." Crystal took out a two-way we both knew she wasn't supposed to have. "What? It's not a bad thing to have around here."

"You were supposed to give them all back after you were finished patrolling," I reminded her. "Do you know the right frequency?"

She smiled at me in a purely competitive female way. "Yeah. I have his number."

Only a moment after she called him, the radio in Grigg's hand beeped. There was no doubt that this was Chase's radio.

I felt like dropping to the dirty floor and wailing like the banshee. It wouldn't do any good, but I felt like it anyway. I kept it together for Chase. We had to figure out what happened to him and find him. *Be strong.* I focused on communicating telepathically with him. *Help is on the way.*

I had no way of knowing if he'd pick up on my thoughts. He didn't answer back. When I was in college, I used to go to the psych department every week to earn easy money doing telepathy experiments with a really cool but weird professor. I never guessed anything right. I hoped that wasn't a signal that Chase wouldn't hear me. Didn't they say that telepathy increased with stress?

"Look over here." Grigg walked toward the red letters on the wall. "You see this smear? It looks to me like someone dragged something through it after it was written."

"You think Chase was trying to tell us something?" Crystal asked.

Grigg touched the red letters and smelled his fingers. "It smells like blood. No way to know without proper analysis whether it belongs to Chase. Sorry, Jessie."

By now my heart had given up beating. It was too exhausted from all that pounding. "But you think I have something to show the police?"

He shrugged. "Probably not before tomorrow morning. I wish I had better news. This might convince them to start a search sooner, but it would take more than this to get them out here tonight."

"There's no sign of a struggle," Rafe said. "I can't believe anyone took Chase from here without a major effort."

"How about with a major gun?" Crystal suggested. "Just because he's big and strong and really knows how to please a girl doesn't mean he couldn't be shot and killed on the spot."

I just *thought* my heart had stopped beating. Now it

zoomed up into my throat at the idea that Chase might have been shot. Not that I didn't know it was possible. I just didn't need reminding. I ignored Crystal's meaningless and inappropriate remark about him knowing how to please a girl. Where did she get off anyway?

"We have to do something now." I paced the dungeon floor. "By the time we find out this is Chase's blood all over the wall, he might not have any left. He must be in the Village somewhere. We just have to find him."

Bart sort of put his arm around my shoulders. It was kind of awkward with him being so much taller and bigger, but it was a nice thought. "This is a big Village. We don't know where to look for him. What can we do?"

"I think you'll have to wait until morning," Grigg repeated. "Whoever did this didn't necessarily want Chase dead. If he had a gun, he would've killed him right here. There must be more to the plan."

"Maybe, but whatever it is, there has to be some way to take action now. Later might be too late." I stared into the faces of the Villagers around me.

"I guess we could rouse the Village and security." Grigg looked from Crystal to Rafe.

"It's not exactly keeping with the pirate code to help the bailiff," Crystal responded. "But what the hell? It would be a bad world without Chase. Let's do what we can."

"And as soon as it's daylight, we'll call Detective Almond," Grigg said in a conciliatory manner that I knew was supposed to make me feel better.

It didn't. I took out my cell phone. "The police might not show up by themselves." I dialed 911. "But they *always* come with the fire department."

Twenty-three

The Myrtle Beach Fire Department made it to the Village in three and a half minutes flat. They came in full gear with two ladder trucks, a fire chief car, and a paramedic unit. It was impressive to say the least. They were accompanied, of course, by two Myrtle Beach police cars.

Unfortunately for the Merry Men, the only smoke visible was from a campfire in Sherwood Forest. The whole group of firefighters and cops descended on the three men sitting around the fire. Let's just say it was *more* than extinguished.

"Where's the big fire?" the fire chief demanded in his gruff, smoky voice. "I know you all didn't drag us out of bed at this hour for a campfire."

He looked at me, Rafe, Crystal, Grigg, and Bart as though he were daring us to admit it was a prank. I was about to launch into my story about Chase when Roger joined us near the main gate with Mary at his side.

"What the hell is going on?" he demanded. "Has someone lost their mind? Why is the fire department here?"

Grigg was closest to him. He muttered, "So the police would come."

"What?" Roger glared at him. "Who thought of that stupid idea?"

He glanced at me and I waved, borrowing Bart's cute little-finger motion.

"Chase is missing." Grigg shrugged. "We think something happened to him."

"Something like what?" Roger leaned heavily on his cane.

By this time, Mary had come to stand beside me. "Okay, Jessie. What's going on?"

I explained everything I knew. "I really think Chase is in danger. The police just blew me off with this forty-eight-hour scenario. I didn't know what else to do."

"Basically you're saying this was a false alarm purposefully phoned in to get us out here," the chief summed up. "Do you realize there's a penalty for false alarms? You could all go to jail."

Grigg responded (in typical police officer fashion), "Actually you'd need to know exactly who called in that false alarm to press charges, Chief. You're not going to get that information here."

I could've kissed him for sticking up for me. Worrying about going to jail was the least of my concerns. We were all just standing around while Chase was somewhere maybe in pain or scared.

"Now you listen here, young man," the chief began, shaking his finger at Grigg until I was afraid it might fall off. "I can lock up the whole kit and caboodle of you. I don't need to know one person in particular."

"There are about five hundred people who live and work here," Roger chimed in. "I think it might be difficult to lock us all up."

The chief gave him a sour-grapes face and did the I-wash-my-hands-of-you wave, then briskly walked toward his men.

"What's so important that you're willing to take a chance on the fire department not showing up the next time you have a real emergency?" one of Myrtle Beach's finest asked. "Is that you in there, Grigg? I'd heard you'd gone native."

"Yeah. It's me, Blackman." Grigg shook the other man's hand. "As long as you're out here, maybe you could take a look at a situation we have."

Blackman's partner nodded, and the two men fell in step with what had become a huge group of Villagers heading back to the dungeon. Grigg filled him in while we walked. "You know, we aren't detectives," Blackman said. "But if it looks like something suspicious, we can get those other guys out here."

Grigg smiled. "That's what I was counting on."

Everyone but Grigg and the two police officers stayed outside the dungeon while they looked around inside. I paced the ground with frantic strides. It was nearly three thirty A.M. Chase had been gone for too long. I felt as if I wasn't doing anything to help him even though the police were finally here. Who was to say he was still alive? If that really was his blood on the wall . . . I couldn't finish the thought.

"It's gonna be okay, Jessie." Mary put her thin arms around me and squeezed tight. "Chase is a tough boy. He won't go without a fight."

Grigg and the officers finally came back outside. Blackman glanced around at the group. "I definitely think something is wrong here. Where's the girlfriend?"

I stepped forward. "My name is Jessie Morton."

"Ms. Morton, maybe we should have a talk in the cruiser." Blackman nodded at me, and his partner moved in closer.

My temper got the better of me. "That's it? We got you out here so you could question me? We're going to sit in your nice little police car while someone might be doing something terrible to Chase?"

"I think it would be better if you come along quietly." Blackman put away his radio. "We don't want any trouble."

I didn't want any trouble either. It just seemed to find me. Without really thinking about what I was doing, I slid the sword from the scabbard. I heard a general indrawn breath from the gathered villagers. Bart was beside me. I jumped behind him and acted as though I might use the sword on him. A ludicrous sight, I'm sure, but the police seemed to buy it.

"We're not going to any police car." I laid down the law. "We're going to call in more police, maybe a few dogs, and organize the Village to go out and look for Chase."

"That's a very good idea," Bart said. "I wish I would've thought of it."

"We can talk about all of that," Blackman said, "as soon as you let that man go."

Bart glanced around the group. "What man?"

I nudged him and showed him the sword. "You're my hostage."

He smiled. "I've never been a hostage before. Sweet!"

"That's enough!" Roger interrupted our moment. "I was with the police for many years and so was Grigg. We'll vouch for Jessie. She didn't have anything to do with this.

And she's right. Everyone needs to look for Chase. The Village is a big place, but with some help, we can figure out what happened before it's too late."

I could tell Blackman didn't like that idea. He wanted to arrest me right then and there. But he looked at the crowd again and backed off. "All right. But she has to give us that sword."

I pushed the tip of it into the dirt and the whole sword bent, then flexed back into shape. "Welcome to Renaissance Village. Nothing is what it seems here, gentlemen. Shall we get started looking for Chase?"

Blackman actually did call in a few more police officers. The Great Hall at the castle became the staging area for the biggest manhunt in Village history. The police went out in pairs with their radios and advised everyone else to do the same.

I handed out every two-way radio I could find, then told each pair of searchers to take at least one cell phone with them. Harry and Livy actually took part in the exercise. Dressed in street clothes, they took a cell phone and prepared to search the castle. Two fools also went on castle patrol. Princess Isabel was unable to participate because she had a headache.

"We've made maps of each part of the Village." Rafe showed each group the part they were expected to search as Bart stoked up the computer and printer to make more copies. "Roughly, we're dividing into pirate space at this end, animal space at the far end, craft space and eating space in between. Robin, obviously you and the Merry Men will search Sherwood. Can you let the Sheriff of Nottingham go long enough for him to help out?"

Robin considered the question, hand to chin. "Of course. Anything to help the bailiff."

"Now we'll have Craft Guild search all craft shops. Food Guild search all food shops. And so on. Everybody report in every ten minutes, even if you don't find anything," Rafe told them. "We don't want to have to worry about anyone else."

"But why is this end pirate space?" Adora asked him. "There are as many mystical creatures and shopkeepers down here as there are pirates."

"Lighten up, Adora," Crystal said. "Let's focus. Chase could be in serious trouble. Who cares who has which end?"

No more was said about the division of the Village. With the efficiency of a well-oiled machine, the teams went out, one after the other, into the predawn to search for Chase.

Bart finished printing out the last of the maps, handing one to Rafe and Grigg. "Are we going out to look for Chase, too?"

Roger answered, "I think it might be better if this group stays here. We might need a small force to be able to go out quickly in case of an emergency."

"Has anyone seen Lonnie?" I looked around, half expecting him to appear suddenly. He had a habit of doing that. "I can't believe he didn't come out to look for Chase."

"I didn't see him," Grigg said. "But he's kind of small. Maybe we just overlooked him."

No one could disagree; with all the other residents crammed into the Great Hall, one or two could easily have been overlooked. Roger looked at maps of the Village while Rafe and Grigg plotted strategy. I wasn't sure when my quest had been taken over by the pirates, but I didn't care as long as Chase came back safe.

About five A.M., Crystal went back to the *Queen's Revenge* to feed her baby, promising to return when she was done. I had already paced the entire sawdust floor in the hall. I'm not much of a waiter.

"I'm going to get some coffee," Bart said. "Anyone else want some?"

"I could use some, too." Rafe yawned. "I'll walk over to the bakery with you. Jessie, you want to come?"

"No, thanks. I'll wait here, but I'll take the biggest mocha they have. Triple shot."

"It won't bring him back any faster if you drive yourself nuts with it," Roger said without looking up from his map.

"I don't care." I smiled at Rafe and Bart. "Thanks, guys."

Rafe shrugged and the two of them walked outside. Grigg continued looking at the map with Roger. I sat down at the computer where Bart had been. I started scrolling through the list of past and present employees that Adventure Land had sent him. Maybe if we'd kept going with that project, Chase would be safe now.

I knew a lot of the names on the list. Joe Worlsey. I remembered him well. He was the Black Knight for a summer. He kept breaking his lances when he lost. They finally had to fire him. Too bad, too. He was a very good-looking guy.

David Murphy. Oh yeah. He was King Arthur for a summer. I thought he looked a little too old. Apparently I was right because he had a heart attack when he forgot the code for taking the sword out of the stone.

Jeff Porter. Chase's assistant who'd disappeared in August. He was in the column of looked-for-employment-elsewhere rather than fired-by-Adventure-Land. His sister, Jennifer, might find that interesting. It wouldn't necessarily help her find him, but maybe some word was better than none.

I continued scrolling through the names, hundreds of them through the last ten years since the Village opened. Chase's name was in there as full-time. He had a permanent character now so that was listed as well. Most people changed characters from time to time.

My name was in there, too. Still employed, part-time. I was followed by Tony, of course, who was full-time but not a permanent character (as evidenced by his Devil persona).

"That's odd," I muttered to myself. "Lonnie Murdock was listed as fired by the company in late August. Maybe it's not the same Lonnie."

But when I searched the employment records, there was the same little rat face. It even showed him working at Sir Latte's, which was where he'd been until coming to work for Chase. "Maybe it's nothing, Roger, but did you know Adventure Land had fired Lonnie?"

"Who?" Roger sounded annoyed.

"Isn't that the little guy who hangs out with Chase?" Grigg asked.

"Yeah. He's been working for Chase since I got here this month. But it says here he was fired in August. Actually around the same time Jeff disappeared."

"Who?" Roger asked again.

"Jeff." Grigg nodded. "Medium height, brown hair. Always smelled like vegetables. He was working here over the summer when I started."

"That's right," I agreed. "Jeff's sister was here looking for him. I met her in the Honey and Herb Shoppe right after you were attached. She said he never came home."

Roger frowned. "Does that have anything at all to do with what's happened to Chase?"

"It could, I suppose." Really, I had no idea.

"I don't see how." Grigg smiled at me in a sympathetic

way. "That little guy didn't take on Chase. I just can't see that happening."

"What about the big-gun theory?" I reminded him. "Maybe Lonnie had a gun."

"Even if it were possible," Roger said, "what reason could Lonnie have to kidnap Chase?"

"I don't know." I took a deep breath and closed my eyes for a minute. "But no one saw Lonnie when we were sending people out. Maybe I'll just go over and check on him."

Roger glanced at Grigg, who said, "Why don't you do that, Jessie. Take a cell phone or radio with you. Report back in every ten like everyone else."

I took out my cell phone (I'd given my radio away). "All right. At least it'll give me something to do." I could tell that's all they were trying to do.

I passed Rafe and Bart on the way out of the Great Hall and took my mocha from them.

"Where are you going?" Rafe asked. "Has something happened?"

"No. Probably not. I'm going to see if I can find Lonnie." I explained the situation. He kind of grunted and kept walking.

"I'd like to come with you," Bart said. "I'm tired of sitting around."

"Great. I wouldn't mind having the company." I'd feel a lot safer with Death beside me.

The sun was starting to creep up over the east side of the beach. The sky was lightening and the birds were singing. It looked as though it was going to be a nice day, at least weatherwise.

"How could Lonnie do anything to Chase?" Bart asked as we walked toward the housing area behind the tree swing; Lonnie's employee file indicated he had lived there for the past two years.

"I don't know. Maybe he couldn't. It just seems odd, doesn't it? I mean, he said Adventure Land wanted him to be Chase's assistant. Jeff seems to have disappeared so there was an opening. Now Chase has disappeared, too."

Bart shook his head. "I don't know. I think if it was me, I'd just squish him."

"Even if he had a gun?"

"Especially if he had a gun. I don't like guns."

I recognized the older building Lonnie was living in. I'd stayed there one summer with a few other girls. It was big by resident standards. Much of the housing in the Village is more closetlike, which is why Adventure Land had felt comfortable shoving five of us into this one. Lonnie had been lucky to get it all to himself.

"What do we do now?" Bart asked as I stared at the door.

"I guess we knock." I followed my words with the appropriate action. There was no response.

"Now what?"

Light mist was forming in the streets, between the houses. It hung like wet wraiths from the chimneys and the doorways, and brought a creepy, clammy quality to the air that smelled like the ocean. I could feel it tangle in my hair as we stood there.

"I don't know. I guess we could find someone with a master key. Merlin has one."

Bart stepped up to the door and pushed at it. The portal swung in at first, then fell completely off its hinges. "Oops."

I grinned. "Oops is right. Don't worry. I won't tell. Let's go inside and look for Lonnie."

But there was no sign of Lonnie, Chase, or anyone else. The two-room structure was completely empty. Only the remains of beer and pizza showed that anyone had been there recently.

"So much for that. I guess he'll be surprised when he comes in from looking for Chase. I'm sure we just missed him at the castle."

"Too bad. I guess I'll put the door back up as we go. It's the least I can do." Bart shrugged.

We started back out of the house when I noticed a red smear on the floor near the door. I didn't say anything to Bart, afraid he'd give it away. Maybe we were wrong about Lonnie not being here. And maybe Chase was here with him.

We looked around again, more carefully this time. We were the only ones there. "Did you see that red smear near the door?" I asked him.

"No. What red smear?"

I pointed to the floor. "What if Lonnie dragged Chase in here?"

"What do you mean? Chase is too big for that."

"No! I mean, what if Lonnie accidentally had some red paint or blood or whatever it was on the wall in the dungeon on his shoe and walked it in here."

Bart scratched his head. "I don't understand."

I got down on my knees to examine the red smear. It started at the doorway and ended abruptly within a few feet of the threshold. "Most blood or paint stains wouldn't end with a flat edge like that, right? Something else must be here."

I could tell Bart had no idea what I was talking about. I ignored him and followed what I hoped was telepathic messages from Chase guiding me in the right direction. I pulled back the pathetic excuse for a throw rug from the front door area, then got down close to the floor again to look at the red smear mark.

"Do you see anything?"

"Not yet. But you can see that edge of the red stuff near the door is like a spill. This end is flat like someone laid a ruler against it. There has to be a reason for that." I stuck my fingernail into the floor (ouch), then moved it over a little. It disappeared into a deep crack.

"It looks like a trap door," Bart said. "Sweet!"

"Help me get it up. Look for something we could stick in there and pull at it." I searched through the room for anything that would fit in the crack.

Bart looked at the spot then brought one foot up and cracked the board with a sharp retort. "How's this?"

"Great!" I took my flashlight out and shined it down into the darkness while Bart cleaned away the fractured wood until there was a perfect square opening. "I'll have to go down there. I don't think your shoulders will fit."

"I think you're right. When you get down there, call me. No, wait a minute. Go ahead and call me now."

I did as he requested, wondering if my cell phone would work as I descended into the hole. "It's like a tunnel," I told him. It was so dark my flashlight beam seemed as bright as a street lamp. "And it's yucky and slimy. I don't want to think about what's down here."

"Just keep talking," he urged. "Where are you now?"

"Still the tunnel thing. You know there are huge spiders down here. Probably some kind of subterranean slugs or something, too. I can't believe I love Chase enough to do this."

The tunnel continued for another twenty yards or so (but who's counting?), then it started climbing upward. "I think this may be going somewhere," I told Bart. "I'm going to be quiet now in case someone might hear me."

Bart didn't respond. Probably staying quiet, too, so I wouldn't get caught. With every step forward, I could feel the tunnel getting wetter and more slippery. I saw a light from above and moved toward it, hoping it wasn't certain doom. But I could only stand so much slime. "I'm going in," I whispered into the cell phone. "Stand by."

Twenty-four

I was afraid the other side of the tunnel might be as hard to get out of as it was to get into. But there was only a plastic piece over this end. I pushed it off easily, then pulled myself out of the tunnel.

The flashlight picked out a bunkerlike setting with low ceilings, rusted bars, and standing pools of water on the cement floor. The smell was awful. Something like a garbage truck and a sewer backup. "We aren't in Kansas anymore, Toto."

I'd never been here before. I couldn't imagine where in the Village the tunnel had led. It looked almost like an old prison of some kind. Weird, since I'd calculated I was crawling toward the dungeon.

I could hear water dripping, possibly from the ceiling. Hopefully I hadn't tunneled under the lake and this, whatever it was, would eventually collapse in on me. *Chase?*

Where are you? I called out to him as telepathically as I could.

Nothing. Either I wasn't much of a telepath (probably true) or I had a wrong number.

"Hello?" I broke my vow of silence just to hear a voice in the eerie place. I looked at my cell phone. There were no bars. Not surprising. Bart probably hadn't answered me back in the tunnel because he hadn't heard me. *Great!* Where were those network guys when you really needed them?

I couldn't see an exit out, and I was afraid of going too far and not being able to find my way back. I was about to go back to the tunnel when I heard a sound, like another person. At least I *hoped* it was another person. As long as it wasn't Lonnie.

I shined the light around the area again. Something rattled, like chains against the floor.

"Hello? Is someone there?" A pitiful voice called out of the darkness. "For the love of God, someone help me."

It wasn't Chase. But evidently someone had heard my telepathic outcry. I followed the sound of that voice for a few yards. I still didn't see anyone. "Say something else," I encouraged. "I can't find you."

"I'm here!" Chains rattled and the voice sounded a little more hopeful. "Come this way. I'm chained to a wall over here."

"Keep talking. I have a flashlight. Let me know when you can see the beam."

He (at least it sounded like a man) started singing "The Star-Spangled Banner." It's amazing what we revert to when we're stressed. He probably hadn't sung it in years, because he couldn't remember most of the words and had to just hum in some spots.

I kept walking and looking around. This place had to

be an old jail or a torture chamber. There were overturned, rusted metal bed frames and broken, dirty toilets. I half expected to see skeletons hanging from the walls and ceiling.

"I see it! I see it! You're close!"

Everything was damp and covered with moss. Water dripped everywhere. I tried to dry my hands on my jeans but they were too wet and muddy. The flashlight was slippery in my grip. I couldn't believe someone was down here. I hoped Chase wasn't here.

"Yes! Look to your right," the voice (starting to sound familiar) instructed me.

I turned to my right and shined the flashlight against the other side of the wall that had prevented me from seeing him. "Jeff? Is that you?" As I rushed over to him, I noticed another form close by.

It was Chase. He was still in his boxers and lying silent on the concrete floor.

"Thank God you found us," Jeff cried. His dirty, heavily bearded face was streaked with tears. He pulled at the rusted chains to show me he was bound to the wall. "He just brought Chase in last night. He's still out. We have to get out of here before he comes back."

"You mean Lonnie?" I shined the flashlight on Chase and took a deep breath before I touched him. He was still warm, still breathing. It might be just as well that he wasn't awake, although we'd have to rouse him somehow to get him back out through the tunnel. I couldn't even imagine how Lonnie had fit him through it.

"Yeah. The little snake. He hit me in the head and dropped me down here. I don't even know how long it's been. He fed me, but that's about all. Didn't anyone even notice I was gone?"

"Of course. Everyone noticed. Your sister came looking

for you. It's just that we thought you'd moved on." I shined the flashlight on Jeff's wrists. I wanted to help Chase, but I would need Jeff's help. My plan was to free him, then Chase, and get us all out of this nightmare.

"What is this place?" I asked, trying to divert Jeff's attention as I examined the manacles around his wrists. "Are we under the dungeon?"

"It's the old Air Force jail. Chase knew it was under here. I guess everyone assumed when they built the dungeon over the top of it, there was no way into it. They were so wrong. Can you unfasten the manacles?"

The manacles attached to the chains that held Jeff prisoner were rusted but still strong. I doubted if even Bart could break them. The skin on Jeff's wrists was bloody and raw. I winced when I looked at it.

"I don't know." I pulled at the chain and Jeff moaned. "Sorry. I just wanted to see how strong they were."

"I thought of that. Actually I haven't thought of much else for . . . how long have I been down here?"

"About a month. It looks like there's a screw thing holding the manacles together. Maybe I can unscrew it."

"Don't you have a two-way with you? Can't you call for help?"

I didn't go into why I didn't have a two-way. Instead I handed him the flashlight with instructions to shine the beam on his left wrist. "I have a cell phone with no bars. We'll have to get out of this ourselves."

The screw thing wouldn't move when I tried to turn it. It was too rusted. I needed to get a better grip on it. I pulled my T-shirt up to use it as a buffer between my fingers and the rusted metal, then tried turning the screw thing again. This time it budged a little. Now I really wished Bart was here. He could probably get this open in no time.

I kept working on it, conscious of every little sound,

worried about Lonnie coming back and hitting me in the head. Who knew someone so small could be so vicious? He had to be strong, too, since he took out Chase and Jeff. I thought about him carrying that heavy keg of ale by himself. *Good going, Sherlock. You could've remembered sooner.* But who knew that would make any difference?

I finally got the first manacle off. It dropped to the concrete with a loud clank.

"Geez, Jessie! Don't make so much noise!"

"Hey, I'm doing the best I can! I didn't know it was going to do that."

Jeff was going to take off the second manacle while I went to revive Chase, but he couldn't move his hand enough to work the screw thing free. "You'll have to get this other wing nut off of here," he said. "And hurry. I don't want to be here when Lonnie comes back."

"Like I want to!" I gave him the flashlight to hold in his free hand while I worked on the wing nut (yeah, like that's a real name).

I heard a sound off in the darkness. "Is that Lonnie?"

"No. That's just the rats. Ignore them. They won't bother us as long as we're moving."

I worked on the wing nut until I felt the manacle loosen. This time I held it in one hand so I could catch it when it opened. I put the manacle on the floor and took the flashlight from Jeff.

He massaged his wrists, probably trying to get some feeling into them. I helped him to his feet. Thankfully he could stand without falling over. "Is Chase chained, too? Let's see about getting him up." I shifted the light to Chase's inert form.

"Whatever. I'm out of here. That lunatic could come back any minute. Don't worry. I'll send help."

"You can't do that! I need you!"

But it was too late. Jeff had already melted into the darkness. I silently called him every foul name I could think of. Not that it did much good. I was so going to hurt him if I ever saw him again. How could he leave me down here with Chase unconscious after I'd freed him?

"I guess that's an important lesson to learn, Jessie," I said to myself. "Never help the other guy before you help yourself."

I turned Chase over so he was on his back. He was manacled as well but only by one hand. Lonnie must have been in a hurry when he locked him up. Maybe there was only one manacle over here. Whatever the case, I applied myself to opening that manacle, going over and over my escape plan in my mind to keep from panicking. *Free Chase. Wake Chase up. Get both of us the hell out of here.*

The single manacle was harder to open than both of evil Jeff's (I guess *that's* why Lonnie used only one on Chase). I fought with it, gritting my teeth and swearing under my breath, but I couldn't get it open and my fingers were already raw and painful from twisting the rusted metal on evil Jeff's manacles.

Chase groaned and moved his hand to his head. I stopped trying to open the manacle and considered that my plan might have to start with *wake up Chase.* I could always go to step one after step two. The important part was getting to step three.

"Jessie? Is that you? What's going on? Why does my head feel like it just had batting practice with the Diamondbacks. Where are we?"

"It's me. Lonnie apparently knocked you in the head and dragged you into some underground military prison. I think that answers all the questions." I tried to resist hugging him, but it was a useless endeavor. I was scared, glad he was okay, worried about Lonnie. No way I wasn't going to hug him.

He groaned again. "Could we hold off on that until we get out of here and I find the back part of my head? What do you mean Lonnie hit me in the head?"

"I don't know how else to say it." I told him about Jeff and that Lonnie had been fired by Adventure Land before coming to work with him. "I don't know why he did it. But he doesn't know I let evil Jeff go or that we're trying to escape. We have to get out of here. Only I can't get the wing nut in the manacle loose."

Chase dragged himself into a sitting position with his back against the slimy wall. "So, where did Jeff go?"

"That's why he's evil. I'm never helping another human being escape from an old prison again. They're just too ungrateful."

"He ran off and left us?"

"Exactly. Oh wait. He said he'd send help. Totally evil. We have to get your hand free."

"Shine the light on the manacle. Let's see what I can do." But Chase's best efforts were useless as well. "It's no good. We need some WD-40, maybe a pair of pliers. You'll have to leave me here and go get them since I'm assuming we have no way of communicating with the outside world."

"No bars. Sorry. I'm so getting a new cell phone company." I leaned my head against his (carefully). "I can't just leave you here. What if Lonnie comes back? There has to be some other way."

He kissed my forehead. "You have to leave me here and go for help, Jessie. It'll be okay. If he wanted to kill me, I'd be dead already, right?"

"Not necessarily." A large flashlight beam hit us.

The sound of another voice, particularly since it was Lonnie's voice, made me jump to my feet. "The police are on their way," I told him. "You're going to jail. Too bad it can't be this one instead of a clean, nice jail."

He laughed at me, an ugly little rat laugh. "You know I always liked you, Jessie. You're so cute and sexy. Otherwise, you might be down here instead of Chase. I guess you *are* down here now, but I wish you weren't. Just don't lie to me. I'm not stupid, no matter what everyone else thinks. Chase wouldn't tell you to go for help if help was on it's way, would he?"

"Why are you doing this?" Chase demanded. "Is there some weird plan or are you a few cards short of a full deck?"

"It's simple, really. Adventure Land fired me. They told me to leave the only real home I ever had. I couldn't do that. So I created a position for myself by putting Jeff down here and becoming his replacement. But I still couldn't forget what they'd done. I just wanted the Village to close down. I thought it might after Death died. Then I thought it might after Roger was attacked. But it just keeps going. I think one more person dying might do the trick. What do you think?"

"You killed Death? I mean Ross?" I asked in disbelief.

"It was an accident, really. We were horsing around and the big guy fell on that piece of rebar. I tried to help him get up. It was too late. Then I looked at him and realized I could use his death to get what I wanted. So I wrote *Death shall find thee* on his chest. I never meant to really hurt anyone. That's why I left Jeff alive."

"You expect us to believe that? Did you beat up Roger, too?" Chase demanded. "Did you have anything to do with those two visitors dying from heatstroke?"

"I don't care what you believe, Sir Bailiff. But it was an accident, and no, I didn't touch Roger. And I sure didn't have anything to do with those visitors. What was really funny is that I only wrote that phrase two other times. Someone else did it the rest of the time. Good thing, too. That pig's blood was expensive. Cool, huh?"

I could feel Chase still working on the wrist manacle,

trying to free himself. I made sure my body shielded his actions from Lonnie's flashlight. I hoped he could do it, but I wasn't sure he could protect us from Lonnie. In any other circumstance, no problem. But he was injured and would probably be unsteady on his feet.

"What do we do now?" I tried to keep the conversation going until I could think of a better plan.

"One of you is going to have a terrible accident." Lonnie's evil smile made me shiver. "I'd rather it be Chase so I can keep you here with me, Jessie. I'm sure in time you'll come to appreciate me."

I wasn't sure how far Chase was from getting loose, but I knew I had to act. I pulled my sword from its sheath in one smooth movement. The light from both of our flashlights gleamed on the silver blade. It was fake, but Lonnie might not know that. He'd seen me use the real thing at the castle.

"You'll have to kill me first," I challenged him.

He stepped back and his flashlight wiggled. "Come on, Jessie. I can't believe a nice girl like you could hurt anybody."

I advanced another step toward him. "Try me."

He retreated, and I advanced another few steps. "Let's talk about this. Are you really prepared to cut me open? I don't think so."

I made a bold move and brought the sword quickly under his chin so he could feel the point. It wasn't real, but I knew it *felt* real. "You're talking about killing the man I love. Think about it, Ratboy. Do you really think I *wouldn't* kill you?"

I could see he was scared and the wheels were turning in his brain. I just hoped he didn't get brave and push against the sword. Maybe he'd just drop down and surrender. I don't think I'd ever been as scared as that moment. Everything was riding on pretense, just like the Village.

"Jessie—" I saw his eyes roll up in his head, then he slumped to his knees and finally to the floor.

I couldn't imagine what had happened until Bart stepped into the light. "I hope you didn't mind that I smashed him in the head."

The sword sagged in my hand and I collapsed on the concrete. "No. I don't mind at all."

"You were doing a very good job considering your sword isn't real," he said. "I just got tired of waiting. Is that Chase over there?"

While there's nothing better than being at Renaissance Village, sometimes even the most die-hard, character-bound actor needs a break. I thought a lot about that while waiting for hours as they examined Chase at the hospital. We both needed a break, I determined, after our experience in the old Air Force jail. If Chase survived all the poking and prodding, we were going to get away for at least a few hours. Just the two of us. Someplace nice.

So, two days later, we were sitting in an oceanfront pool at a swank hotel on the Grand Strand. A friend of ours (and part-time actor at the Village) leaves the sliding glass door open for us a couple nights a month. We have the whole place to ourselves. The hotel (not mentioning the name so our friend stays anonymous and employed) has an excellent pool and huge lazy river. You can float in it all night long looking at the stars through the glass roof.

Unfortunately, Chase and I weren't the only ones who needed a getaway. It wasn't as romantic as I wanted it to be, but I floated in the warm, chlorine-scented water with Chase beside me and decided it wasn't too bad.

You haven't seen anything until you've seen Death in a bathing suit floating in an inner tube. But I'll always love Bart for the gentle way he lifted Chase off the cement floor in that old jail and carried him out the secret trap door that led back into the dungeon. Thankfully, we didn't have to crawl back out through the tunnel.

Bart had been watching the dungeon and had seen Jeff run out. He didn't get very far before Bart caught him and he pointed to the trap door.

"The one thing that puzzles me," Rafe said, still wearing his pirate bandana as he floated in the lazy river, "is how that little guy got you into that jail, Chase. Come on! You had to help him out, right? He's half your size. I mean, a good swat with one hand would've taken care of him."

"How about he hit me in the head with a piece of concrete and I fell down the opening that led into the old jail." Chase nudged my inner tube and smiled at me. Lonnie kept using the banshee to try and keep people from noticing what he was doing in the dungeon.

Chase's head was in pretty good shape, according to the doctor. They'd tried to get him to stay at the hospital at least overnight, but he'd refused. I'd promised to keep an eye on him. So far, he seemed okay to me. Maybe a little too quiet. Was he still thinking about when he woke up in the old jail?

"Maybe we should fill that jail in or something," Grigg suggested. "It's a hazard. Someone else could fall down there, or the whole place could sink in."

"Already taken care of it." Merlin had refused to take off his robe (probably just as well) and was drinking a martini as he came down the waterslide. Of course, when he hit the bottom, the water splashed up and took care of the drink. But he ate the olive, then set the glass to the side and whooped as he ran up the stairs to go down again.

"What's going to happen to Roger's nephew?" Crystal cuddled her baby on her lap as she floated.

"Who knows?" I answered. "Roger says he'll testify against him and won't give him bail money. Mary's trying to talk him around. I guess we'll see."

Chase and I hung around for a while with all the other Village lunatics that had managed to escape for the night. They were too busy enjoying the benefits of living in two worlds to notice when we left. That's part of the beauty of being in the Village instead of really living in the 1500s. You can always call out for pizza, watch TV, or go out to play the lottery at Phil's Convenience Store on the corner.

We drove back from the hotel silently. Traffic was heavy on Ocean Boulevard, but we made good time back to the Village. I turned off the car (first time I ever drove Chase's BMW—sweet ride!), then I turned and looked at him. "A gold doubloon for your thoughts."

He smiled at me, but his eyes were still sad and thoughtful. "I don't know if they're worth that much."

"What's up? You've been really quiet, and you didn't even get your hair wet in the pool." I traced the shadows on his face with my finger.

"Nothing. Nothing *really*. I guess I've been wondering what would've happened if you hadn't crawled down that tunnel and rescued me."

I thought so. Latent survival thoughts. LST. It will get you every time. "You would've figured out something else to do. I'm sure it was easier because I was there. But you would've been okay. I have faith in you."

"Faith, huh? Does that mean next time I get to save you?"

"You already did. I wouldn't be here if you hadn't saved me from the pirates. That makes us even. Your turn next. Okay?"

He smiled and pulled me close. "Okay. Maybe not tonight. But later."

The zombies were trying out the spiderweb idea again when Chase and I walked back into the Village. The night was cooling rapidly, a stiff breeze blowing in from the ocean. The smell of salt air mingled with burning pumpkin flesh and roasting barbecue. Tomorrow would be another big day at the Village with the news of Lonnie's capture and the underground-jail hostages. Jeff had been on the news at least ten times in the past forty-eight hours.

"Don't you just love to watch the zombies at work?" Chase wrapped his arm around me as we walked to the dungeon.

"Why yes. I find them quite colorful. Maybe we should stay outside for a while and take in the sights, Sir Bailiff." I kissed the side of his face and neck.

"Yes. Forsooth. We shall take in the color, my lady. What say you to a turn in the Swan Swing?"

"My lord." I curtsied deeply. "I would do anything to please you. But art thou certain to be up to the experience?"

He smiled. "I believe I am. Wouldst thou fetch the Joan of Arc garb?"

Ye Village Crier

Greetings and salutations to you, faithful reader! You've made it to my official newsletter for Renaissance Faire Village!

Halloween at the Village

Halloween was observed much differently during the real Renaissance in Europe than it is at Renaissance Faire Village. There was far less partying and far more torture and other unpleasantness, which we won't go into here. Suffice it to say, not many self-respecting Renaissance villagers ever celebrated Halloween (*samhain,* as it was known then) without hiding their revels.

But for today's modern Renaissance revelers, Ren clothes are a great way to dress for Halloween. Ladies may enjoy the long, flowing dresses and skirts matched with peasant blouses. Men may want to be knaves or varlets (even knights if you don't mind the clanking). Men and women can dress as monks, jesters, or sorcerers.

The Renaissance was known for each tradesman and every noble dressing according to certain dictates. Fortunately for you, good folk, there are no such strictures. You can dress however you like. But truly, Renaissance fashions are an excellent choice for Halloween wear. You can even decide if you want to be a live peasant or a dead monk.

Here are a few Renaissance fashion terms to get you started:

snood: a type of hood or hairnet worn by women (now a video game)

chemise: a smock or shift worn next to the skin to protect your expensive clothing from oils and sweat (they didn't do laundry much back then)

doublet: a man's snug-fitting, buttoned jacket (also a type of refractive lens—go figure!)

corset: an undergarment used to mold and shape the female torso (many times made of whale bone, ouch!)

jerkin: a man's short, close-fitting, sleeveless jacket, usually made of leather and worn over the doublet (check it out on almost any picture of Sir Walter Raleigh)

A Little History

The term *renaissance* means rebirth. It describes the life-altering changes that took place in the fourteenth, fifteenth, and sixteenth centuries.

One of these changes was the Black Plague, which occurred between 1350 and 1450. The disease killed more than half of the population in Europe in really awful ways. No one, rich or poor, saint or sinner, was spared. People turned away from the church that had no answer to the disease. They left their families and abandoned their lives. Even governments fell during this time as wars and economic depression took their toll on humanity. It wasn't a pretty picture. But it ushered in a time of bounty and radical free thought that the world had never seen before.

THE PRINTING PRESS

One of the greatest inventions of the Renaissance was the printing press, as I'm sure you'll agree since you're reading printed matter at this very moment! Up until this time, books were only in the hands of the rich and the church. The printing press changed all that by putting printed material into the hands of the masses. There was more information than people knew what to do with (kind of like the Internet now), and suddenly, even peasants wanted to learn to read.

Johannes Gutenberg was responsible for all of it. He invented the printing press in 1445. It didn't take long before everyone wanted more. Almanacs, travel books, romances, and poetry were all being published and sold throughout Europe. It was the beginning of literacy for everyone, not just the few who could afford it.

FOOD

Exploration changed the way people ate during the Renaissance. Europeans enjoyed precious spices like pepper, nutmeg, mace, and cinnamon that weren't known to their forbearers. So they made cinnamon couscous like this recipe! Enjoy!

CINNAMON COUSCOUS

> ½ cup sugar
> 2 teaspoons ground cinnamon
> ¼ cup melted butter
> 1 cup almond milk
> 2 cups couscous, cooked according to package
>   directions
> 1 cup raisins
> 1 cup chopped pitted dates
> 1 cup chopped dried apricots
> 1 cup chopped blanched almonds
> ¼ cup pine nuts

Stir sugar and cinnamon into butter. Add almond milk. Pour over couscous. Stir in fruit and nuts. Cool and eat!

Check out these Ren Faire sites:

> http://www.mzrf.net/
> http://comp.uark.edu/~dupton/NWA_Festival/
> http://www.calcityrenfair.org/

Huzzah! See you at the Faire!

—Jessie